MW01229465

"I don't u
It's been three
the library.

Her father glanced up impatiently. "You are wearing a hole in the rug. Sit down, for God's sake. Mayhap when he observed the condition of the castle, he had second thoughts about his marriage."

"Don't be ridiculous, Father. Lachlan has no money concerns. If the castle cannot be made livable, we'll return to Lochleigh. I quite like it there."

Her father didn't answer, and Elspeth continued her pacing. "I wish Hamish were here. He'd know what to do. I'll send a message to Abhainn."

"Stop this foolishness!" her father bellowed. "Clearly your husband has chosen to abandon you. He has seen the wreck of a castle he dreamed about when he married you and has gone on to greener pastures!"

He got up and stormed out of the room.

Elspeth stared after her father, speechless. He had no idea of who or what Lachlan was, or what their marriage meant to them.

She had to get a message to Abhainn. Her father must have writing paper somewhere. She walked around to the other side of her father's desk and opened the top drawer. There, on top of bills and scraps of paper, sat Lachlan's ring. The ring he never, ever, removed from his finger.

She sat in stunned silence. If her father had Lachlan's ring, Lachlan was dead. He would never have parted with it while still he lived.

The MacInnes Affair

by

Blair McDowell

The MacInnes Affair

Cover Art by *Debbie Taylor*

The Wild Rose Press, Inc.
PO Box 708
Adams Basin, NY 14410-0708
Visit us at www.thewildrosepress.com

Publishing History
First Crimson Rose Edition, 2019
Print ISBN 978-1-5092-2714-3
Digital ISBN 978-1-5092-2715-0

Published in the United States of America

Dedication

To Jeanette and Sherry,
the two women who keep me writing

Acknowledgements

To all the innkeepers, taxi drivers, waiters, and tour guides in Scotland who took the time to answer my tiresome questions, and most particularly to Hamish MacPherson, owner/operator of the Skeabostview B&B on Skye, thank you.

To Cindy Clarke and Cathy Lesperance, thank you for sharing with me your knowledge about horses.

To Peter and Mairi Blair for helping us plan our research trip to Scotland.

To Jeanette Panagapka and Sherry Royal, for your constant support and belief in me.

And finally, my deepest thanks to my Editor, Kinan Werdski. It has been a rare joy to work with someone whose mind is so attuned to my own.

~*Blair MacDowell*

It is not while beauty and youth are thine own,
And thy cheeks unprofan'd by a tear,
That the fervour and faith of a love can be known,
To which time will but make thee more dear!
No, the heart that has truly loved, never forgets,
But as truly loves on to the close;
As the sunflower turns on her god, when he sets,
The same look that she turn'd when he rose!

~*Thomas Moore, 1775*

Chapter One

The Present

Lara gaped at the forbidding stone fortress before her. This was not at all what she'd expected of a bed and breakfast. She turned to the taxi driver. "Are you sure this is the right address?"

"Aye, lass." The driver was unloading her luggage. "You said Athdara. There is only one Athdara, Athdara Castle. That'll be twelve pounds."

Lara counted out the fare and added a tip. Was one supposed to tip in Scotland? She should have found that out before leaving Canada.

She climbed the wide marble stairs to the entrance. Beside the massive front door was a small hand-lettered sign, "Please ring and enter". She pressed the button and heard a clamoring that would have awakened the dead. Hitching her backpack up on her shoulder and wheeling her one small bag behind her, she opened the door and stepped inside to a square, high-ceilinged, oak-paneled hall. A massive stag-horn chandelier illuminated what would otherwise have been a very dark space.

An austere, middle-aged woman bustled in and introduced herself. "Welcome to Athdara Castle, Miss MacInnes. I'm Mrs. Murchison, the housekeeper. Lady Glendenning asked me to apologize for not being here to greet you. She will see you at dinner. Just leave your bags here in the hall. Ewan will take care of them. Come this way, please."

Lara followed the tall, dignified, and rather forbidding Mrs. Murchison, up a flight of stairs with polished wood bannisters that felt like satin under her touch, down a series of a long, dark corridors lined with portraits. Past Glendennings? At the end of the hallway, Mrs. Murchison opened a door with an old-fashioned brass key and stepped back to allow Lara to enter.

Lara caught her breath. Dominating the tower room was a massive four poster bed draped in plaid and dressed in crisp white linens. She could almost see Mary, Queen of Scots in that bed, awaiting her lover, Bothwell. How could she, a cowgirl from Alberta, possibly sleep in such a bed?

Her gaze slid past wainscoted walls of dark oak to the stone fireplace. Its blaze was welcome after the damp of the day. She strolled over to warm her chilled hands in front of the flames. She had not expected Scotland to be so cold in June.

Turning, she ran her hand across the soft leather of a wing chair placed in front of the fireplace, a lap robe haphazardly tossed over its high back, dark blue squares on a bright green field. The Clan Glendenning tartan? She would enjoy sitting in that chair, in front of the fireplace with the lap robe over her knees.

On the other side of the room, pallid sunlight poured through six narrow, leaded-glass windows set in the circle of the tower. Weren't tower rooms used to house prisoners in the past? She was sure she'd read something like that. Pretty sumptuous surroundings for a prisoner.

"Will there be anything else?"

Mrs. Murchison's question brought Lara back to the present with a start. "No, thank you. This is lovely."

"Dinner is at eight. Drinks in the drawing room at seven." Mrs. Murchison withdrew.

Her bags were already in her room. How had they done that? Back stairs?

She was staying in a castle. Nothing her mother had said about her friend's bed and breakfast had prepared Lara for this opulence. She gazed out the bank of windows. A manicured stretch of lawn was defined by boxwood and low stone walls, and beyond the walls, a forest of pine and birch beckoned enticingly. In the distance, high hills were covered in intense green and yellow.

She had grown up in the shadow of the Canadian Rockies. These foothills of the Scottish Highlands were very different. They had rounded tops rather like upside-down bowls, not the jagged peaks of the mountains she knew. And although they were very green, the green appeared to be some kind of ground cover. The castle grounds were edged by forest, but the distant hills were largely denuded of trees, and they gave the impression of being ancient. No other houses were visible. How large was this estate? She would enjoy exploring the grounds. Perhaps she had time for a short walk before dinner. She was tired from the overnight flight but was too keyed up to rest. Some fresh air might help clear the cobwebs from her brain. Hastily she took off her wrinkled travel clothes, pulled on a pair of jeans and an oversized sweater, and tucked her long dark hair up into her Calgary Stampede baseball cap. She met no one as she made her way back through the hallways with their many dark portraits, down the winding stairs, across the broad entrance hall and out the front door. She was really here. She was in Scotland.

She glanced back at the inn. Athdara was definitely a castle, even though it lacked the moat, the multiple towers and battlements she had seen in pictures of Scottish castles. Built of square-cut gray stone, four stories high, it sported a fat round turret on each of its four corners. Her room was in one of those. The narrow windows in the turrets would at one time have been for shooting arrows down on the enemy. In her mind she could see red-coated British soldiers surrounding the castle, and the Glendennings at those narrow windows, bravely defending their castle. She laughed. She had a habit of letting her imagination run away with her.

Which way should she go? She stood and gazed around her for a few moments. The grounds were beautiful, but the forest beckoned her.

Soon she found herself surrounded by trees, fragrant pine and slender birches and feathery rowan trees—mountain ash—with their shiny red berries. The Scots Broom was in full bloom, its clusters of brilliant yellow flowers lighting the forest. She followed a narrow ribbon of pathway lined with plump junipers and wild cranberries and bog-myrtle. She broke off a small twig of bog myrtle and inhaled its bitter-sweet scent.

Birds chattered in the trees. Ravens? She glanced up as a heron took flight, its blue wings spread wide as it soared out over the treetops.

Entranced, she continued along the increasingly rough trail. Abruptly, she emerged from the wood to some kind of promontory. Below her, a swift-flowing river bubbled over rocks, shimmering in the setting sun. On the other side, trees were reflected in its cool green depths, the sun casting long shadows as it settled behind the hills.

She'd better be heading back. Mrs. Murchison had said "drinks at seven." She studied the terrain. To her surprise, there was a broad, well graveled path along the cliff's edge that disappeared into the wood in the direction of the castle. It might be faster than the overgrown track she had followed here. With a last glance at the beauty of the setting, she set out at a brisk jogging pace.

She heard the drumming of hooves before her mind registered what the sound was. A magnificent black stallion came thundering toward her out of the forest, its rider oblivious to her standing in the middle of what she realized too late was a bridle path.

She threw herself to the side, out of the way of the oncoming beast, and landed in the middle of a large yellow flowering bush.

"*Whit ye daein, ye dunderheed!*" The man brought his horse to a halt. The horse began to sidle, and the rider tightened his grip on the reins, bringing him firmly under control. "This is nae a footpath!"

Painfully, Lara tried to extract herself from the bramble. Her right hand was already bleeding from a long sharp thorn embedded in it, and another thorn had pierced the seat of her jeans. She struggled, unable to get a foothold. A thorn pushed through her shoe into her right foot. The sharp penetrating thorns were everywhere. Her cap fell off and her dark hair tumbled around her shoulders.

5

"Jesus! Yer a lass." He was off his mount in a flash, kneeling by her side. "Stop struggling. Yer only making it worse. I'll have to lift ye out. Gorse is a painful bed."

He reached into the bush, carefully slipped his arms under her shoulders and knees, and lifted her free of the clinging barbs. He set her down on her feet only to have her knees give way. Quickly his arms came around her, supporting her.

"I'm sorry," Lara said. "I should have been more attentive. I should have realized this was a bridle path. I was just so entranced by the woods and the river and…what is that horrible bush? I thought it was broom."

"Nae." He shook his head in apparent disbelief that anyone could be so naive. "It's gorse. Any Scot knows the difference. The blooms appear alike, but the gorse is mean. I knew a man once had to be lifted out of a large patch of gorse by a crane."

Tears filled her eyes. She hated herself for it, but this was just the last straw. It had been an endless overnight flight from Calgary and a long train trip from Edinburgh, and she had just arrived here, to be very nearly run down by the biggest horse she'd ever encountered. And to top it off, she'd fallen into a gorse patch and been yelled at in a language she didn't understand, although the sentiment had come through loud and clear.

"Dinnae dae that! Please don't cry. I canna stand a woman's tears. Come. Ye ken how to ride?"

"I grew up on a ranch," Lara said, searching unsuccessfully for a tissue in the pocket of her jeans. "I've been riding all my life."

"Here." He took a large linen square out of the pocket of his jacket. "Here. I'll take ye back to the house and me mother will tend to yer scratches and wounds. I'm that sorry. I dinna expect anyone to be on the path, and I was giving Thunder his head."

"Thunder?"

"He was a wee bit difficult to break. But he's a fine ride now."

Lara stared up at the horse that stood a good seventeen hands. They had never had one as big on the ranch. Then for the first time she examined the rider. She didn't think she'd encountered one that big on the ranch either. He was well over six feet tall, with broad shoulders and long legs. He had a thick shock of auburn hair, some strands of which fell over his forehead. His eyes were so dark a blue they bordered on black. He appeared as dangerous as his horse.

"So can ye stand?"

"Certainly, I can stand," Lara said, propelling herself to her feet. She wobbled and almost toppled, but his arms came around her before she could once again land in the gorse.

"My foot…"

He lifted her in his arms.

A few minutes later, Lara was mounted behind the horseman, with her arms around his waist, as they traversed the bridle path at a sedate canter. At the stables, he dismounted, then lifted her down.

A stable hand appeared instantly.

"Ewan, can you take care of Thunder for me? The lass is injured."

"Of course, milord."

Lara was almost sorry their ride was over. She had

enjoyed being pressed against his broad back, every bounce of the horse making them bounce together. Who was he? The stable hand had referred to him as "milord."

Over her protests, he carried her across the broad lawn and into the house, through a big stone kitchen, through a butlers' pantry and formal dining room, to a large drawing room at the front of the castle. He was about to deposit her on a yellow silk damask sofa when Mrs. Murchison came into the room.

"What happened to Miss MacInnes? Good heavens, she's injured!"

Lara glanced down. Indeed, her hand had been more than scratched. Blood was dripping from it. She held it against her shirt to keep the blood from ruining the blue and cream oriental carpet.

"I found her in the wood. Is it she belongs here?"

"She's our personal guest. If you ever listened to what your mother said over breakfast ye'd know that. She's Miss Lara MacInnes, arrived this afternoon from Canada."

"Aye. I do remember somethin' of the sort now. Where shall I put her?"

Lara listened as the man referred to her as if she were some sort of package to be deposited. He was insufferable. Her face flushed with embarrassment. "Put me down, please. Don't disturb yourself with another minute. I can make my own way to my room."

He stared down at her wriggling in his arms, and a slight frown creased his forehead. "Dinna be daft. Ye canna stand."

"She's in the west tower room," Mrs. Murchison instructed. "You can take her there. I'll let your mother know. Then go clean yourself up and dress. You're expected in the drawing room in an half hour and you know how your father is about tardiness."

With a grunted acknowledgement to Mrs. Murchison, the man carried Lara up the stairs and to her room. There he deposited her carefully on her bed.

He headed toward the door, then turned back. "I'm that sorry," he said. "I dinna mean to run ye doon."

Lara laughed in spite of herself. "Apology accepted."

Her eyes followed him as he beat a hasty retreat. She let out the breath she hadn't realized she was holding. It was an incredibly sexy experience, being carried by a man.

A few minutes later Aileen Glendenning came rushing into the room. Her mother's friend, Aileen, was a tall, slender, willowy blond, exactly as Lara's mother had described her.

"I'm so sorry I wasn't here to greet you when you arrived this afternoon. Are you injured? My son said he nearly ran you down on the bridle path."

"I'm fine except for a few scratches I managed to get when I fell into the gorse. The jeans and long sleeves protected most of me."

"There's a nasty gouge on the back of your hand."

"My foot is more of a problem. I think a thorn may have pierced my shoe."

Aileen examined Lara's foot. "Right. The thorn has penetrated your shoe. I'll have to extract it before we remove your shoe. I'll try not to break it off in the process."

"Thank you. I hate to be a bother."

"It's no bother. I was a nurse before I married

Duncan and moved to Scotland. Your mother must have told you that's how we came to be friends. We were in nursing school together." Aileen was carefully working the thorn out of Lara's shoe as she spoke. "There it is." She held up the lethal-looking spike. "Now you can take off your shoe."

Lara did as instructed. Her foot was sore where the thorn had penetrated, and her shoe was wet with blood.

"I'll get you fixed up. I can't tell you how sorry I am. What an introduction to the Highlands! That son of mine with that half-wild stallion no one else can ride. He's a danger, that horse."

"He's the biggest horse I've ever seen," Lara said, thinking that Aileen's son was as much a danger as the horse. They were a well-matched pair.

Aileen poured peroxide on Lara's wounds to cleanse them. Then she applied antibiotic cream and bandaged them. "I think they shouldn't cause you any trouble. Are you sure there aren't any other thorns in you?

Lara sat up and winced. She had a thorn in her behind. How embarrassing.

Aileen laughed. She gently edged the thorn out. "There. That should be better. I'll just clean and dress it like the others. But you may be a bit uncomfortable sitting this evening."

Wonderful. It hurt to stand, and it hurt to sit. What an impression she would make at dinner. So much for grace and elegance.

Aileen put the first aid supplies back in their box. "I could have a dinner tray sent up to you if you're uncomfortable."

"Thank you, but I'd prefer to join you downstairs."

No way did she want to miss this opportunity to observe Aileen's son when he wasn't shouting at her or carrying her. Was he always so overpowering?

Aileen smiled. "Good. Oh, and we do dress for dinner. The tourists expect it."

Lara recalled reading something online about Scottish Castle stays. They were elegant, upscale lodging, where well-heeled tourists could stay and play and pay.

Alone in her room Lara pondered. What exactly did "dress for dinner" mean? Was it like they did on *Downton Abby*? Too bad if it did. There wasn't much call for that at home on the ranch. She was relieved in retrospect that her mother had insisted she include a serviceable long skirt and a couple of nice dresses. Left to her own device, she'd have traveled with nothing but jeans and sweaters. She pushed through the offerings in her bag.

She chose a soft swinging blue dress, and with it, wore an antique gold and amethyst necklace, a gift from her mother five years ago, on her twenty-first birthday. She brushed her hair, so it hung to her shoulders, thick and dark, with just enough natural wave to make it bounce. She took time to touch lipstick to her lips and to apply soft eye shadow in a shade that made her eyes an even warmer brown than they were. She tried to tell herself that taking time over her appearance had nothing to do with the very attractive man who had nearly run her down earlier.

Fifteen minutes later, she limped down the stairs and followed the sound of voices to the room where her rescuer had first taken her. She realized she didn't even know his name.

He was standing when she entered the room. She froze, mesmerized by the sight. He was wearing kilts. They were both wearing kilts, father and son, and they were as alike as two peas in a pod, both tall, with legs like young tree trunks, broad shoulders that strained their formal black jackets, both overpoweringly masculine while wearing skirts. Extraordinarily handsome men. Aileen's husband's hair, soft amber shot with silver, was not quite the blaze of his son's.

Aileen, dressed in a simple long black gown, hurried forward and drew her into their circle. "Duncan, this is Eileen MacInnes' daughter, Lara. Lara, my husband, Duncan. And I believe you've met my son, Iain."

During the next few minutes, Lara answered Aileen's and Duncan's questions about her mother and the ranch in Alberta, and about her own work as a kindergarten teacher. She responded automatically, her mind buzzing and her eyes feasting on the richness of her surroundings. The huge stone fireplace surmounted by what she took to be the Glendenning crest, the rich dark colors of antique tapestries on the walls, the high-backed oak chairs with their barley-twist arms. And portraits, more portraits wherever she turned.

Other guests were drifting into the drawing room now, the men in dinner jackets, the women in long gowns or short elegant cocktail dresses. Duncan and Aileen greeted them each in turn, making them welcome and offering them small glasses of whisky.

Lara found herself alone with Iain. "How old is this castle?" she asked.

"This new one was built in the late seventeen hundreds," he answered. "The original fourteenth-century castle was sacked, and the land confiscated by the Crown in the aftermath of the Jacobite Rising in 1745. Our branch of the Clan Glendenning fought for King George. But marauding gangs of the king's soldiers had no way of knowing we were not Jacobites. We were Scots and that was enough." He spoke as if he had personally witnessed the events of some three hundred years ago. "The land was restored to my family in the late seventeen hundreds. They lived in a small stone tenant house on the property until they recouped their fortunes through trade toward the end of the century, and this new house was built."

Lara laughed. "You can't imagine how strange it is to me to hear a castle dating from the eighteenth century referred to as 'this new house'."

"By the time they were married, me mother and father that is, the castle was once again in a pretty bad state of repair. They started working on it a bit at a time, installing central heating and hot water, private bathrooms, all the things tourists expect. And finally, twelve years ago, they listed the property as a Castle-Hotel. The income from that has allowed us to complete the restoration, and to maintain it. Can you even imagine what it costs to heat a place like this?"

Lara regarded the blazing fireplace. "But you use fireplaces, don't you?"

"They're more for show than for warmth. Our guests come from everywhere, and they pay verra well for the privilege of stayin' in a Scottish castle. They expect fireplaces and plaids and bagpipes, but they also expect heat and hot water on demand." His voice held a slightly bitter edge.

"You don't like it, do you, having to share your

home with strangers?"

"Can't say as I do. On one hand I hate puttin' on a show, but on t'other, it's only four months a year. And it helps majorly with the expenses of keeping this place together and with running the other parts of the operation."

"The other parts?"

"We have some seven hundred acres here and we run long-horned Scottish cattle. Ewan helps out, but I pretty much run that part. Then there are the stables. They're Ewan's and my responsibility with the help of some of the local lads. We have some of the finest horseflesh in Scotland."

Lara burst out laughing. "I grew up on a ranch in Alberta. Horses and cattle and cowboys. I can't believe I'm here on a ranch in Scotland, with horses and cattle and cowboys."

"Well, I canna' say I've ever heard Athdara Castle referred to as a ranch, and I've most certain never been called a cowboy." For the first time a grin lit his face.

There was a sudden din from the hallway. "That'll be our Ewan to pipe us in to dinner. Ye are with me."

The man Lara had last met in the stables, now dressed in kilts, entered the drawing room and stood for a moment, playing bagpipes, feet marching in place in time. He crossed the room as double doors to the dining room opened. Duncan Glendenning took his wife's arm and led her in, followed by Iain and Lara. The rest of the guests, some twenty in all, followed.

Later that night, Lara sank into the comfort of her bed, her head buzzing with the excitement of the evening, with all that had happened in the last six weeks. Had she done the right thing? Breaking her engagement to Edward, running off to Scotland?

She remembered Iain Glendenning and the tension and excitement she experienced just being in his arms as he carried her to her room, and her heart answered with a resounding "Yes!"

Chapter Two

The next morning, a large Scottish breakfast was set out on the sideboard in the dining room for people to help themselves. The Glendennings were not present, but Mrs. Murchison was in and out of the dining room, pouring coffee for the guests from a silver coffee urn, or tea from a Staffordshire china teapot, while making sure the chafing dishes were kept full.

In chatting with the other guests, Lara found they were a very international group, from Sweden and France and Spain, and the U.S., and even from her own country, a couple from Toronto. They were all leaving that day, continuing on their bus tour of Scottish Castles.

After breakfast, Lara wandered through the public rooms and found a small book-filled room with sunlight streaming in through long narrow windows, each with a cushioned window seat. A room too appealing to resist. She scanned the shelves for something to read and selected a novel by Sir Walter Scot, *Waverly,* an appropriate choice, written two hundred years ago about events of three hundred years ago in the Scotland of the Jacobite uprisings. She nestled into a window seat and was soon immersed in the pages, taken back to the time that had left its indelible mark on this small, unique country.

She was so deeply into the story that she wasn't

aware of him coming in.

"Hrumph."

Startled, she glanced up. Iain Glendenning loomed over her.

"Might ye care to go ridin' with me? That is if yer foot…"

She closed her book with a snap. "My foot is fine this morning. And yes, I'd love to go riding with you. I can't think of a better way to enjoy this beautiful countryside. If it's no bother."

"Nae bother. I must inspect the boundary lines and check on some of the distant cattle. It's the time of the year for the calving. I've chose a nice little mare for ye."

"Give me five minutes to change." Lara put the book back in its place in the shelf and left him standing there gazing after her.

Her heart pounded as she climbed the stairs. Why did he always appear so abrupt, so almost angry? Had his mother put him up to taking her along on this ride? Would he have preferred her to say "no"? Too bad. Lara loved riding and there was no way she was going to give up a chance to explore this countryside on horseback. Fortunately, the wound where the gorse had penetrated her behind was well padded with bandage and was high enough not to be in her saddle area. It shouldn't make riding uncomfortable.

She slipped into jeans and a sweater. There was a nip in the air. She'd packed her riding boots, hoping there might be opportunity to wear them. She combed her hair back in a ponytail and topped it with her Calgary Stampede cap. Glancing in the mirror, she decided she would be just fine, Alberta cowgirl that she was. If Iain Glendenning supposed she was going to appear in some fancy top hat riding gear, too bad. What had he been wearing when he accosted her in the library? She had no idea. Not kilts. She'd have noticed that. But she had been too flustered at his invitation to take in what he was wearing. She hadn't been aware of anything but those blazing blue eyes and that strong face and tousled, amber-colored hair. She wondered what it would be like to run her fingers through that hair.

Enough. Iain Glendenning could barely tolerate her presence. He was cordial to her only because she was a guest of his family. With a last quick glance in the mirror at her jeans—they did show off her long legs rather well, and her oversized sweater effectively hid everything else—she was out the door.

He was waiting in the front hall. "We'll gae out through the kitchen," he said. "It's closer to the stables." Without waiting for a reply, he headed for the back of the castle and out through the kitchen door.

Lara almost had to run to keep up with him. Once outside, he paused and waited for her. "I think ye'll like the stables. We have some very fine horseflesh here. I'm breedin' Thoroughbreds, both racin' horses and ridin' horses, and we now have a waiting list of clients who want them. We sell privately, of course, but once a year we hold an auction. 'Tis a fine time. People come from as far away as England and France and Spain for a chance to bid on our horses."

Lara was stunned. That was the most words she had yet heard out of Iain Glendenning's mouth. "You care about your horses."

"Aye, that I do. They are the best part of me life."

"If your Thunder is any example of what you're breeding, I don't wonder they're in demand."

"Well, Thunder now, he's a special case. I found him runnin' loose in the hills, his flanks scarred and bloody. Managed to capture him and fetch him home with me, bucking and rearing all the way. When I finally got him into a stall, he near kicked the door down. Our vet calmed him enough to treat his wounds and I put out the word, trying to locate his owner. Notices in the paper, his picture on billboards. Meanwhile, I was tryin' to gentle him."

"Gentle him?"

"You know. Speaking to him soft-like, in a loving way. Offering him carrots and apples. At first, he bit me, but I kept on trying. The day he let me stroke his nose I realized I had won the hardest part of the battle."

"But how… It isn't easy to break even a normal horse to the saddle. But one who had been maltreated?"

"Patience. That and determination. Finally, the day came when he let me harness him and lead him around the trainin' circle. I was that pleased."

Iain's voice turned dark, and he frowned. "That evenin' I got a phone call from his owner. His idea of breaking a horse was to beat him into submission. The idiot ended up in the hospital with several broken ribs and lucky to be alive. He told me to put the horse down."

"Oh no. What did you do?"

Iain smiled. "I persuaded him it was to his benefit to sell the beast to me. But to this day, nobody's been able to mount Thunder but me. He shies away from anyone else who approaches him. Horses have a long memory."

Lara had been so engrossed in Iain's tale she had failed to notice where they were. She turned from Iain to a compound with three long, low, concrete buildings.

Ewan was there to greet them. "I'm that glad ye are walkin'. That was a nasty fall ye had yesterday. Ye'll be wantin' the grand tour, then?"

Lara smiled at Ewan. "Yes, if you have the time. I'd love to see everything."

"Well, we raise Thoroughbreds here, as the laird may have told you. Most are sold as ridin' horses, but some end up as racehorses. The stallions are all housed in this building in the winter, but they're let out to pasture at this time of year. Better for them."

The familiar smells of hay and axle grease and harness oil assaulted Lara's senses. A deep whinny came from a stall halfway down the building.

Iain laughed. "Coming," he called. Turning to Lara he said, "Thunder is in his stall. He has what ye might call a wee problem playing well with others. Come and meet him."

Lara followed Iain. He took an apple out of his pocket and offered it to the horse, who nibbled it and brushed his head against Iain's hand.

Without thinking Lara raised her hand to stroke the horse.

His ears went back, flat against his head. She drew her hand back slowly, then, murmuring soft words, stroked him.

"He let you touch him. That's incredible."

"I've been around horses all my life. I think they sense when someone likes them."

Leaving Thunder munching on his apple, they followed Ewan out of the stable to another building.

"This is where we house the mares due to foal. We can monitor them more closely this way, and deal with problems if they occur. This larger stall is a special foaling stall." Ewan pointed to the corner of the stall. "The webcam? That was Iain's idea. It's connected both to the house and to my rooms over the stables. We can observe when a mare lies down in a position to foal. I have some trainin' as a large animal vet, but if there's a serious problem, we have a vet nearby on call." There was pride in Ewan's voice.

"Our mares generally foal out in the fields in the spring," Lara said. "This is amazing."

Iain took her hand and led her down the aisle to the farthest stall. "Here's our newest addition."

"Oh! She's beautiful." A tiny, wobbly foal stood nursing as its mother licked and nuzzled it. Lara stood, enchanted at the sight.

"Ye really like horses, don't ye?" Iain sounded surprised.

"Of course, I like horses. I've been around them all my life."

"It's just I never met a lass before who liked horses. Oh, some of them know how to ride, but they don't much care for any of the rest of it." He led her out of the stable. His hand was large and warm and comfortable on hers.

"Now this next smaller building," Ewan said, once outside, "is the breedin' shed. Nothing goin' on there now. But when they come into season, mares are brought here to be bred to our best Thoroughbreds."

"It all sounds very scientific. I'm afraid our horses usually breed in the wild as they do everything else. But of course, most of ours are Quarter Horses. They come from rugged stock."

"There's a lot to be said for rugged stock." Iain smiled down at her. "Whether it's horses or people. Quarter Horses are a smaller breed, aren't they?"

"Small but incredibly tough. They're solid muscle. They have to be tough to survive Alberta winters."

A few minutes later they had their horses saddled and ready. Iain put his foot in the stirrup and swung up onto Thunder's massive back.

Lara did the same with her considerably smaller mare. She stroked her mount's neck. "What's her name?"

"Flora."

"Nice to meet you, Flora."

The sun had burnt off the morning mist, leaving the air sweet and clean. The scent of wet earth and leaves surrounded them as they cantered across the green fields. In the distance, the hills rose in a purple haze against a fierce blue sky.

"Here we are. The first of the herd."

Lara's mouth dropped open. They were like no cows she had ever known. Smaller than any cattle in Alberta, they were covered with long shaggy red hair, hanging almost to the ground, and they had snub noses and long, long curved horns.

"They're Highland cattle, and they have a history as old as this country's. When I was a boy, these were almost the only cattle you found in Scotland. But somewhere along the way, farmers discovered they could make more profit from bigger, heavier cattle. More meat to be had from Hereford and Angus. Gradually our unique Scottish breed began to disappear. There are a few on Skye. But if you want to find a real herd, you pretty much have to visit Balmoral. The Queen keeps them."

"So?"

"So, I decided we would have only real Scots cattle here. They're going to disappear if someone isn't purposely breeding them."

"Do you sell them for their meat?"

Iain laughed. "Weel, that was the plan. But so far, I'm just trying to increase the herd. Someday when the herd is of sufficient size…"

Lara laughed. "They're pets. They're not beef cattle, they're pets!"

Iain had the grace to blush. Then he said, "They are a passion of mine. I dinna want them to them disappear from the Highlands as so many other species have. I hope to interest others in raising them. But no. I won't be selling them for their meat anytime soon."

"That's what you meant when you said the B&B helps support other parts of the operation."

"Aye. That's what I meant. But I wouldn't want you to think I don't contribute. The Thoroughbreds I raise bring in a goodly profit every year. It's a fine balancing act, keeping a property like this solvent."

Lara was reminded that this was work for Iain as he stopped periodically to check on the herds grazing on the hillsides among the gorse, bracken, and heather.

On their way back to the stables, Lara spotted a small stone cottage in the distance. "What is that building? It looks very old."

"It is. It dates from the fourteen hundreds, originally a tenant house," Iain told her. "I grew up in it. At one point there were thirty or so tenant houses like it on Glendenning land. They were all destroyed by the British in the aftermath of the Jacobite Rebellion of 1745. You can find their foundations outlined in stone. Not sure why they left the one standing."

"But they didn't destroy the castle?"

"They mucked it up a bit, but in the end, they left it standing. Me Glendenning ancestors restored it in the eighteenth century, but by the twenty-first, the castle was again uninhabitable. Me mother and father renovated it, room by room, until it's as it is today, and we lived in that cottage while they did it."

Lara considered what he'd said. He knew where he came from. His ancestors had inhabited this land for centuries. Where had her family, the MacInnes, been four hundred ago? In Scotland, but where?

They rode on, Lara's mind chewing on what Iain had told her.

A sudden shower caught them unaware. "It happens all the time here," Iain laughed. "Think on it as wet sunshine."

They took shelter in a grove of trees, dismounting and tethering their horses. They sat on the stump of an old felled pine.

"Is it verra different where you come from?" he said, peering down at her.

"Alberta? Oh, it's very different. In the first place this shower would probably have been snow in Alberta. Or worse, hail."

"That sounds very harsh."

"It's not so bad. We don't usually have heavy snow. It's a dry climate. And the light in the prairies is brilliant. You can see for miles. There is a sense of endless space."

"Aye? It is hard to imagine. The endless space I

mean. Here, we're all about boundaries. And the horses and cattle thrive there?"

"We don't raise horses the way you do. At least not on our ranch. Our Quarter Horses are work horses. We mainly raise cattle. My family has had a cattle ranch since the mid-eighteen hundreds. My very-great grandfather, Lachlan, came to Canada from Scotland in eighteen fifty-five. He landed in Quebec, and when the government offered land grants in the west to settlers, he traveled west to Alberta and pioneered the ranch I grew up on."

Iain was quiet for a few minutes. When he spoke, his voice held a trace of bitterness. "In the years after the last Jacobite Uprising, many Scots emigrated to Canada or Australia. Some were deported. They were the lucky ones. They were deported instead of being hanged. Others left because their homes and livelihood were destroyed by the British." Iain rubbed his jaw. "Do ye ken what took your ancestor to Canada?"

"Not really. That's one reason I'm here. I want to find out what I can about Lachlan MacInnes, about the MacInnes Clan in Scotland. I don't think he left because of the lost Jacobite cause. He left more than a hundred years after the Battle of Culloden."

"Ye ken yer Scottish history."

"Only as it touches on the MacInnes Clan. It's been passed down in the family."

"Then ye must know yer family was from the Highlands. And in all likelihood, they were Jacobites."

"What about the Glendennings?"

"Ach…we're a mixed bag. Some of us were Jacobites, most were loyal to the Hanoverian King Geordie. It's thanks to the ones who fought for the

English King that Athdara Castle is still standing."

"And now? What do you think about the possible separation of Scotland from England now?"

"We lost that chance with the referendum." He tone was neutral. "Although we well may have another chance. Brexit is no' popular with Scots."

He stood and offered her his hand. "Enough about politics. The sun is shining again. We'd best get gaeing."

Six hours later Lara was back in her room, grateful for the hot water available for her bath. She ached in every bone. Since starting to teach, she had ridden only on weekends, and never for so long at a time or over such hilly terrain. Still, it was an exhilarating experience, riding beside Iain Glendenning.

For one brief moment, when he was helping her dismount Flora, she had been sure he was going to kiss her. But the moment passed. What would her reaction have been? She wasn't sure. He was a very attractive man.

****

There were no B&B guests that night, and Mrs. Murchison had the night off, so Lara joined the family at the big pine table in the kitchen. Aileen put the warm serving dishes on the table to be passed family style, while Duncan poured cider or ale into the glasses.

"I'm surprised you have a night with no guests during the tourist season," Lara commented.

"We arranged Mondays to be our free night. All of our business comes from bus tours, so we were able to negotiate that."

"Don't you ever get independent travelers?"

"We choose not to. The tours keep us full. And

truthfully, tour groups are much less trouble. Their guides take care of any and all problems. All we have to do is provide them with bed and bath and a suitably Scottish surrounding."

Lara laughed. "The kilts and the bagpipes."

Duncan broke in, "I wouldna' want you to think we use our kilts and our pipes only for the entertainment of tourists. They're a part of our heritage and a part of our lives. When we celebrate Christmas with our friends and neighbors, we all wear our colors. And we have pipers as well as some local fiddlers for the dancin'."

Iain grinned. "It's a grand occasion. I wish ye could be here for it."

Later, Lara helped Aileen load the dishwasher and wash up the pots and pans. "I've enjoyed the last three days here more than I can say. And I'm so grateful to you and Duncan for taking me in. But I know I'm taking up space you need for your tour guests. Tomorrow I must start searching for someplace else to stay."

Aileen draped the tea towel over the handle of the Aga. "It's been a pleasure having you here, but I'm afraid your room is booked, beginning next Friday." She paused. "Duncan had an idea…"

"Yes?"

"The stone cottage…the one we lived in while we were renovating the castle…"

"You mean I could rent it? How absolutely wonderful!" Lara hugged the older woman impulsively.

"Rent it? Absolutely not. It's in no condition to be rented. There's no heat but from fireplaces, and no hot water unless you run the generator or heat it on the stove. I'm afraid it will need a thorough cleaning, and all in all it would be more like camping than like staying in a B&B. I told Duncan you're a Canadian lass who's used to all the modern conveniences, but he said you might enjoy the experience. But as to renting it? No. It's yours for the summer if you want it."

"Oh, thank you. I do want it. A cottage all my own! Iain said the original part of it goes back to the fourteen hundreds?"

"That it does. It's a solid house, built to last. But it hasn't been lived in for quite some time. Iain says he'll help you get it cleaned and fit for habitation if you're interested."

Lara laughed. "Great." The mere notion of working side by side on the house with Iain set a tingling down Lara's spine.

Chapter Three

The next morning Iain was waiting in the kitchen when she came down to breakfast. "Ye sleep late for a cowgirl. We'll no get the cottage fit to live in by Friday if ye don't get a move on."

Lara laughed. "It's not yet eight o'clock. How long have you been waiting?"

"Let's just say I'm almost ready for lunch." He held up a basket. "I've packed it for us, so we won't lose any more of the day."

"You packed us a lunch?" Lara laughed. "Then I'd better eat breakfast fast so we can be on our way."

"There's porridge, hot on the stove, and fresh coffee made and some scones in the warming oven." He examined her from head to foot and nodded. "Ye are dressed for the job. Ye'll need that warm sweater. The cottage has been closed for a long time. It will be cold and damp until I get the fireplaces going."

He strode to the kitchen door. "I'll saddle the horses and bring them around while ye eat."

Lara settled for a scone with jam and a quick cup of coffee. From the sound of it, lunch would be early. She grabbed another scone to eat on the run and opened the door just as Iain arrived on Thunder and leading Flora.

An hour later they were at the stone wall and picket gate to the cottage. Iain tethered the two horses as Lara stood and gazed at the little stone house. Ivy traced over the walls, and the old slate roof had some moss on it. Chimneys rose on both sides of the cottage. A study in symmetry, the house had windows placed in mirror image of each other, two dormers equally placed on the upper level, and a front door squarely in the middle. Very Scottish; solid and enduring, like the Scots.

Iain joined her and saw her eyes on at the roof. "That's new," he said. "Put on sometime in the last hundred years to replace the old thatched one."

"Of course. New." The Scottish view of what was new and what was old never ceased to amuse Lara.

Iain took a large iron key out of his pocket. "I suggest you always keep this key on a peg in the kitchen. 'Tis original to the house and it would be verra difficult to replace it today."

"You can't mean this key is six hundred years old?"

"Aye. It is that."

"But it has no rust or deterioration."

"It's been kept well cleaned and oiled. The lock as well. But in truth ye don't need to lock yer doors. Nobody will bother ye here. We only had it locked because no one was living in it." He turned the key in the lock and swung the door open, ushering Lara in, and put the key on the hook by the door.

She stood just inside the front door and glanced around. Dust motes danced in the sunlight streaming through the two front windows. She was standing in one big room. Furniture was shrouded in white dust covers, giving the whole a rather ghostly appearance. A large stone fireplace dominated one wall. The floor was stone. It would be cold underfoot. She'd need to think about getting some small rugs for warmth.

A doorway led to the back of the house. She headed for it, Iain following. She found herself in a kitchen almost as large as the front room. Here the floor was brick. Against the stone outer wall of the house stood a stove, an Aga almost as large as the one in the castle. Lara loved these huge old iron stoves. So different from anything she had ever cooked on in Canada.

Iain followed her gaze. "We'll get the Aga workin' tomorrow. It's a newer model. Operates on propane, it does."

"Your mother said the Aga stays on all the time?"

"Aye. Once up and running, it stays on the ready. And it keeps the whole kitchen warm. That rocking chair nearby? That was me mother's favorite spot when we were living here."

Lara sat and rocked for a moment. "I think it may well be mine. Bedrooms?"

"Two bedrooms upstairs. And an attic above. If ye need any furniture, check the attic first. It's crammed full of old pieces me mother and others before her didna' want to dispose of but were clutterin' the living space."

A flight of narrow wood steps, each worn in the middle, circled up from the kitchen to the floor above. The floors on this level were made of wide pine planks, mellowed with age.

He led her first to a room at the front of the house.

"Oh!" Lara gave an involuntary intake of breath. "Lovely." A four-poster bed had what appeared to be a feather bolster for a mattress. Beside it, a small table held an oil lamp protected by a tall glass chimney. The stone walls in this room had been plastered over, and someone, probably a hundred or more years ago, had papered them in a soft rosebud design. A very feminine bedroom. Best of all, there were two dormer windows opening out to the view. In her imagination, a warm rug covered the floor by the bed and white cotton curtains fluttered at the deep-set windows. She was going to have fun with this house, even if it were hers for only two months.

"No chest of drawers, but there is this." Iain pointed to a tall piece of furniture on the wall opposite the bed. The exterior of the dark oak cabinet was embellished with barley twist sides and round fat finials at the corners.

She opened the doors. Inside there were four shelves and a narrow bar for hanging clothes. "That is far more storage space than I need. I didn't pack many clothes. And this room is lovely."

"I think the feather bed will have to go." Iain said. "I'm afraid some wee critter has taken up residence in it in the last ten years."

"Oh, dear. It's so inviting."

"Aye. I'm sure the mice found it inviting, too." He picked it up and showed her a fist-sized hole with feathers trickling out.

Lara laughed. "Point taken."

They strolled back into the hallway. There was a small bathroom, with a washbasin, toilet, and shower. Lara turned on the sink tap. Nothing happened.

"Ye'll no get water until I've turned on the generator and the pump. I'll do that as soon as we go back downstairs."

The other bedroom was a mirror image of the front

one, but simpler, with dark oak furniture and walls of stone.

"This was my room." Iain examined the bolster on the bed. "Me feather bed appears to have fared better. We can hang it out the window to air out and then decide whether it's usable." He opened the casement window wide. "It's a bonnie day. The sun should freshen it." He hoisted the large feather bed up and set it across the window sill. "If you still want a feather bed, this one will fit on the frame in the front room."

"Thank you. I'd like to give it a try."

"Well, if ye decide ye want a modern mattress, we can take a trip to Edinburgh to buy one."

Both bedrooms had fireplaces. She remembered Iain's mother telling her fireplaces were the only source of heat. She'd probably use the one in her bedroom. Even in June, the night temperatures were low.

"Let's start with the kitchen." Iain headed downstairs. "I'll scrub down the floors while ye tackle the stove and sink. The windows could use a washing, too. But first I'll need get the generator and pump goin'."

Lara followed him outdoors to a small shed by the side of the house.

"They had no power and no runnin' water here or in the castle when me da' was a boy. Water had to be pumped from a well, candles and kerosene lamps provided light, and fireplaces, heat. Me da' put in the generator and pump here when he married me mother. There was electricity to the castle by that time, but it needed so much work they chose to live here while they renovated the castle."

The generator started with a loud hum and Iain

plugged in the pump.

"Ye should be quite comfortable here now. Ye'll have light and runnin' water as long as the generator is runnin'. But ye'll have to use fireplaces for heat. There's a stack of wood just outside the back door. Ye ken how to start a fire?"

"Of course. Camping was a part of my childhood. I can build a fire."

"If ye have trouble with anything, just let me know. Now let's get to work."

They returned to the house and Iain found buckets and scrub brushes. Two hours later, the kitchen was gleaming.

Iain scanned the area. "Ready to tackle the parlor?"

"Sure."

Lara yanked off the closest dust cover. Immediately dust filled the air. She coughed and sputtered until her eyes watered. "Sorry!"

Iain laughed in the middle of a cough. "Slowly. Take them off, folding them inward as ye go, to contain the dust. Then put each one outside before tackling the next. No sense in adding to the dust already in the air here."

"You've done this before."

"Aye. We had a mammoth job to do on the castle. We had considerable outside help but still"—he grinned—"ye might say I have a master's degree in house cleaning."

At four in the afternoon they stopped for the day. Iain had set up and lit the fireplaces both upstairs and down. The pervading dampness of some hours ago was dispelled.

They plopped down in two chairs in the kitchen

and Iain opened the basket of food he had assembled. He set cider, cheese, bread, sausage, and shortbread out on the table. Lara lit into the feast with gusto.

"I like a woman who isn't afeared to eat," Iain said, munching on a chunk of bread with sausage. "So many are forever dieting." He inspected her up and down. "Ye for certain have no need to diet."

Lara laughed out loud. There was nothing subtle about Iain Glendenning. He said what he was thinking without worrying about how socially correct it might be. He was a breath of fresh air after her ever-so-proper ex-fiancé.

He looked puzzled. "Did I say something wrong? Me mam says I have the manners of a dock worker."

"No," Lara laughed. "I love the way you speak without worrying about what you say. It's natural and unaffected."

Iain put his food down on the table and then took hers out of her hand. He leaned over and touched her face, his fingers gliding over her features. Then his lips touched hers, gently, experimentally.

He sat back. "Sorry. I've been wantin' to do that ever since I pulled ye out of the gorse."

Flustered, Lara said, "It's quite all right. I've been wanting you to do that ever since you pulled me out of the gorse."

"That's good then." He stood. "We have to get back and change. Drinks at seven, dinner at eight. Tourists."

"I'd almost forgotten. Thank you for all your help today."

"'Twas nae bother. I enjoyed it." He grinned. "Especially the last bit."

****

By the end of the week, the cottage was ready, and Lara settled in. Aileen had invited her to continue taking dinners at the castle, saying one more made no difference when they were serving so many. Lara accepted, because it gave her more time with Iain.

Iain had given her the gentle little mare, Flora, to use while she was there.

She was going to miss Iain. She'd been with him all day every day while they were working on the cottage, but now the work was done, and he no longer had any reason to be here with her. He had his own work to do. She could still be with him, chat with him, when they were waiting for Ewan to pipe them in to dinner. But their conversation was brief and stilted, surrounded as they were by his mother and father and eighteen or twenty other people.

She had been staying in the cottage four days when he said to her over dinner, "I'm gaeing to the village tomorrow to pick up some supplies. Would ye care to come with me?"

"I'd love to, thank you. I need everything in the way of groceries. The supply your mother gave me has just about run out."

"That's settled then. I'll pick you up at nine in the Land Rover."

****

Glendenning Village consisted of one long strip of houses and shops along a center street. At the far end, a narrow stone bridge crossed a rushing stream. A few houses straggled up the hills on either side the main road, alongside the stream. Lara was struck by how similar all the Scottish houses were to one another. All were made of flat cut gray stone. All had symmetrically placed doors and windows, as if one architect had designed the whole country.

She surveyed the main street of the village. There was nothing remotely resembling a supermarket. In its place, there was a greengrocer, a butcher shop, a florist, two tea shops, a pharmacy and a bakery.

"Where's the seafood shop? Where do you get that wonderful salmon we've had on the menu almost every night, fresh or smoked, as either a main course or an appetizer?"

Iain laughed. "Yon river. Ye might say we have a perpetual source."

He led her from one shop to the next, three roasts of lamb for tonight's dinner, a huge sack of potatoes, fresh cream and butter, four dozen eggs. All would be delivered before noon.

"What about salad greens? They've been wonderful every night."

"Aye. They're from our kitchen garden."

****

Lara had been living in the cottage a week. Her days had taken on a particular rhythm. She'd take an early morning ride into the village on Flora. There she'd buy warm fresh bread and fruit and cheese for her breakfast. She did not share the Scots' love of porridge. Then she'd return to the cottage and, if the day was not too brisk or raining, she'd take a kitchen chair outside and have her breakfast where she could eat her bread and drink her coffee with the warmth of the sun on her face. Where she could gaze at the brilliant green hills, splashed with purple heather and yellow gorse, so different from the stark, rugged mountains she had grown up with.

She had started keeping a journal of her days. Knowing they would come to an end with the end of summer, she wanted to record both the beauty around her and her reactions to it. And she wrote about Iain Glendenning. They had been together frequently since that day, the day he kissed her. Often, he stopped by to ask if she'd like to go riding with him as he checked on his far-flung herds. She always said yes. On their rides he could be silent for long periods, but she never minded that. They enjoyed each other's company without needing to talk. He had never kissed her again, never made reference to what to her had marked an important change in their relationship.

She wasn't sure what she expected, but she had not expected this—his acting as if nothing had happened.

She was sitting outside her kitchen door, writing in her journal, absorbed in expressing her frustration at Iain's behavior, when a shadow fell across her page.

He leaned down and brushed her hair away from her face. "'Tis nae a good position for writing. Ye have need of a desk, or at least a small writing table."

Flustered she stared up at him. "How did you get here? I didn't hear you."

"Ye wouldn't have heard a herd of cattle on the move, ye were so engrossed in what ye were writing. Thunder's tethered by the gate."

Lara closed her journal with a snap. "Do you have time to come in for a coffee or a cup of tea? I have fresh bread from the bakery, and I have some honey from the village."

"Aye. I have time." He brushed her hair back again. He kissed her. A light brush of his lips across hers. Then a more lingering kiss. "I wasn't sure I remembered correctly. I did."

"Oh?"

"Shall we see if we I can find ye something to write on? Ye can put the kettle on. I wouldn't object if ye could put together something for me to eat while I'm in the attic."

"Not on your life! I've been dying to explore the attic, but I didn't think it right with you not here. I'll feed you after."

They climbed upstairs together, Lara pausing just long enough to put her journal on the table beside her bed.

The door at the top of the stairs creaked when Iain opened it. Dust rose in clouds as they stepped into the small space. "Watch yer head. We're under the eaves."

Furniture was piled everywhere.

"Over there." Iain scrambled across two upended chairs. "There," he said. "Behind that chest. Help me shift the chest."

Lara did as instructed, but her attention was riveted on the chest, old, very old, made of wood, with frayed leather straps around it. A discolored brass latch sat squarely on the front.

"Here." Iain hauled a delicate wood desk out and set it down in front of Lara. "Will this do?" He took a handkerchief out of his back pocket and rubbed it across the top of the table, displaying swirling patterns of inlaid wood, lighter wood against darker.

"It's absolutely beautiful."

"Do ye have need of a chair?"

"No. I have several chairs downstairs." She answered almost absently, her eyes returning to the chest. She was drawn to it for some reason.

Iain's eyes followed hers. "Would ye like to know what's in it?"

"Oh, yes."

"Nae problem." He took out his penknife and jiggled it about in the keyhole. The lock gave a satisfying clunk and sprang open.

Iain lifted the heavy lid.

Lara leaned forward and gently unfolded a layer of tissue. A faint scent of lavender wafted up from folds of pale blue silk. She lifted it out of the trunk. A woman's dress, in a size not unlike her own. She held it up against herself. The low neckline was encrusted with seed pearls, and lace fell in a cascade from the sleeves.

Iain drew his breath in.

"What's wrong? I'm sorry. I shouldn't have disturbed the contents of the trunk."

"No. It's nae that. It's just for a moment I was sure I'd seen that dress before."

"Unlikely." Lara laughed. "I think from the style it dates from the mid-eighteen hundreds."

"Aye." He shook his head and a frown crossed his features. "But I've seen someone wearin' that dress. I need to think on it. It will come."

He touched the silk of the dress. "Would ye mind taking it downstairs? Hang it up so the folds fall out. I'd like to see ye wearin' it sometime."

"Do you really think I should? I don't know much about period clothing, but I think this should be in a museum."

"What else is in there?"

Lara put the blue dress carefully aside and lifted another. "This one's pale pink muslin. Our lady was into pastels." She held it up against her. "Do you recognize this one?"

"No."

"Or this one?" She took out a confection of peach-colored sarcenet and lace.

"No. Anything else in there?" He peered in and took out a thin white garment with tight short sleeves and a low neckline. "What's this?"

"I think it's worn under the dress, like a slip, or petticoat. The tucks and lace on the hemline? They're meant to show. Remember, streets were not very clean in those days. A woman had to lift the delicate silk of her dress to get into a carriage or to get from her doorway to her carriage. Her petticoat showed, hence the lace and tucks."

"How do ye ken such things?"

"I've read Jane Austin."

"Well, ye'd best take that along, too, if we're goin' for authenticity."

He reached in again and came up with a short, laced-up garment with stiff stays covered by cotton padding.

Lara laughed. "That's meant to make the waist smaller and push up the—" She stopped, embarrassed. "There is no way I'm putting that on, no matter what. You can just forget it." She took the garment from him and buried it deep in the trunk. Her fingers touched something…a book? She drew it out. Not one book, five books covered in frayed silk and tied together with pink satin ribbon. She untied the ribbon.

"They're journals. Diaries." She opened the first volume. "*Edinburgh, 1850,* and a name, *Elspeth Glendenning*. She must be an ancestor of yours."

"Could be. There were a pile of them."

Lara thumbed carefully though the first one. Suddenly her eyes riveted on a page. "My name is in here. My great, great, grandfather's name I mean, Lachlan MacInnes. I should love to read these. Do you think your parents would mind? I mean, they could be rather personal."

"There's no reason my parents would object. After all, they were written well over a hundred and fifty years ago. Any scandal they might contain is long forgot. By all means read them."

He hoisted the little table up. "But maybe ye could help me get this down two flights of steps first. I'll take it outside and clean it."

Later, with the little desk polished to a soft gleam and placed against a window in her bedroom, Lara and Iain sat at the kitchen table near the warmth of the old Aga to share a lunch of fresh bread and cheese.

"Have ye cooked anythin' on it yet?"

"The Aga? Of course I have. I love the way it's never off. There's always an oven ready for baking and another to keep food warm. And two large cooking surfaces on top always at constant temperatures. And as if that weren't enough, it keeps this whole part of the house warm. I sit in your mother's rocking chair beside it and read by the hour."

"Aye. But can ye cook on it?"

"You could come for dinner tonight and find out for yourself. After all, it's Monday, your free night. No tourists to have to put on a show for."

Iain sat back and grinned.

Lara burst out laughing. "You were just angling for a dinner invitation, weren't you?"

"Seems to have worked. What time?"

Lara's mind raced. She'd have to go back to the village to get the ingredients for whatever she decided to make. "Maybe seven o'clock?"

"Seven it is. And now I'd best get back to work or I'll be hearin' about it from Ewan."

He stood and gazed at her for a moment, then he was gone.

She gave a little laugh. What an exasperating man.

The dinner that evening was a rousing success. Lara had prepared some of the old favorites from her days helping out in the ranch kitchen. Two large steaks, baked beans, corn bread and spinach, barely cooked, just immersed in hot water and then dressed with a bit of bacon fat and vinegar.

Iain ate every bite on his over-filled plate. He ate with total concentration and no conversation. When he had finished everything, he eyed the half steak pushed to one side on Lara's plate. "Are ye no goin' to eat that?"

"I'm afraid I can't. I'm much too full."

Without a word he took it onto his plate and demolished it.

He pushed his chair back with a sigh. "'Tis a relief to eat without having to make idle chit-chat with guests who always have the same questions. Do ye nae teach history in those schools of yours in America?"

"Not America, I'm from Canada. And not much. Certainly not much about Scottish history."

"Aye. Weel, we're a small country. And nae even properly a country. We sit under a British flag." The corners of his mouth turned down.

"But you do have your own Parliament."

"Aye. There is that. And we print our own money, too, the Scottish Pound." He took another piece of corn bread off the serving dish. "This is a peculiar substitute for scones, but I like it."

Lara laughed. "So, you now know I can cook on an Aga."

"Aye, lass. That ye can."

Side by side, they washed and put away the dishes. Lara's mind flashed briefly back to her former fiancé, who would never have dreamed of lifting a hand in the kitchen.

As if he could read her mind, he asked, "How is ye are neither wed nor pledged at yer age?"

Lara laughed. Whatever Iain Glendenning was, he was not subtle. "I was engaged to a doctor in Calgary. I broke off our engagement in May. I took this trip to get away from the repercussions."

"How'd ye do that? Break yer word to marry, I mean. It can't have been easy."

Her mind drifted back to that last unpleasant scene with Edward. No. It had been anything but easy. "My fiancé wanted to set the date of our wedding to coincide with a medical conference in Toronto. No consultation, no conversation. That was just the last straw. I'd been aware for some time I didn't love him, didn't want to be his wife. Why did I wait so long to break off the relationship? Pure cowardice. I was afraid there would be a scene."

"Aye. I know what it is to be afeared of a scene." Iain's voice broke through her reminiscences. "But what did ye actually say to him?"

"I told him I'd considered it for a long time, and he was just the wrong man for me. Then I slipped the

diamond off my finger and slid across the table to him."
She gave a wry laugh. "His main concern was what
people would say."

"But what made ye finally break it off?"

"Some antiquated notion of romantic love," Lara
said, smiling. "At least that's what Edward called it."

"Do ye regret it?"

"Not for a moment," Lara replied. "Do you believe
in love? I don't mean affection, or friendship, or a long
history together, or even sexual attraction. I mean the
kind of intense, deep love that makes two people *have*
to be together? That *not* to be together is unthinkable?"

Iain was silent for a long time. Then, without any
of his usual bantering tone, he said, "I would nae have
believed so until verra recent. Did ye no love him?"

Lara sighed and gazed directly at Iain. "Not like
that. Not the way I want to love the man I marry. My
fiancé was unused to being thwarted. More than once
he swayed me by sheer force of his will. I realized if I
wavered, I was lost. So, I told him I was not going to
marry him…and then I ran like hell before I could
change my mind."

Iain slapped his hands on the table and laughed
until he had tears in his eyes. When he had his laughter
under control, he wiped the tears of mirth from his eyes
and said, "I can for certain understand the runnin' part!"

He stood. "I've laid a fire in yer bedroom. All ye
need to do is light it."

"Thank you. I meant to do it myself earlier but…"

"But ye were cooking. And a fine meal it was. I
must be gaeing now. I have an early mornin'
tomorrow."

At the door he kissed her. The kiss started out as a

gentle, almost perfunctory one, then he sighed and bent down to take more. Pulling her against him, he kissed her until she was breathless. Her arms came around him of their own volition. When he broke away, they stood speechless, staring at each other. Then he turned and strode swiftly to the gate where Thunder was tethered. He rode away without a backward glance.

The man was insufferable. Could he not say anything about what was happening between them? Or perhaps nothing was happening from his perspective. From hers, she admitted ruefully to herself, she was falling in love.

Slowly she made her way upstairs. She shivered in the chill as she knelt to light the fire Iain had laid for her, and then lit her bedside oil lamp. Snuggling under the down duvet, she picked up the first volume of Elspeth Glendenning's diaries. The year was 1850. Lara skimmed through the early pages describing household duties and social calls and rather dull days until she came to June 30th.

Today is my birthday. I am twenty-two years old. It is hard to believe I have been able to avoid the pitfalls of marriage for so long. Dear Papa has not been too happy with my desire to remain single, but I know he would be lonely without me. How fortunate I am that Great Aunt Hermione left me a trust with a small annual income that makes it possible for me to be truly independent. To say 'no' to the suitors Papa parades before me. They are fewer in number each year. And now I am almost beyond marriageable age.

I fail to understand the desirability of marriage. I have watched my girlhood friends succumb to it. Some have fared well enough, but it appears to me, at best, a form of servitude. I observe that wives are expected to not to have opinions, to defer to their husbands in all things, to run their households and bear their children and have no life of their own. I believe Mary Ellen's husband, duke that he may be, abuses her. I have seen bruises on her face and arms. No. Not for me wedded bliss.

I oversee Papa's household but that takes little time. Of course, I am expected to make social calls and entertain occasionally as Papa's hostess, but by and large my time is my own. I am free to wander in the countryside with only my maid, Kincaid, with me. To sketch and paint as I love to do. What matter if no one ever sets eyes my work? I paint for the sheer joy of doing it.

July 1, 1850

How annoying! Just when I had such a nice routine that allowed me freedom every morning after breakfast, I find I must now pack up and take myself off to Nairn. Of course, Kincaid will do the packing, but it is such a nuisance to have to leave home. Cousin Cumina will expect me to attend soirees and teas and will introduce me to every eligible male in the vicinity and I shall never have a moment to myself.

But it will be fun to go shopping there. The boats cross regularly from France with goods we don't have in Edinburgh. I need new gloves. I quite ruined my best ones last week by spilling watercolor paint on them.

Father has given me an errand...there are some papers he wants me to retrieve that he doesn't wish to entrust to the post. It is little enough to do for him. He is so patient with my foibles.

Lara yawned, closed the diary, and placed it on her

nightstand. Elspeth Glendenning appeared to lead a very ordinary life considering that she lived in the mid-nineteenth century. Lara blew out her lamp and snuggled down into her bed.

Sleep would not come. She kept reliving Ian's kiss and thinking about Elspeth Glendenning's desire to remain single, a rather unusual attitude for a woman of her period.

Lara gave up trying to sleep, pushed herself up in the bed, lit her lamp and opened Elspeth Glendenning's journal again. She leafed through the pages.

18 July 1850

Today was most the most exciting day of my life, if I am to admit the truth. And I met a man. A man different from any I've met before.

Chapter Four

The Past

18 July 1850

I met a man. A man different from any I've met before. I was on the way home, from Nairn to Edinburgh, when the most terrifying event occurred…

****

Lachlan MacInnes sat still as a statue on his stallion, Bailoch, on the crest of the hill, his gilly, Hamish, close behind him, on an only slightly smaller horse. The Highlander surveyed the MacInnes lands, as far as the eye could see, to the winding carriage road and rushing river below him. The mountains in the distance were a brilliant green against the azure of the sky. It promised to be a bonnie day.

He had turned his mount's head toward home when a loud clattering rose from below. He stopped and scanned the carriage road. Some fool driver was traveling much too fast. He was likely to end up in the river at the far bend if he wasn't careful.

Motioning for his gilly to follow, Lachlan started weaving his way through bush and bracken down the almost perpendicular face of the hill. As he watched, incredulous, a ponderous old landau rounded the first curve on two wheels. Where the driver should have been, controlling the horses, the seat was empty.

Driverless, the panicked horses were racing full tilt toward destruction.

Once on the coach road, Lachlan urged Bailoch to a full gallop. If he could overtake the runaway horses, he might be able to bring them under control before they flung themselves and the coach into the river. He was alongside the horses, trying to grasp their reins when the old-fashioned carriage careened around the curve, tilted precariously, and plunged down the bank. The air was filled with the high-pitched screams of panicked horses.

Dismounting Bailoch, Lachlan scrambled down the bank, Hamish close behind him. Hamish cut the whinnying horses loose from their harnesses with his dirk. One of the bays scrambled up and stood, trembling, as the gilly patted her and soothed her with soft Gaelic phrases. The other shuddered her last breath and was dead where she lay in a twisted mass of harness and splintered wood.

Lachlan surveyed the overturned carriage. No sounds from within. Were there no passengers? He brought Bailoch closer to the coach and mounted so he could get to the door, resting high in the air, face to the sky. Had the passengers been knocked unconscious in the accident? Or was there no one inside?

He climbed on top of the landau and wrenched the door open. At first all he could see was a flurry of petticoats. With shock, he registered there was a woman trapped between the seat and the far wall.

"Ho down there! Are ye injured?"

Where he expected hysterics, the voice answering him sounded merely annoyed. "I have no idea. Not seriously in any case. I became stuck in here when the carriage overturned." She stared up at her rescuer imperiously. "Well? I shall need some help extracting myself."

The haughtiness of her manner was so in contrast with her position, wedged as she was between the seat and the far door, her feet in the air, her petticoats thrust up, showing shapely ankles and much more, that he laughed aloud.

"I do not find anything amusing in this situation!"

"No, of course not, m'lady." Swallowing his laughter, Lachlan lowered himself into the cab and stared down at its sole passenger. Her bonnet had fallen off and a mass of dark, silky hair was falling loose around her face and shoulders. Hair the color of raven's wings. The bench seat had come loose in the accident and trapped her against the wall. Lachlan took hold of the bench and, yanking it down, freed the young lady from her undignified confinement.

She took a moment to straighten out her rumpled and torn skirts and her pelisse. Then she stared up at him with liquid brown eyes that made his heart lurch. "Thank you. Now how do you propose we get out of here?"

"Nae fash y'rself. I'll hand ye up to me gilly and then climb out after ye."

He stood staring at her. How could she be so unaffected by what she had just been through? And why had she been traveling alone? She had no lady's maid, no male escort?

"If you are through appraising me, perhaps we might proceed?"

"Of course, m'lady. Hamish! Come take the lady as I hand her up."

His gilly's face appeared in the open door above them. "Aye."

Lachlan lifted her in his arms, and, bracing his legs on the seat, deposited her gently outside the door into Hamish's waiting arms.

She bit off a cry as Hamish climbed down from the coach and sat her on a stretch of mossy bank.

She started shivering once the ordeal was over. Wordlessly, Hamish unwound the plaid from his shoulder and wrapped it around her.

Lachlan climbed out after her and stood, legs akimbo, hands on his hips, staring down at her. "Would ye ken what happened to yer driver?"

"There were shots. I'm not sure what happened to him." She shuddered.

"I'll send men back down the road as soon as I have ye to safety. It's possible they were highwaymen, but 'tis a rare thing to be bothered by highwaymen here. It's not all that profitable a route." He hesitated. "Ye were travelin' alone?"

"I was not alone when we started out two days ago. My maid, Kincaid, was with me, and my Aunt Abigail, and then there were the coachman and his boy. Just a young boy. I hope he's all right."

"What happened?"

"My aunt became ill and I left her with relatives in Nairn. At my urging, Kincaid stayed behind to take care of her."

"But surely yer relatives cannot have condoned ye traveling alone through this desolate part of the country?"

She colored, the blush staining her cheeks. "They didn't exactly know I was traveling on alone. Somehow they believed my cousin, Jared, would be joining me."

"But there was no cousin."

"Oh, there is a cousin. I just chose not to bother him with my travel plans. I don't care very much for his company."

Lachlan threw back his head and laughed.

He studied her. She was a tall woman. And she was definitely a woman, not a girl. While she appeared delicate, all soft curves, encased in her cashmere pelisse, her torn silk and lace, she was calm and unruffled in a situation that would have left most women and some men he knew in hysterics. "Can ye stand?"

"Of course I can stand." She pushed herself to her feet, gave a cry of pain and would have fallen except for Lachlan's quick arm solidly around her.

"Which leg is it?"

"My right. I can't put my weight on it."

"Sit." He lowered her gently to the ground again. "Hamish knows about injuries."

The gilly knelt beside her and carefully turned her foot. She winced and involuntarily cried out. "Sorry, lass." His hands then slid gently over her lower leg.

Hamish stood and reported to his laird. "The ankle and leg are some swollen, and it's possible there may be a break in the smaller of the two leg bones, though it feels to be in line. I think I'd best strap her leg and ankle before we try to move her."

So saying, he took a length of muslin and a few short straight lengths of birch from his kit and proceeded to enclose her ankle and lower leg in a protective casing of cloth and wood. "With a bit o' luck, she'll no have permanent damage. That is, if ye can keep her off her feet for a few weeks." He peered doubtfully at his patient.

The young woman grimaced at the pain and bit back a moan. "A few weeks? But that's not possible. I must be in Edinburgh."

"Edinburgh is it? Weel ye'll no be gaeing far on that leg, and that's a fact." Hamish said.

Lachlan MacInnes studied the young woman. "Ye'll have to ride afore me on my horse. Can ye manage that? There's no other way to get ye to help quickly and I'd prefer not to leave ye here while I fetch some."

"I know how to ride." She frowned. "But will the coach horses be all right left here?"

Lachlan had the fleeting notion that, under these circumstances, only a rare woman would give a thought to the horses. "One didna' survive the accident. I'll put t'other on a lead. We'll take her back with us. She has a few scrapes and bruises, but she has survived the fall better than her mistress."

She gave a shaky laugh. "And to whom do I owe my rescue?"

"We have no one here to make a proper introduction so I'll have to do it m'self. Lachlan MacInnes, at your service, Madam."

Her eyebrows shot up. "MacInnes?"

"Is that a problem?"

"Not at the moment, no." She gave a crooked, utterly charming smile. "But my father may take a different view. I'm a Glendenning. Elspeth Glendenning."

"Ahh! Well, Mistress Glendenning, since there is no help for it, and since you are on MacInnes lands, I think the rules of hospitality must precede the feud between your clan, with its past ties to the Hanoverian Court, and mine, with its former loyalty to the Stuart kings. Perhaps for a time we could just lay down our claymores."

"I'm not sure my father would agree."

"Nor my brother," Lachlan conceded. "But needs must."

Hamish helped lift the lady onto Lachlan's horse, careful of her injured leg, and Lachlan mounted behind her. They neither of them said more as the horses wound their way up the steep hillside.

Lachlan's body responded in an uncomfortable manner as Elspeth leaned back against him, her eyes closed, her long lashes dark against her milk white skin, her hair, blowing against his face, carrying the faint scent of lavender.

They traversed across moor and over rocky crag to the far valley where the MacInnes had lived for more than six hundred years. Lachlan meditated on the good fortune of his clan. Lochleigh Castle had been unimportant enough and far enough off any known trail to keep it from the notice of the Sider Roy, King George's marauding forces in the aftermath of the Uprising of 1745. It had miraculously escaped the destruction that monarch loosed on clans suspected of Jacobite sympathies. It had been passed over during the Highland Clearances, later, when land farmed for generations by Highlanders was appropriated by the crown for raising sheep. Sheep would not find much nourishment in the rocks and moors around Lochliegh Castle.

And now, under Queen Victoria, there was a period

of general amnesty. Plaids were once again allowed, even encouraged. Bagpipes again sounded in the glen. The MacInnes Clan was fortunate to have survived the terrible years following the Battle of Culloden Field.

Unfortunately, the old animosities survived. Clan against clan, sometimes brother against brother, former Jacobites, supporters of Bonnie Prince Charlie, against the former supporters of King George and the English Court. Catholics against John Knox's Kirk of Scotland. He glanced down at the lovely girl riding in front of him. Hard to think of her as the enemy, whatever her family's political and religious persuasions.

They clattered across a drawbridge and through the raised gate into a busy cobblestone courtyard. The smithy was at his anvil, hammering a red-hot horseshoe into the right shape for a horse that stood nearby, held in place by a groom. Groups of men stood around in conversation, while women were gathered around the well, gossiping, and children played at dueling with wooden swords. A busy, cheerful scene.

Lachlan dismounted, lifted Elspeth Glendenning down in his arms, and nodded to a groom standing nearby to take Bailoch. Men and women alike stopped what they were doing and stared at the newcomer in their midst. The women immediately surrounded Lachlan.

"The lady is injured. She can't stand on her own. We need…"

A large rotund woman, more swathed in clothing than dressed, pushed the others aside and scooped Elspeth out of Lachlan's arms. "We'll attend to the lass, ne'er you mind. The laird's been asking for ye."

"Look after her well, Brighid. She's our guest and

she's been hurt."

"We'll see to her."

Hamish was already busy organizing a party to return to the scene. They would try to locate the driver and his young helper first. Then they would bury the dead horse and try to right the old landau. If it could be made drivable, they'd hitch up horses and get it to a stable in Nairn for repairs. They could not transport it to MacInnes Castle. The narrow dirt tracks through the mountain passes and over the moors were not designed for the likes of such a large coach.

With a last hesitant glance at Elspeth Glendenning, Lachlan headed into the castle. He found his older brother, Abhainn, holding court in the Hall. Abhainn sat on a slightly elevated, elaborately carved oak chair with a swath of MacInnes plaid thrown across its back. The chair was by no means a throne, but it spoke clearly of its occupant's importance. The Laird's chair. No one else sat in it, ever.

Abhainn was settling disputes among clan members, accepting small offerings from tenants, dispensing justice as needed. Lachlan stood and observed him for a few minutes. His brother's uncanny ability to settle differences and leave all believing justice well served left him in awe. How did he do it? He was possessed of a deep well of understanding and patience. Lachlan was grateful, not for the first time, that he was the younger rather than the older MacInnes brother. He was not cut out to be laird.

With a nod and a wave of his hand, Abhainn signaled the audience was over for the day. Slowly the great hall emptied of people.

"Come." Abhainn led his brother to a pair of chairs

by the massive stone fireplace and poured them each a whisky.

They downed the draught in one swallow.

"Ye have brought the enemy into our camp."

"Have ye even seen the wee thing? Aye, she's a Glendenning, but what was I to do? She was hurting. Her coach was destroyed or at least severely damaged. One of her horses dead, the other crippled. Do we war on helpless women?"

His brother sighed. "No. We do not. But I wish I didna' have a foreboding this willna' end well."

Lachlan shook his head in denial. "Our women will tend to her injuries and we'll send her on her way as soon as she's able to travel. Surely no fault can be found wi' that."

Abhainn continued as if Lachlan hadn't spoken, "We must send word to her family that she is safe and in our caring. Do you think for a moment they'll believe us? They'll more likely believe we're responsible for the accident. It *was* an accident?"

"I dinna ken. We'll know more when Hamish and his party find the driver and his boy."

"Inform me the minute there is any information. Find out where we should send word and to whom. And after that, stay away from the Glendenning lass."

Lachlan repaired to his rooms, his senses overflowing with the beautiful young woman whose hair smelled of lavender. She weighed nothing when he lifted her in his arms, but she was far from a weak, hysterical female. With a chuckle, he remembered her imperious command, "Get me out of here!" For all she appeared to be a wee mite of a thing, she was a woman. A woman unlike any he had met before. His brother, the laird, had ordered him to stay away from her. Well, perhaps not ordered, perhaps advised. Advice he intended to take. But just in case their paths crossed inadvertently, he should rid himself of some of the smells of blood and horses and mud. He called for a tub.

****

A day later Hamish returned with a small frightened boy in tow. He took the child straight through to the kitchen. Brighid was stirring a pot suspended on a hinged iron brace over the huge brick kitchen fireplace.

"What in the name o' God is this?" She stopped her stirring and glared at the dirty, shivering, mud-splattered object before her.

"Can ye feed him and get him bathed and clothed? The Laird is going to want to speak wi' him and I don't think he'll get much out of him in his present condition. He hasn't eaten in two days."

"Oh, the puir laddie. What can I do?"

"Ye could start by giving the both of us some of that fine soup yer making."

"Gladly. Soup, and fresh warm bannocks to go with it."

"Sit ye doon right here, boy." Gently Hamish steered the child onto the bench at the long kitchen table and sat down beside him.

Brighid took a damp kitchen cloth and wiped the boy's face and hands. Then she placed steaming wooden bowls of the thick broth in front of them. "Eat first. Then we'll clean ye up properly and find ye some clothes."

The boy crammed the bannock into his mouth.

When the last crumb was gone, he puzzled uncertainly at the soup bowl and wooden spoon. He looked at Hamish.

Hamish picked up his spoon, dipped it in his soup and brought it to his mouth.

The boy tried to do the same, grasping the spoon in his fist, spilling most of it on his already filthy clothes. Then with a side glance at Hamish, he picked up the bowl in both hands and began slurping up the soup.

Hamish sighed. Manners could come later.

They finished their meal and Hamish left the boy in Brighid's hands to bathe and dress. "Mind yer manners and do what Mistress Brighid tells ye to. I'll be back for ye in an hour."

****

Abhainn was in his chambers with his wife, Fiona, and his brother, Lachlan, when Hamish came in. "I'm glad ye are all here together. It is not good news I bear."

"Sit." Abhainn poured a generous dram of whisky and handed it to his brother's gilly. "What can you tell us?"

"I retraced the path of the landau back. I found the driver first. He was dead, shot through the head. The boy was sniveling in the bushes. He fought like a tiger when I tried to take him. Right terrified he was. And half starved. I gave him some bits o' bannock I had in me kit and he calmed down enough to tell me some of his story."

Hamish took a swallow of his whisky. "Two men on horseback came out of the forest and chased them. They shot the driver and the horses panicked and went careening down the roadway. The lad was terrified and jumped off his perch at the back of the landau to hide in the bushes. He said her ladyship was screaming, but he didn't know what to do. The horsemen pursued the carriage but then turned heel and raced away when the landau lurched over the cliff and the two of us," he nodded to Lachlan, "came onto the scene."

"Two men. Unlikely to have been highwaymen then. They work alone. Why would anyone give chase to a carriage carrying only a woman?"

Fiona put her hand on her husband's arm. "Perhaps they didn't know it carried only a woman. It is most unusual for a young woman to travel alone. Who or what was originally supposed to have been in that landau? Clearly something or someone valuable enough to risk a daylight raid on the coach. Perhaps we should question Mistress Glendenning?"

Her husband nodded. "Lachlan, ye should do that. She has reason to trust ye. Learn what ye can from her."

"As ye wish. I'll discover what she has to say on the matter."

****

Lachlan could not hide his dismay as he headed for the women's quarters. He had determined to avoid Elspeth Glendenning. She aroused sensations that were new to him and that were quite hopeless under the circumstances. For all his words to her about burying the past, the enmity between the MacInnes and the Glendenning was long, deep seated, and bitter. It would not be casually set aside for anything so unimportant as a young man of his clan who loved a young woman of hers.

Loved? Where had that word sprung from? He didn't even know Elspeth Glendenning. Still, he remembered all too well the warmth of her body as she leaned against him on the ride back to Lochleigh. He could close his eyes and recall the silk of her hair blowing against his face, her scent…

He had no evidence that Elspeth Glendenning even noticed him, beyond thanking him for his services. He contemplated the beautiful, courageous young woman he had rescued from the carriage, the calm way she had reacted in a terrifying situation. He had never met anyone like her. So soft and sweet-smelling and vulnerable while at the same time showing nerves of iron. All his life he'd known only three kinds of women. Married women who, although sometimes very appealing, were not to be touched; simpering, rather silly young girls, who didn't interest him in the least; and widows who were generally grateful for any attention. Without the help of the latter, he mused, he'd still be a virgin.

In Mistress Glendenning he perceived something else entirely. She was a woman, not a girl. A woman of daring, strength, and beauty. He could easily be lost in those liquid brown eyes He remembered the way her hair brushed his fingers as he lifted her out of the landau and imagined how it would feel spread across his naked chest.

Good Christ! He could not let her see him in this condition. He'd best cool off first.

****

Elspeth thanked the young woman who had helped her bathe and put on a nightdress. Her torn clothing had been taken away to be cleaned and mended. Her leg throbbed in its braces and wrappings. The MacInnes surgeon had examined her, confirmed Hamish's diagnosis and bandaged her leg again. He was insistent that she stay off the leg for at least six weeks if she wished to walk normally again. Six weeks before she could even consider resuming her trip to her home, to her father.

Her father. She could hardly imagine his wrath when he learned she had been making this journey alone, without attendant or companion of any kind. And then to be placed in danger for her life and rescued by a member of the hated MacInnes clan, forced by circumstance to accept their hospitality.

A young woman entered the room with her hands full of clothing. "I'm Mairi MacInnes, Lachlan's sister. Ye might be more comfortable in some looser clothing, something without stays." She held up a long loose garment of soft blue wool. "It hasn't much style to commend it, but it's warm and comfortable. I wore it the last few weeks before my wee bairn was born."

"Thank you." Elspeth allowed the other woman to undress her and slip the garment over her head. She wriggled it down her body. "It's lovely. Warm and cozy. How old is your baby?"

"Oh, he's no babe anymore. He's four years, and a holy terror." The smile on her face belied her words. "I must be about me duties, but I'll be sending one of the kitchen maids, to help ye as needed. We're no much for lady's maids here."

The last was said not unkindly, but as a simple fact of life on the MacInnes lands. Mairi took a small blue bottle out of a cloth bag hanging from her waist. "I have something here to ease yer pain. I'll give ye two drops now and I'll return with it again at bedtime."

"Thank you, Mairi. My leg does throb."

When Mairi had left, Elspeth snuggled down on

her couch, near a paned glass window. A distant hillside was ablaze with summer color. How she longed to be able to ride through that wood, free. Free of her aunt, free of her father, free from their constant bullying, their pushing first one man and then another into her path. She did not want to marry. At least in her father's house, unlike her aunt's, she was free to pursue her own interests. Her life was not made up of endless, useless social calls. She could read, she could paint. No husband would allow that. If she were to marry, she would be expected to manage a large household and start producing heirs. She shivered. While the mysteries of the marriage bed intrigued her, the rest of it, belonging to a man, being his property to be used or abused as he wished…the idea was appalling.

She'd join a nunnery first. But, of course, the Glendenning were Kirk of Scotland, not Catholic, so that wasn't really an option. On the positive side, there was the modest income from her great aunt. One no husband could touch. And she was almost past marrying age. A maiden still at twenty-two, she was most likely heading for a life of taking care of her father's household and her sister's children. She sighed. That would be infinitely preferable to marriage.

There was a tentative knock at the door. "Come," she called.

A wee mouse of a girl entered, her very posture apologetic. "I'm Agnes, mam, sent to help ye. Do ye need anything? Would ye like use the…" her hand indicated the screen concealing the chamber pot and washstand.

"No, thank you. I'm fine for the moment."

"Very well, mistress. I'll just be here if you need

me." The child started to sit on the floor by the door.

"Don't do that."

"What, mam? Am I doin' something wrong?"

Elspeth softened her tone. "No, of course not, child. There's a chair beside you. Sit in it, not on the floor."

The girl gazed at the chair, then back at Elspeth, and finally perched gingerly on the edge of the padded seat of the oak side chair.

"That's better," Elspeth said.

Agnes's small pinched face broke into a wide grin. "It is that, mam."

There was another knock at the door and Agnes bounded to answer it. "Milord." She bowed her head and scurried backward into the room.

"You may sit on the chair again, Agnes."

With a hesitant peek at Lachlan MacInnes, Agnes once again slid onto the chair.

Turning to Lachlan, Elspeth said, "I'm so glad to have opportunity to thank you. Please come sit by me."

"Ye appear a bit better than the last time I saw ye." Lachlan placed a chair close to Elspeth's couch. "Ye have more color." He had an almost irrepressible urge to touch her soft hair, to cup her pale, lovely face in his hands, to kiss those ripe lips. Instead, he said, "Did Mairi give you some of the draught she uses to ease pain?"

"Yes. And it does help, although it leaves me a bit drowsy. What news have you?"

"We found the driver's body. He was shot through the head. We buried him. And we found the boy alive." Lachlan smiled. "Cook has taken a liking to him, so he's clean and well fed and has a corner to sleep close to the stove."

"Thank God for that. Do you know whether my boxes and trunks are here? They were lashed onto the carriage. It's not so much my clothing, but there were some documents I was carrying to my father from his agent in Nairn. There appeared to be some urgency in getting them to him. That, in fact, is why I continued the journey alone when those attending me were unable to carry on. There was a parcel in my reticule that I think must be particularly important. Did anyone find my reticule?"

"Not to my knowledge. Where was it?"

"I had it with me inside the carriage."

"I don't know about your reticule. Everything my men retrieved will be taken to your room, but between the time we rescued you and the time my men got back to the landau, your boxes were searched. They were opened and their contents scattered about. Someone was looking for something."

She gave a small gasp and a frown crossed her features. "I hope they didn't find it. It's always possible they were searching for any jewelry I might have been traveling with, but…"

"You think it more likely they were searching for the contents of your reticule."

"Yes."

"When I hauled you out of the landau, the bench was pushed against the wall. Your reticule could still be wedged in there. I can search for it in the morning."

She put her hand on his arm. "Would you please? I don't know the contents of that case, but my father needs it most urgently."

Her touch scorched him. Instead of pulling back as

every caution urged him to, Lachlan brought his chair closer and placed his hand over hers "I will do what I must to recover it for you." His eyes held hers. He resisted the impulse to lean in and taste her lips.

"Have you been able to send word to my father?"

"Not yet. Hamish will be leaving tomorrow morning. Perhaps ye would care to write a letter to him? I suspect something in your own hand will reassure him more than any message we can deliver."

"Of course." She hesitated. "If you find my reticule, do you think Hamish could carry a small package to my father? I don't know its contents, but I was assured of its urgency. Do you trust him?"

"With my life. If I ask him to do this, he will, ye may be sure."

Forcing his mind back to the purpose of his visit he drew back. "If ye don't mind my askin', why were ye travelin' on this remote way? Ye said you were goin' from to Nairn to Edinburgh. The road ye were travelin' is no' between Nairn and Edinburgh. Ye were headed toward Skye."

"What? Skye? That's not possible. The coachman said the usual road between Inverness and Edinburgh was washed out by heavy rains and might be impassable for several days. He suggested we take this longer route." She hesitated. "I had to get the packet entrusted to me in Edinburgh and to my father with all due haste."

"There is no way this road could have taken ye to Edinburgh. Not travelin' in the direction ye were goin'. And I know naught about severe rains to the south of us. Could it be your driver was workin' with the men who attacked you?"

A frown crossed her features. "That possibility had not occurred to me. Our regular coachman was taken ill in Inverness. This man was a replacement. But if he was part of some plot, why would his colleagues have shot him?"

"Perhaps they no longer needed him?"

****

The next afternoon, Lachlan decided to discover for himself what progress had been made in righting the coach. He saddled Bailoch and rode to the site of the accident.

Hamish was overseeing the work. The men had attached ropes to the coach and were heaving it upright. Miraculously, the wheels were intact, if a bit wobbly.

They dragged it onto the road just as Lachlan arrived on the scene.

"Well done!" he called out.

The men threw themselves down on the bank, brushing sweat from their brows. Hamish passed a flask of whisky to the nearest of them, who drank from it and passed it on.

Lachlan approached the landau and tried to open the door. When it refused to open, he braced his foot against the side and tried again. It would not budge.

"Can you help me get this door open? It's jammed."

Two men jumped up and added their weight to his effort to no effect.

"What about the window?" Hamish suggested.

"Too small to crawl through. How about the other door?"

They trooped around the carriage.

The door hung open. They laughed as Lachlan

grabbed the frame and hoisted himself into the vehicle. The bench was still jammed against the wall. He yanked it down and a fur-trimmed, brown velvet bag fell to the floor.

He held it up like a trophy and the men all laughed. "Goes weel with yer plaid," Hamish shouted, to a further roar of laughter.

Later that evening Lachlan reported to his brother that the coach was on the road again and with some work on the wheels it might be possible to drive it as far as Nairn.

"I think we'll just keep it here for a while. Ask Hamish to get it off the road and out of sight, and to have our men repair it." Abhainn said. "And about the reticule Mistress Glendenning asked ye to retrieve? Have ye returned it to her?"

Lachlan tried to suppress his surprise. How did his brother know about the reticule? But then Abhainn was aware of everything that happened in Lochleigh.

"I did not wish to disturb her this late in the evenin'."

"Just as well." Abhainn adjusted the plaid over his shoulder. "Have ye examined the contents of the reticule?"

"No. It is a woman's most personal belonging. It did not seem fitting I should…"

"Please fetch it."

Lachlan left without further remonstrance and returned a few minutes later with the fur-trimmed velvet bag.

Abhainn held out his hand. He opened the reticule and withdrew a large, linen-wrapped package sealed with red wax and an official stamp. He held it out to

Lachlan. "Ye fought alongside the English in France. Ye can read French. What does it say?"

Lachlan examined the seal. "It's the official seal of a French bank."

Abhainn studied the seal for a few moments, then used his dirk to slide under it and open the package, carefully so it would be possible to re-seal it.

They both drew in their breath. Bank notes. A considerable number of bank notes in large denominations.

"Weel. Now we know why the carriage was attacked." Abhainn carefully refolded the linen around the bank notes, and using a candle to soften the wax seal, reattached it.

"What else have we here?" He reached into the reticule again and drew out a leather case. Opening it, he withdrew a folded parchment. "Some sort of legal document?" He spread it out on the table.

Lachlan skimmed the page. "It appears to be a loan agreement. Four thousand pounds, at an annual interest rate of forty percent. This is his copy of the transaction. He used his house in New Town, Edinburgh, as collateral. Why would he borrow money from a bank in France?"

"Perhaps he has already borrowed to the hilt in Scotland. To use his house as collateral…that indicates some level of desperation. I wonder if his daughter is aware of her father's financial situation."

"Why, in God's name, would he use his daughter as courier?" Lachlan stood and paced the room. He stopped in front of his brother. "Surely he must have realized the danger he was placing her in?"

"Not necessarily. Who would expect a young

woman visiting her family of having so much money on her? But someone found out."

Lachlan nodded. "And that someone made sure she would be traveling on a seldom used road and then set up an ambush."

"They didn't count on you and Hamish appearing on the scene." Abhainn sighed. "I do not like being party to this, even accidentally. I wish the Glendenning lass had chosen some other place to injure her leg."

He carefully refolded the document and placed it back in its folder. "Return the reticule to Mistress Glendenning tomorrow morning. We will see what she says."

"She has already asked me to send the case on to her father. Along with a letter from her."

"Then that is what we shall do. Better to act as if we hae no knowledge of it. It will bring trouble to him soon enough."

Abhainn stood to leave, then looked at Lachlan. "Who will be delivering it?"

"Hamish could go."

"Very well."

Lachlan left the hall, his feet slowing as he neared Elspeth Glendenning's chamber. Light showed under her door. She was still up. If he visited her now, Hamish could start off at daybreak tomorrow morning rather than mid-morning, he rationalized, knowing full well that his wanting to be with her had nothing to do with Hamish's departure time.

Before he had time to reconsider, he knocked on the door. The child—what was her name? Ah, yes, Agnes—stood in front of him, effectively barring his way.

"Who is it, Agnes?"

"It's the Laird's brother, my lady. Lachlan."

"Well, show him in. Then you may take your chair and sit outside my door until he leaves."

Lachlan stepped around the kitchen maid and in one sweep swung her chair into the hall. He noticed she now had a straw mattress with a warm cover on the floor. Mistress Glendenning had a kind heart.

Elspeth was stretched out, half sitting, half lying on the couch, her leg, with the wood braces and bandages, elevated on cushions. The rest of her was swathed in creamy silk that clung and revealed every nuance of her generous figure. Over her shoulders she wore a pale pink shawl, loosely woven of some soft fuzzy material. The effect was shattering.

"I must thank you for returning my trunks to me. Your sister Mairi has been most generous with the loan of her clothes, but one is always more comfortable with one's own, don't you think?"

Lachlan laughed. "I can't say as I've ever been in the position of needin' borrowed clothes. And considerin' my size, that's probably a good thing."

She laughed with him. "Come. Move that chair over here closer to me."

Lachlan did as directed. "I should not be here in your room without any female in attendance."

"No one need know. Mairi has already given me my evening dose of laudanum. It's here in a glass on my table. But I have no wish to sleep yet. There is no reason anyone should know you are here."

"Still…"

"You have my reticule." She held out her hand for it and examined its contents. "Everything's here. Will you be able to get this packet and these papers to my father?"

"Hamish will start out with them early tomorrow morning."

"Good," Elspeth said. "I've written a letter explaining my predicament and telling Father I will be unable to travel for some weeks. I've also told him of the kind treatment I've had at the hands of the MacInnes, and that the doctor is sure I'll be able to walk normally in a few weeks."

They sat in silence for a few moments.

"I should go." Lachlan stood, only to have Elspeth place her soft white hand on his large callused one.

"Don't go. Stay a while and talk to me. Tell me about your life here. What do you do to fill your days?"

Lachlan sat down again. "The days are full enough. We run cattle on the hillsides, and deal with our tenants' needs, and hunt, and keep a watch on our borders. I suppose to one who is city bred it must appear to be a dull existence, but it suits me."

"It doesn't sound dull at all. I cannot imagine such freedom. My life in the city is confined by so many things. Endless social calls, dinners to give and dinners to attend, tea and gossip. And always the pressure to marry, the sense of being paraded before every eligible man with the hopes of making a 'suitable' alliance. How I envy your freedom."

"I'm not sure our women here have much more freedom. They may not be attending balls or making 'pointless social calls' but they are important cogs in our wheel. They keep our lives running smoothly. They feed us and see to our comfort. They are certainly expected to marry, and they don't often have much choice in the matter. They grow up knowing they have an obligation to the continuation of the clan. But perhaps in your life, you have no such sense of obligation?"

"The name is passed on only through male heirs. Why should I marry? I have no wish to cease being a Glendenning. I have no desire to become subject to any man other than my father, and he is very lenient. I like my life as it is. I prefer not to marry."

He hesitated. "But do ye never yearn…"

"No. That is, I never yearned until…" She glanced down and twisted the silk of her gown in her fingers. Then she gazed directly into his eyes. "Until you fetched me out of that carriage and carried me here."

His heart pounded so she must surely hear it. He leaned in for the kiss. The kiss he'd been dreaming about for the last two days and nights. There was a brief moment when he sensed she was going to resist and then her arms were around him, the contours of her body through the thin silk of her gown more enticing than if she had been nude. The kiss lingered, gentle, exploring. She opened her mouth to his, tongue entwining with tongue. He was almost faint with desire. His hand slid down her body to her breasts. They rose in peaks at his touch.

He gasped and sat back. "We cannae be doing this. Yer an unmarried lass." He eyed her suspiciously. "Unless yer thinkin' to marry. Now *that* I think might be a fine idea. Is it marriage yer seeking?"

Laughter bubbled up. "Marriage is the last thing I want."

Lachlan frowned. "What then?"

Elspeth settled back into her chair. "I'm twenty-two years old, and since I was sixteen my father and my aunt have been trying to marry me off to first one man and then another. I have no intention of becoming the property of any man. A chattel, whose only life lies in running a household and bearing children. I shall live and die single. And I can do that because my great aunt Hermione left me a small income in my own name. She lived and died a spinster. I intend to do the same."

"But…"

"But I have a certain curiosity about what happens between men and women. I don't want to grow old and die without ever having experienced what happens in the marriage bed."

"And I'm to be the guinea pig?" Lachlan pushed his chair back, shock written on his features. "No thank you, Mistress Glendenning. As you have no interest in having children and running a household, I have no interest in serving as your stud. At twenty-seven, I've avoided marriage even longer than you. Mind, I have not avoided the more intimate aspects of marriage, but single I am. Being with you, I could easily succumb to marriage. But I will no hae a casual rut with ye. Ye'll have to seek elsewhere if that's what ye want. I'm sure there are men a plenty who would be happy to instruct ye in the mysteries of the marriage bed without benefit o' priest."

"Not men I want."

Lachlan stood and scrutinized Elspeth for a moment. He was being a fool. All that lush beauty, his for the taking? But what then of the morrow? He had a foreboding he would not survive the morrow. He took the contents of her reticule and strode to the door. "Goodnight, Mistress Glendenning. Agnes, you may come in now." He placed the child's chair back into the room and closed the door behind her.

****

Elspeth stared after him. Her face flushed at the wanton way she had offered herself to him, only to be coldly refused. There had been nothing cold about his kiss or the way he had caressed her body. Her very skin tingled at the recollection of it.

She had been considering this action for a long time, waiting until she met a man she believed she could trust. It had never occurred to her that the man she chose would refuse her offer. How could she ever face him again? He wanted marriage? That was an odd turn-about. Most of the men who courted her in the past would have been only too happy to bed her without benefit of a wedding ring.

Marriage to Lachlan MacInnes? She smiled. Her father would have apoplexy. A Glendenning married to a MacInnes? She supposed they would have rooms in this castle, miles from anyplace. Life as she had always known it would be turned upside down. She would be expected to help with women's chores, whatever they were. And, of course, children. There would undoubtedly be children. She who had sworn never to marry, never to have children, now wondered if she had been a bit hasty in her decision. Those few moments in Lachlan's arms had undermined her steadfast decision never to marry.

He would probably avoid her in the future. It would be best if he did. Her resolve never to marry would not hold up long in his presence.

Her entry in her diary that night was detailed. When she finished writing she had almost come to the conclusion she would marry if that was what it took to get the Highlander into her bed. She wanted him with a deep visceral yearning she had never experienced before. Was this love? This uncomfortable, uncontrollable longing, this aching? This sense the ground was giving way under her feet?

She took the draught Mairi had left her and settled down to sleep. To dream about the handsome Highlander who had so unexpectedly invaded her life.

Chapter Five

The Present

That evening Lara was invited to the castle for dinner. She often took dinner with the Glendennings and their B&B guests, but for this evening, Aileen had made a point of inviting her. "It's a festive occasion. There's someone we'd like you to meet," she'd said. "Someone special."

Lara wasn't sure what "festive occasion" meant, but she took considerable care dressing. She wore a long full skirt of shimmery blue with matching sandals, and a high-necked, long-sleeved white silk blouse, clothes she had bought on a recent shopping foray in Edinburgh. It was, she decided, very pretty in an old-fashioned way. For warmth, she donned the large wool square in the Glendenning Plaid Iain had given her. She touched her eyes with shadow and even used some very pale pink lipstick. Glancing at the overall effect in the mirror she decided, *Not bad for a cowgirl*. Then she giggled.

Normally she rode Flora and came in through the kitchen door when she had dinner at the castle, but tonight Ewan was coming for her in the Land Rover. As they bounced along the dirt track, Lara tried to pump him about tonight's special guest. He deflected her questions and said, "Just remember, lass. The deed isn't done yet. And I for one hope it never is."

"What on earth are you talking about?"

He closed his mouth firmly and said not another word.

The floodlights outside were blazing, shining up on the ramparts and imparting a sense of grandeur on the castle. Lara had never approached it at this time of day, when the sun had fallen behind the hills and twilight was turning everything to a silvery glow. She was Cinderella, being deposited at the massive front door to meet the prince.

Ewan hopped out and opened the door for her. "I have to go get me pipes. I'll be back soon. Remember lass, hold yerself straight and don't let them know what ye may be thinkin'."

Lara paused for a moment in the hall, gathering her wits, then straightened her shoulders and followed the sound of voices coming from the drawing room.

Aileen spotted her the moment she arrived. "Lara, dear. Come join us."

Lara's eyes were riveted on Iain. Iain, with a tall shapely blonde draped on his arm. Iain, looking as if he would like to disappear through the floor. His face was flushed, and his eyes refused to meet hers.

As if from a great distance, she was aware of Aileen saying, "This is Iain's fiancée, Allison Macaulay. Allison is with a law firm in Edinburgh, so we don't get to have her with us often. But she has three days off and we're delighted she decided to spend them here with Iain."

"How very nice to meet you." Lara wanted to cry or scream or just disappear into the earth. Ewan's voice echoed in her head. *Hold yerself straight and don't let them know.*

She straightened her shoulders and, totally ignoring Iain, spoke to the woman he was engaged to marry. "Have you known each other long?" she asked.

"We grew up together. My father was the headmaster of the village school."

"It's is an interesting field you've chosen, the law." Lara found herself babbling. "It must be hard to contemplate giving up your urban law practice to live here in what is essentially a hotel and a cattle ranch."

Allison gave a short silvery laugh. "I'm afraid we haven't quite worked that out yet, but I assure you I won't be giving up my law practice and we won't be raising either horses or cattle. My practice requires an urban setting. Besides, Iain is much too highly educated to spend the rest of his life here. He needs to find a suitable career in the city. Isn't that so, Lord Duncan?"

Duncan appeared reluctant to be drawn into the dispute. "Weel, Aileen and I hae been verra happy here. I ken country life is no' for everybody. Iain must make his own choices. But he is the next laird of Athdara. There's no escapin' that."

"Of course he is. And I'm prepared to be his lady, but surely that doesn't mean we have to spend all our days living here at the end of nowhere."

Ewan entered at that moment and started to play. "Ye are with me tonight," Duncan said, taking Lara's arm and leading her into the dining room.

Dinner was endless. Lara forced herself to make a show of eating. Duncan appeared to sense her discomfort and made just enough idle conversation to get her through the meal. Iain, across the table from her, sat in mute silence, his food untouched, his face a mask.

Finally, the ordeal was over, and she was at the front door, thanking Lord and Lady Glendenning for their hospitality. Iain and Allison had disappeared.

Ewan was there waiting to drive her back to the cottage. They drove in silence to the gate. As Ewan got out to see her to the door, he said, "That lass is all wrong for him, ye know."

Back in her room, tears burning behind her eyes, Lara undressed mechanically, pulled on the oversized T-shirt she customarily slept in, and climbed into her feather bed. She tried to sleep. She resolutely plumped up her pillow, rearranged her duvet, and got a drink of water. Nothing worked. Her mind kept replaying the moment she set eyes on Iain with Allison Macaulay, the way the statuesque blonde stood beside him with her arm so possessively linked through his.

Betrayal. The shock of betrayal. Then embarrassment mixed in equal parts with the anger. She had made a fool of herself. Iain had never committed himself to her in any way. Clearly, she had read more into their budding relationship than he intended. Still the sense of his treachery remained, a tight fist somewhere in her middle.

Over her morning coffee, Lara became more resigned to her situation. She had overreacted last night. After all, there'd been nothing between them except a few chaste kisses. It's not as if she'd been ravished. Her choice of word had laughter bubbling up.

She remembered the frank diary entry she had read last night. Elspeth Glendenning had shown remarkable bravery for a woman of her time and upbringing. Imagine, asking a man to become her lover. And then to be rejected. If she, Lara, had been embarrassed and confused last night over Iain's behavior, imagine how much more embarrassed and confused Elspeth must have been. And to think an ancestor of hers, a MacInnes, had turned down her wanton offer. It was enough to make her lose faith.

Still smiling, she took her coffee outside the kitchen door to sit in the sunlight of a *bonnie day*, as Iain would have put it. She was not going to spend it indoors sulking. No indeed. In fact, she might take a little excursion. Where were the places Elspeth had mentioned in the diary? Nairn was one of them. She'd go to Nairn. Perhaps spend a couple of days sightseeing on the way.

Before she could change her mind, she ran upstairs and threw a few clothes into her backpack. At the last moment she noticed Elspeth's journals, and placed the first volume carefully in her computer case. Back downstairs, on her way out, she shut off the propane tank and generator. Finally, using the ancient key, she locked the front door and turned her back on the little cottage which, until Iain's deceitfulness, had afforded her so much pleasure. Would she be coming back to stay? She wasn't sure.

She rode Flora over to the stables and asked Ewan to take care of her for a few days.

"Of course, lass. Getting away is a good idea. Give the lad cause to remember what it's like around here without ye."

Impulsively, Lara leaned over and kissed Ewan on his cheek.

He blushed a deep red. "Go on now. And have a guid time!"

"I intend to."

Lara's next stop was at the castle. She had to tell Aileen she would be away for at least a few days.

"Nairn? What a lovely idea. You'll have to go to Edinburgh by train and then take a bus. I wish you had said something a little earlier. Iain and Allison left for Edinburgh in her car this morning. You could have gone with them. But no matter. Duncan will take you to the train station. There's a 10:50 to Edinburgh. Where will you stay?"

"I'm not sure. I'll find something."

"There's a nice little inn on the beach in Nairn, I think called The Invernairne. Duncan and I stayed there last spring for a few days."

"Thank you. And thank you for all you've done for me in the last month. It has been wonderful being here."

"It has been our pleasure to have you. I've never known Iain so happy…" her voice trailed off and a frown crossed her features. "But you'd better go if you're going to catch the 10:50."

As if by magic Lord Duncan appeared. He regarded Lara and her backpack. "Ye are not leaving us?"

"Only for a little sightseeing," Lara replied. "Lady Aileen suggested you might be able to run me to the station?"

"With pleasure. Wait at the front steps while I get the car."

On the ride to the station Lara was quiet. When they arrived, Duncan took her hand. "Don't stay away for too long. Iain has been a different man since you came. I've never known him so content. So happy."

Lara's eyes filled with unshed tears. "He never told me he was engaged."

"That was verra wrong of him."

"I must go." Lara ran into the train station.

****

Lara decided to rent a car in Edinburgh and drive to Nairn. Perusing a map, she tentatively planned to stop at the little village of Pitlochry for the night, and then the next morning continue on through a huge national park and the Cairngorm Mountains on her way to Nairn. She was a little nervous about driving on the left-hand side of the road, but if she got an automatic, she could manage. The idea of trying to shift gears with her left hand did not appeal.

At the rental agency she found in order to get an automatic with a built in GPS she would have to rent a much larger car than she wanted or needed. "Oh well," she said to the agent, "in for a penny, in for a pound."

He laughed. "I would never have taken that for an American expression," he said.

"Canadian," she corrected.

Fifteen minutes later she found herself behind the wheel of a Nissan X-Trail, on the dual-lane highway that encircled Edinburgh.

As she left the city her gaze took in the huge hillsides covered in the bright yellow bushes, she in her innocence had thought were broom. She knew better now. It was gorse, and God help anyone who fell into it.

When she came to her first round-about she almost panicked. Then she remembered what the man in the rental office had said. "The best thing about roundabouts is you can just keep going 'round until you decide which is the correct exit." She discovered the worst thing was by the time she made the circle a third time, the voice on her GPS was screaming at her. With a British accent. By the time she came to the fourth roundabout she was getting the hang of it. She found her exit on the first try.

Two hours later there was a sign pointing to Pitlochery. "The Gateway to the Highlands," it proclaimed. She glanced at her watch. Only four o'clock, but she was tired. It had been a long day since she left Athdara Castle, and she was yearning for a glass of wine, a good meal and a bed.

She exited the highway and drove into the little town. As in Edinburgh, the houses were very uniformly made of hand-cut gray stone, but there the similarities ended. In Pitlochery, houses were charming, highly individual, many with peaked roofs and cornices and decorative gingerbread touches. Some were two stories, others three.

Following a hotel sign, she headed up a one-lane road. At the end of the road a sign said "The Pines."

Before her was a manor house. A large elegant private residence. Probably expensive. She hesitated, then decided, so what? She had hardly spent anything so far. She could afford a little splurge.

She marched into the inn.

"You're in luck," the middle-aged man behind the reception desk said in answer to her query. "We've just had a cancellation for a room in the carriage house. But it's just for two nights. It's booked for Monday"

Lara hadn't planned to stay two nights, but why not? "Two nights will be fine."

Lara counted out the three hundred thirty-five Scottish pounds the innkeeper requested. He insisted on carrying her backpack as he led her outdoors and down a gravel path to a second building. There he showed her a ground floor suite with views out over the gardens.

"This is wonderful," Lara said.

"You're fortunate you came just when you did," he said. "We're full because of the celebrations at Blair Athol Castle tomorrow and Sunday."

"Celebrations?"

"Ah, yes! A trooping of the colors, with pipe band tomorrow, and then Highland Games on Sunday. The town is full. There's not a room to be had."

"Well, thank you for this one. It's lovely."

"You are most welcome. Will you be taking dinner with us?"

Lara hesitated only briefly. "Yes, thank you. Seven o'clock." That would give her time for a shower and a little lie-down. It had been a long day since Lord Duncan had dropped her at the train station.

She had driven through so much history today. She remembered Iain and the way his face closed when he spoke of the history of his country. There was pain mixed with resignation in his voice on those rare occasions when he spoke about the distant past, as real to him as today's news.

How could he have betrayed her so? He was honest to the point of brutality on most occasions. He kissed her as if his whole heart was involved. And all the while he was engaged to someone else. Tears burned behind her eyes again. They had been threatening all day. She threw herself down on the bed and sobbed.

She must have drifted off. She woke at six-thirty and she'd booked dinner for seven. Quickly she showered and changed into her blue dress, the only one she'd packed. Somehow, she had the notion that this inn was a dress kind of a place.

At the entrance to the dining room she caught her breath. The wainscoted walls, the portraits, the white linen tablecloths and silver service, all spoke of a past elegance, of a time when this was a private residence and princes might have dined here.

The headwaiter approached her and said, "Miss MacInnes? Please follow me."

Normally Lara hated eating alone, but the man placed her at a small table set for one beside a window with a view of the gardens.

"May I get you a drink?"

"No, thank you. I might have some wine with my dinner."

Lara perused the menu. Breast of pigeon? Roast of boar? Calling herself a coward, she opted for a baked salmon with Sauce Béarnaise and ordered a glass of white wine to go with it.

After the sumptuous meal she retired to the bar and settled into a deep leather armchair next to a fireplace with a roaring fire.

"May I get you an after-dinner drink?" The young waiter was courteous and subdued in his manner.

Lara paused for only a moment. "Glenfiddich" she said. "Straight up, no ice, no water.

The waiter gave her an admiring glance.

Lara never drank anything stronger than wine, and she usually stopped at one glass of that. But tonight was different. She was on her own, and she was going to have a glass of real Scotch whisky. To hell with Iain Glendenning.

An hour later she stumbled back to her suite and, after fumbling with her key, managed to get as far as taking off her dress before falling into her bed.

The next thing she was conscious of was sunlight streaming through her windows. Ten o'clock? The Blair Castle events were scheduled to start at noon.

Hastily she dressed in jeans and shirt and threw a sweater over her shoulders. After a quick breakfast of scones and coffee, she headed for her car.

Her GPS took her directly to the castle grounds, where she paid a small entrance fee and parked in a field beside a number of other cars. Following the crowd, she rounded a bend in the road to a fairy-tale castle, a huge white structure with multiple turrets and a middle section that was for all the world like a giant chess piece. She glanced at the brochure given to her with her ticket. The castle was more than seven hundred years old, built before even the earliest explorers came to the Americas.

She found a place to sit in the grass among many others and had almost no time to wait. The drone of the pipes and the boom of the drums echoed across the hills, in a sound that stirred her soul. There must be something to this business of genes. Bagpipes were a part of her genetic make-up. She stood for a better view. Over the crest of the hill, the pipers appeared, at least forty of them, marching in perfect time, kilts swaying with every step, with drummers behind, swinging their fur-capped batons in the air between drumbeats. Lara laughed aloud at the joy of it all.

The regiment marched behind them. Lara's brochure said this was the only private army in the entire British Isles. A hundred or so years ago, when Queen Victoria visited, the then Duke had greeted her with the same display Lara was now observing. The Queen was so impressed she bestowed upon Blair Athol

Castle the right in perpetuity to maintain a private army, a document still in force today. The Blair Athol Highlanders had fought for the Empire in two World Wars.

Lara sat through the next two hours of speeches and awards, only half listening. This was Iain's Scotland. A land with a long history and unique traditions. She had been dreaming to think she could fit in here. Of course, he would marry someone with a background similar to his own. Allison Macaulay had grown up here. They had a shared history.

So, he had stolen a few kisses. It wasn't the first time she had been kissed. She was not a child. He'd never said anything—not a word—to indicate his kisses were more than a pleasant diversion.

The people around her began to stand and gather up their possessions. She joined the other spectators as the pipes and drums marched around the parade grounds before finally leading the regiment off the field. Sighing, she followed the crowd back to the parking lot and headed back to The Pines Inn.

That evening she vowed she would cry no longer over Iain Glendenning. She had an early dinner and settled into bed, propped up on pillows to watch the news on television. Amazing how different the news was here. How could "World News" be so different in Scotland than in Canada? She guessed the answer was probably that each country in some fashion picked and chose what would most interest the population to whom reported.

She woke around midnight to find the TV still on. Groggily she got out of bed and turned it off.

The next morning, after a full breakfast that

included haggis, which she discovered she rather liked, she headed back to Blair Castle for the Highland Games. Mild chaos was how she remembered it later. There were pipers in booths being rated by judges. The cacophony of so many pipers all playing different things in close proximity to each other would have turned a less devoted fan off bagpipes forever, but Lara loved it. There were Highland dancers competing against each other. On a large open field, Highlanders, really big, burly guys in kilts, were tossing telephone poles—the taber-toss, a man near her told her. Each contestant picked up a huge pole, ran a distance with it and then threw it forward. The winner was the one who threw it the farthest.

In the middle of everything the pipe band marched in, playing.

Food stands offered the same kinds of fare Lara might have found at the Calgary Stampede, hot dogs and hamburgers topping the list. She bought a very large hot dog and then realized Iain was not here to eat the half of it she couldn't. She wondered idly if Allison shared her food with Iain. Somehow it did not seem in character.

At four o'clock, exhausted and longing for quiet, Lara headed back to the hotel. Iain had not crossed her mind all day. Well, not much.

She got an early start the next morning. An hour later she was in the Cairngorms. The green hills rose all around her as the road wound round and twisted through them. There was almost no traffic. Slowly she relaxed into driving on the left. It began to be natural and right. She laughed. No. Not right, left.

Sheep grazed on the hillsides. Hundreds of them,

thousands of them. Some were like the ones she saw in Canada, but many had odd black faces, and some were entirely black. This was the time of year of the birthings, and young lambs romped in the fields or huddled close to their mothers, nursing. A bucolic scene, almost unreal in its pastoral peace.

What had Iain said? The English had confiscated the land and deposed the owners in what was known as the Highland Clearances, to raise sheep? It certainly appeared to have succeeded. She had never in her life seen so many sheep. Or so few people.

She wondered at the sparsity of dwellings. Occasionally there was a little white or stone house perched on a hillside. The owners or caretakers of all those sheep, she supposed.

The few houses were all two stories. They all had windows perfectly matched above and below and a center entrance. Their uniformity astounded Lara. In Canada even tract houses were built with different rooflines and shapes and facades.

There were churches, too. Also small, made of gray stone like the Scottish houses. Each had its perfectly centered steeple. And each was empty, no longer functioning as a church. Iain had told her about the Scottish Reformation, when John Knox succeeded in making his church the official Church of Scotland, the one and only "Kirk," and the Catholic religion was outlawed. What was it about religion that those who practiced one faith could not allow others to pray in a different way? She must ask Iain's opinion about that.

But Iain was not hers to ask. And she should be thinking about moving on. She did not want to live every day, seeing him, knowing he was promised to another woman.

She'd been driving only an hour or so when there was a sign, *Balmoral Castle*, pointing off to the right. The Queen's Scottish residence. She took the exit and a short while later slipped into one of the parking spaces provided for visitors. The castle itself was not open to the public, but the grounds were when the family was not in residence.

The castle was not particularly interesting architecturally, and blinds were drawn at every window, giving it a closed, unwelcoming appearance.

There was a rose garden and a maze. Otherwise there was not much of interest. Then she raised her eyes to the surrounding hills and spotted them. The Queen's cattle. Iain's cattle, with their long reddish-brown coats and their snub noses and long horns. Her eyes blurred with tears and the happy mood with which she had started the day fled as quickly as it had come.

Damn it, she told herself. *Get a grip. It's not the end of the world and he's not the last man on earth.* Resolutely she squared her shoulders and headed back to the car to continue her trip. She was going to enjoy this day and to hell with Iain Glendenning!

And surprisingly, she did. The endlessly winding road, the high green hills and low mountains, all with their unique rounded tops, all green clad but without any trees, were a totally new experience to her. At one point she came to a sign saying "Weak Bridge Ahead." She laughed aloud. What was she supposed to do about a weak bridge? Just before the bridge she pulled the car to the side of the road and got out to examine it. Constructed of stone and only one lane wide, it appeared sturdy enough. She got back in her car and edged slowly over it, with a sigh of relief when she arrived safely on the other side.

What was the purpose of the sign? She had come a long way on this road through Cairngorm National Park. There were no possible detours. Would some motorists just turn and retrace their paths?

Five hours later she was in Nairn and soon after, at the entrance to the inn Aileen Glendenning had recommended. Getting out of her car, Lara stretched her shoulders, tired from the long day, and, backpack in hand, strolled in to enquire whether they had a room for her.

A little boy sat on the floor in the front hall, pushing a toy truck back and forth. When he saw her, he ran into one of the rooms, calling "Mommy!"

A somewhat distraught looking young woman emerged and said, "I'm Annie, the innkeeper. How may I help you?" Then her eyes widened. "You're the one!"

"The one?"

"The one he's been waiting for, for three days. Davie, run tell Iain she's here."

"Iain?"

"I don't know what kind of disagreement you two had, but he's been nearly out of his mind ever since he arrived." She eyed Lara as if to say, "What did you do to him?"

Davie came running back from the lounge. Lara glanced up to see Iain stopped dead in the doorway. His shoulders sagged, his hair was tangled, and he had a three-day growth of beard. When he spoke, his voice was hoarse. "We need to talk."

"You should have done some talking a considerable time ago."

He held out his hand in supplication. "Please, Lara."

She nodded.

"My room?"

"No. I don't think so." She turned to the young woman. "Is there someplace private…?"

"Why don't you go out in the garden?" She nodded to a door beside the registration desk. "There are benches and you'll have a view of the sea, and all the privacy you want."

Lara nodded and stalked to the door. Iain stood, frozen in place. "Coming?" she said.

He followed her silently.

She chose a bench in the rose garden and sat down.

He stood for a moment uncertainly. Then he sat, his head down, his arms leaning on his legs, his body hunched as if in pain.

Lara longed to reach out to him, to take away his pain. But she had been in pain, too. Pain he had caused. "So," she said, "talk."

"I should have told ye. I was sure of it from that first time we rode together. No, even earlier, when I carried ye into the house after ye fell into the gorse. And then when I kissed ye the first time…"

"Yes?" Lara said, remembering that first kiss.

"I realized I loved ye. I wanted to spend the rest of my life with ye. It was a shock. Like being struck by lightning."

Lara held her breath. So, he had sensed it, too. She waited.

"But I was engaged to Allison and I didn't know how to get out of it. That day when I asked ye how ye broke off with a man ye were pledged to marry? I was hopin' for help. I needed to know how to do it."

Lara remembered that conversation, all the questions Iain asked. A small smile touched her lips.

"After that last time we kissed, I resolved to go to Edinburgh and tell Allison I couldna' marry her, that I loved someone else."

"So why didn't you?"

"Before I could, she showed up unannounced and uninvited. I couldn't break up with her there, in my home. That would have been grossly unfair to her. I needed to tell her in Edinburgh, where she was in her element, where she had friends to fall back on. So, I drove to Edinburgh with her the next morning, and when we got to her flat, I told her that I was in love with someone else and couldna' marry her. I also told her that the life she envisioned for us could ne'er have happened. I would never leave Athdara, me horses and me cattle."

"What did she say?" Lara was drawn into his story in spite of her resolve to remain cold and distant.

"She laughed." He gazed at Lara with a puzzled frown on his face. "Of all the responses I expected that was the last one. I'd braced meself for tears or shouting, and she laughed. She told me she'd been expecting this for some time, but she'd decided to wait and see how I would 'play it out.' She also said if I hoped she was going to return my ring I was dreaming." He shook his head. "Why would I have wanted that ring? A big, ugly, square cut diamond. She chose it. I would ne'er put such a ring on yer finger."

Lara listened in amazement. He was assuming they would marry.

"Anyway, I'd said all I needed to, so I took yer

advice and ran. I couldn't wait to get home and tell ye. And then when I got there and ye were gone…" His voice broke.

He gazed into Lara's eyes. "Ewan told me to come after ye. He said ye were headed for Nairn and would be traveling by bus. Me mother told me she recommended this inn. I got here three days ago and every day I've had less hope. God, Lara, I was so afraid I'd never find ye again." He put his head in his hands, the picture of despair.

Lara longed to put her arms around him, to comfort him, but she held herself in tight rein. She waited until he had himself under control. Then she said, "So where do we go from here?"

"Marry me, Lara. I can't begin to imagine me life without ye."

"No," she surprised herself by saying. "I won't marry you. Not yet, anyway. We'll go on as we have for the present. Later, if this thing between us is real, if it lasts, we'll talk about marriage. Neither of us is in any emotional space right now to make a decision that will shape the rest of our lives. You've just come out of a relationship you decided was wrong for you, I've come out of one that was certainly wrong for me. This is not the time to make such a commitment."

"That sounds to me like a maybe."

Lara laughed in spite of her resolve not to. "Yes. I suppose it's a maybe."

They strolled back into the inn. Iain had an irrepressible grin on his face.

"You've worked things out," Annie said with an answering smile. "So ye'll be staying tonight?"

Lara said, "If you have a room for me."

The innkeeper frowned. "I'm afraid I don't. We're full up. But Iain's room has two beds."

Lara studied Iain. He appeared to be truly exhausted. He should not be driving in this condition. "That will be all right."

She looked at Iain. "Have you had anything to eat in the last twenty-four hours?"

He appeared to be puzzled by the question.

"No. He hasn't," Annie answered for him. "Why don't I send a couple of sandwiches to your room? And something to drink?"

"Thank you. Perhaps a pot of tea?"

A half hour later, with nothing left but crumbs on his plate, Iain stretched out on his bed and was asleep in moments.

Lara covered him with a blanket and gazed down at him. All signs of strain were gone from his face. Even with a three-day stubble on his chin and hair that hadn't been combed in days, he still was the handsomest man she'd ever known. And he was all hers. Happiness welled up in her. Was she going to marry him? Of course she was, in time. Live in Scotland with him? Yes, a thousand times, yes. Be Lady to his Laird? Naturally.

Living in Athdara Castle would not be so very different from living on the ranch in Alberta. Horses were horses and cattle were cattle, although she wasn't sure what her brothers would make of Iain's "Heeland" herd.

How long should she make him suffer? Not long. She couldn't keep up the pretense of not loving him for very long. It required better acting skills than hers. She'd see what the next days brought.

She crawled under the covers and was asleep in moments.

The next morning, she was awakened by the sound of the shower running and a really good baritone voice loudly singing, "*Scots wha hae wi' Wallace bled, Scots wham Bruce has aften led, Welcome to yer gory bed, Or to victory!*"

He could sing? Scotland had no national anthem, but *Scots Wha Hae* was as close as it got.

She was out of bed and combing her hair when he emerged from the steaming bathroom wearing only a towel.

"Good mornin', my love," he said, giving her a smacking kiss on the cheek as he strolled by her to put on the clothes he had discarded in a heap on the way to the shower.

She could not help the smile that lit her face. He was irrepressible. "Did you not pack any fresh clothes?"

"I dinna figure on bein' gone so long. I expected ye to be here when I arrived."

"And you would apologize, and I would go meekly back with you?"

He squirmed uncomfortably. "Aye. Somethin' like that. Ye gave me a harsh three days, lassie."

She softened. "They were no easier for me."

"What say we make a pact."

"A pact?"

"We will ne'er again lie to each other. Not even a wee lie of omission. There will always be the truth between us. And we will ne'er part in anger."

"I like that."

"Shall we kiss on it?"

"Not while all you're wearing is a towel." With that parting shot she closed the bathroom door.

They ate a hearty Scottish breakfast. Lara observed in amazement as Iain ate the two eggs, grilled tomato, haggis, and toast, and then eyed the remains of her breakfast. Wordlessly she exchanged her plate for his, and he demolished all that was left of hers. How did he stay so fit eating like that? Come to think of it she had observed no obese Scottish men. It must have something to do with their active lifestyle.

They checked out and only realized when they got to the parking lot that they had two cars. "I'll drive the rental back to Edinburgh and we can continue on together from there."

"No, ye won't. I'm not about to let ye out of me sight now I've found ye. What was the rental agency?"

"Hertz. But…"

He was already on his phone. "They have an office in Inverness. That's a half hour from here. We'll return it there."

Lara smiled. The Scottish male. Ever in charge. In this instance she really didn't mind. She wanted to be with Iain.

"Ye know we're a half hour from Culloden. We really shouldn't leave without ye visiting it."

"I had no idea it was near here." The battle that changed forever the path of Scottish history.

Lara was surprised when they got there. Culloden Field was just that, a field where a horrendous battle took place, but just a field. As she wandered through it, she found occasional rough stone markers where men fell. McDougal, Stewart, McKenzie. She trod more slowly, Iain somewhere ahead of her. He had stopped at a particular marker. She joined him. *MacInnes.* Her breath came out in a whoosh.

"Someone from my family, someone from my clan, died here on April 16, 1746."

"Aye, I know. That's why I wanted ye to come here. I told ye the MacInnes were Highlanders."

She knelt down at the marker and the tears came. She brushed her eyes.

He rested his hand on her head. "The battle lasted only an hour. Prince Charlie's men were exhausted and hungry. They were no match for the British forces."

Lara stood and came into the circle of his arms, burying her head against his chest.

He continued speaking, his voice neutral as he recounted horrors. "That's not the ugliest part of the story. After the battle, when by tradition women were allowed onto the field to carry away the dead and tend to the wounded, the British Commander sent men out onto the field to kill all the wounded. No man survived, except the Prince. He was spirited away early in the battle, perhaps even before it began. The story of his escape with the help of a woman has become a myth. For my money, he was a coward who deserted his men in battle." His voice had turned harsh.

Lara realized Culloden was as real and present to Iain as today's news. That it had shaped him, perhaps shaped all Scots.

"Ye must visit the Information Center before we leave. Read everything on the walls."

Lara nodded. She left him standing in the field.

In the Information Center, both sides of the conflict were presented in written and pictorial form, with absolute impartiality. Red for the British side, blue for the Jacobite side. It took Lara more than an hour to go through the exhibits and read the information. It took as long to read the exhibits as it did the British troops, well fed and rested, and armed with cannons, to defeat the exhausted, hungry Scots, armed with swords and knives. As Iain said, Bonnie Prince Charlie appeared to have been the only one who escaped…dressed as Flora MacDonald's maid.

An hour later they were on the road to Edinburgh. They took the fast route, the highway. The traffic was considerably more than Lara had experienced on the road through the Cairngorms, but she didn't have to drive, so she just relaxed and gazed at the scenery. Iain drove easily but with total concentration. There was no chit-chat. That he saved for their stops along the way. They had scones and tea at their first stop. Small, delicate, melt-in-your-mouth scones. Iain ate four, Lara two.

"Ye don't eat enough to keep a bird alive," he observed.

"Good thing, since you always need more than you're given."

"Aye, I hadna' thought of it that way." He grinned. "I guess ye'll just have to keep me around to clean up all yer scraps. When we marry"—he gave her a speculative glance—"that is, say, just suppose we marry…"

"Yes," she encouraged.

"What would ye say to livin' in the cottage fer a time? It would be, I don't know, a wee bit more private."

"I would say, supposing we should marry, living in the cottage would be a fine idea. Although I would want to update it. Bring in electricity and running water. And some good heating source other than just the fireplaces."

"I think that might be possible. Did ye have any timeline in mind?" He kept his eyes on the road.

"I haven't said I'd marry you."

"I know, but just supposin'…"

"Change of subject, Iain. Who is taking care of your prize horses and Highland cattle while you're here chasing after me?"

"Ewan said he get some extra help from the village. There are several young boys who've worked with us in the past. Ewan told me to go find ye and to do whatever I had to, to get ye back, up to and including crawling to ye on me knees. Would ye like me to crawl to ye on me knees?"

"I don't think that will be necessary. We seem to be managing without any crawling. Although a little more supplication might be in order."

"I have me own idea of what's in order."

He turned off the highway onto a small country road and came to a stop beside a fast-running stream.

There he pulled her roughly to him and kissed her, putting his whole soul into it.

She at first tried to push him away, then no longer wanted to. She gave herself totally to the passion and yearning of his kiss. Her treacherous body simply overrode her determination to remain objective. She responded with her whole heart.

Was she going to marry Iain Glendenning? Of course she was. But he didn't have to know that yet. She had to preserve some small semblance of control.

When he came up for breath, he said, "Even better

than I remembered. God, I love kissing ye, Lara. I'm afraid if we ever get around to really making love, they'll find nothing in our bed on the morrow but cinders."

She laughed. She wanted to hold on to her anger, but she just couldn't. He was so completely lovable. And, she admitted to herself, she wanted him in her bed as much as he wanted her in his. How much longer could she hold out?

Later, back on the highway, he asked, "Have ye seen Edinburgh?"

"Not really. I've been through it twice and I spent half a day shopping there, but I've never visited any of the sights."

"What say we spend a couple of nights there? That way we'd have a full day for sightseeing. It's a wonderfully old city. The Royal Mile is something every visitor to Scotland must see, and there is something else I want to show you. A picture in the Royal Portrait Gallery."

"Of whom?"

"Ye'll see."

That afternoon they checked into the Royal Scots Club, two single rooms.

Lara was surprised and a little disappointed he had not asked for a double. But he had effectively told her the next move was up to her. He had laid his heart, his soul, at her feet. If she wanted him, she would have to tell him so. And she was not yet ready. Some residual sense of betrayal still lingered.

They dropped their bags in their rooms and met again in the lobby. "We'll take a cab," he said. "We'd never find a parking space where we're goin'."

The front desk called a taxi for them. Lara laughed aloud when she viewed the big, boxy, old fashioned vehicle.

"They're copies of the London cabs of the 1930's," he said. "The city ordered a fleet of them for Edinburgh to add to the local color—as if there weren't enough local color already here."

"Take us someplace where my friend here can buy some clothes," Lara instructed the driver. "Then wait for us, please. It won't take long."

"What?" Iain started to say something and then changed his mind. "Right. I've been in these clothes for four days now. A pair of jeans and a shirt and some underwear shouldn't take long to find."

"Marks and Spencer," the driver said.

On arriving at the store, Lara said, "I'll just wait with the cab."

Fifteen minutes later Iain was back, wearing all new clothes. Only his runners were the same.

"New from the skin out," he said.

"Where are the ones you were wearing?"

"I told the sales clerk to burn them," he said. "To the National Portrait Gallery," he instructed the driver.

"You didn't!" she said.

"That I did," he replied, smug and self-satisfied. "They were the clothes of a defeated mon. I had no wish to wear them again."

"So, if you are not a 'defeated mon,' what are you?

"Why, on the path to victory. Not there yet, mind ye, but I think on the right path."

"You're as crazy as a…" Lara was lost for words. His high spirits were contagious.

Ten minutes later they were there.

It was obvious the building had once been a church. In its day it must have been an important one, because it took an entire city block. To enter it they had to go through a security screening much like those in airports.

After being thoroughly checked, they strolled through to an impressive high, square foyer surrounded by gothic arches. Above the arches was a complete pictorial history of Scotland through its men and women. It began with the Stone Age and ended with what Lara assumed, from the clothing, to be the early twentieth century. She stood in awe, examining every step of the epic story displayed high above her.

"I love this room."

Iain said. "Aye. I do, too. But this is not why I fetched ye here.

"No?"

"Come with me." He took her hand and led her into the main part of the museum, past portraits of men in kilts and in military uniforms and women in various styles of long period dresses. In the third gallery Iain stopped before a portrait of a young woman.

"Recognize the dress?"

"It's the blue dress! The one hanging in my room."

"The one we found in the trunk and I told ye I had seen it before? Here it is."

"But who is she?" Lara squinted at the small brass plaque beside the portrait. "It says *Lady Elspeth Glendenning Ballantyne, 1856*. It's Elspeth Glendenning. The woman whose diary I'm reading. She's beautiful!"

Iain studied the portrait. "She's clearly one of my ancestors, but I've never been told anything about her.

Odd that her portrait should be here instead of hanging in the castle with the rest of the Glendennings. I suppose the fact the painter was George Hayter, one of Scotland's greatest painters, might have somethin' to do with it."

Lara said, "She was an incredible woman, you know. Far ahead of her time. She was fearless, and adventurous."

"How do ye ken?"

"It's all there in her diaries. Read them. I'm not halfway through the first one yet, but maybe we could read some of it together. I can tell you, she's headed for trouble."

"How so?"

"She's a Glendenning and she's fallen in love with a MacInnes."

"Now ye have me interested. That's us. A Glendenning and a MacInnes."

"But there was a feud between the families then."

"Aye. The Glendenning were split in their loyalties at the time of Culloden. One son fought with the Jacobites, the other with the British. The MacInnes believed, rightly or wrongly, that Sean Glendenning killed Dougal MacInnes. It started a clan war that didn't stop until the late nineteenth century. And it stopped because there were no more MacInnes left in Scotland.

"You think you and I would be the first Glendenning and MacInnes to wed?"

"Aye. Romeo and Juliet. Only, I hope, with a happy ending."

He took her hand and they left the gallery. "Do ye think we could read a bit of that diary tonight?"

"Of course. But I'm hungry right now. Where can

we go for dinner?"

"There's a place I like near the Scots Club. Are ye up for a little walk?"

"After sitting all day in a car? Of course."

Fifteen minutes later they were at an Italian restaurant. The owner greeted Iain warmly and seated them at a quiet table for two in the back of the room.

"They know you here," she said.

"I like pasta," he said.

"Is there any food you don't like?" she said.

"Broccoli," he answered without hesitation. "And ye rarely find broccoli in an Italian restaurant."

Iain was right about the food.

They strolled back to the hotel and Iain accompanied her to her room "Let's read a bit of Elspeth's diary tonight. On my honor I'll behave meself."

"Of course. Come in."

Lara took the diary out of her case and sat in the only chair in the room. Iain sprawled on the bed, propped up on pillows.

With the diary in her hands, Lara recounted the story up to the point where Elspeth offered herself to Lachlan only to be rejected. He was willing to marry her, but not to have an affair. She was now considering marriage to him. A Glendenning and a MacInnes. The long feud between the two families made that an unlikely choice. How could they marry under the circumstances?

01 August 1850

I think my views on marriage may be changing. Marriage to Lachlan MacInnes has a definite appeal. But I'm uncertain how it can be accomplished. Our two families have been locked in a pattern of hatred and division for more than a century. Can we be the ones finally to change that?

Chapter Six

The Past

Elspeth waited all that day and night hoping Lachlan would come to her room. Finally, she wrote a brief note and sent Agnes to find him, with instructions to be sure he was alone when she delivered it.

An hour later, there was a knock at her door and Lachlan entered.

Agnes, without being told, took her chair outside the door and closed it behind the Laird's brother.

"Ye sent for me?"

"Come sit beside me."

Lachlan placed a chair close to where Elspeth lay, her damaged leg resting on pillows. "How is the leg? Are ye still in pain?"

"No. The throbbing has stopped. I think it is healing nicely, thanks to you and your family."

"So…?" He gazed at her.

Elspeth plunged in, speaking quickly lest she lose her nerve. "You said you might consider marrying me."

"Aye, that I did."

"My answer is yes. That is if you're still of the same mind."

There was silence in the room so thick it could have been cut by a knife.

Lachlan leaned back in his chair. "Are ye sure,

lassie? It will nae be easy. What will yer father think? A Glendenning marrying a MacInnes? Even me brother will have plenty to say."

Tears threatened. "I don't care what they say. I've thought of you day and night since you rescued me. And I'm afraid my thoughts have not been maidenly ones. I love you, Lachlan MacInnes. And I don't care about some silly feud over something that may or may not have happened more than a century ago. If you'll have me, I'll be your wife."

Lachlan was stunned speechless for a moment, as if she had spoken in some foreign tongue.

The tears threatening Elspeth spilled over. "Oh God. I've made a fool of myself again. You don't want me."

Swiftly his arms were around her, his hot kisses on her hair, her eyelids, her neck and, finally her mouth. His very soul was in that kiss. His hand ranged over her body, arousing wherever they touched.

She exulted. He was hers!

Visibly shaken, he sat back. "We'll save something for the marriage bed. I love ye, Elspeth. It may not be easy, but I promise ye, on my soul, we will be together."

****

His brother was in the Hall, finishing up the day's business when Lachlan found him.

"I would speak with ye privately in your rooms when ye are done here."

Abhainn nodded.

Lachlan paced back and forth, waiting for his brother. Abhainn had been after him for the last five years to marry. However, marriage to a Glendenning

110

would not be welcomed.

But Elspeth was the first, the only, woman Lachlan ever met he wanted to marry. She had such spirit, such an unconventional wildness that found an answering spirit in his. She was his other half, the completion of his soul. The mate he had sought for these last many years. He had almost despaired of ever finding her, and then she had literally dropped into his arms. If that wasn't fate, what was it?

Abhainn entered. "Ye wished to speak with me?"

"I mean to marry."

"That's good news indeed. Who is the lass?"

"Elspeth Glendenning."

To his credit, Abhainn did not shout or bang his fist on the table. "Ye know this is not welcome news. It is not what I had hoped for."

"I love her, brother. I love her to the depths of my soul."

Abhainn was silent for so long Lachlan began to wonder if the interview was over. Then he said, "How do you propose to get her father's agreement to this union?"

"Elspeth is beyond the age that requires her father's consent, and she has some money in her own name. She needs no approval to marry. Nor, I remind you, do I. We mean to be wed. I ask ye to give us your blessing."

"Ye know I will, brother. But do ye not at least intend to do her father the courtesy of asking for her hand?"

"We both know full well what his answer would be. No. I do not intend to make that pointless journey. This feud between our clans has gone on long enough.

We mean to be wed here, as soon as the banns can be read. We will be tellin' her father, not askin' him."

Abhainn sighed. "Very well. It will have to be a Highland marriage, a handfast ceremony. There is no visiting priest due here for another three months. Ye will stand before me and all our clansmen and declare yer intention to marry each other. It's a binding marriage in the Highlands, as ye know, but if yer young miss wants the kirk and preacher, ye'll have to wait."

"I'll talk to Elspeth. Explain things to her. I doubt she'll want any ceremony that means waiting." A smile lit his lips as he remembered Elspeth's passionate response to his kisses. No. She would not want a long, chaste engagement.

****

Elspeth wrote ecstatically in her diary that night that their marriage was all arranged and would take place ten days hence in the Great Hall of MacInnes Castle.

She and Lachlan saw but little of each other in those ten days. The women of the castle were busy cooking and cleaning and sewing. Seamstresses were working on Elspeth's wedding dress, a simple frock with short puffed sleeves, made of light blue silk taffeta, low necked, and gathered under her breasts to fall in graceful gathers to the floor. Embroidered Scottish Thistles encircled the neckline and sleeves. She found a pair of long white gloves in her boxes to go with the dress, and she carefully snipped the seams of the third finger to bare it to receive her wedding ring. She found, also from her boxes, blue silk slippers she had worn only once before. She was altogether pleased with the ensemble, for this, the most important day of her life. If she had occasional twinges of conscience about her father not knowing, not being present, she thrust the thought aside, and resumed her happy preparations for the wedding.

The day before she was to marry, Mairi came to her room bearing a beautiful blue paisley cashmere shawl. "Ye might like to wear this for your wedding. I wore it for mine. The Hall is cold and ye don't want to be shivering through the ceremony.

Elspeth burst into tears.

"What's wrong, my dear?"

"Nothing's wrong. It's just I'm so happy I can hardly bear it. I keep fearing something will go wrong."

"Pre-wedding nerves, Elspeth. Naught more. Every bride is that way."

"Mairi, what happens in the marriage bed?"

"Oh dear. Did your mother ne'er talk to ye about such things?"

"She died when I was only three."

Mairi took a deep breath. "Men and women are made different. He has a dangle here—" she placed her hand over her mound "—that will fit into you here," she touched Elspeth, "to put his seed into your body so you can have a child. For the rest, I shall leave such instruction to yer husband. But I can tell ye, it gives much pleasure to a woman who loves her mon. It can be as close to heaven as we get on earth. Now stop fretting. Have ye been able to take a few steps on yer own, now that the braces have been removed?"

"I pace around and around the room. I do those strengthening exercises ye taught me. But my leg is still swollen and"—tears welled up—"I cannot wear my silk slippers. My right foot is too swollen to fit in them."

"Slippers are not a requirement. Ye can be wed in yer stockings, no one will notice or care. Everyone knows of yer accident. We're all just relieved ye can walk again."

Finally, the day came. Abhainn came to her room to escort her to her intended. She held tightly to his arm as they approached the Hall. She could hear the babble of voices before she saw the guests. There must have been two hundred people present. For a moment she wanted to run away. Abhainn sensed her fear and hesitation. He smiled down at her. "It's all right, my dear. These people are your assurance that your marriage did indeed take place. With no preacher, we need many witnesses."

Then her gaze fell on Lachlan. He was standing before the Laird's chair, dressed in his plaids and a very formal, very new black jacket, with the MacInnes plaid across his shoulder. All fears fled. She was about to marry the man she loved.

Abhainn, standing in front of his Laird's chair spoke. "Is there any man here knows any reason this man and this woman should not wed?"

The crowd was silent.

"Then we shall proceed."

The ceremony was simple. They each pledged their troth, their faithfulness and fidelity to each other.

They spoke simple words. "I, Elspeth Glendenning, in the eyes of God and before these assembled people, do take thee, Lachlan MacInnes, to my lawful wedded husband from this day forth, as long as we both shall live."

"I, Lachlan MacInnes, in the eyes of God and before these assembled people, do take thee Elspeth

Glendenning, to my lawful wedded wife, from this day forth, as long as we both shall live."

He slipped a ring on her third finger, a smaller version the large clan ring he wore on the first finger of his left hand. The MacInnes motto, *fortiter et recte,* boldly and rightly, was engraved around an amber cairngorm stone.

Abhainn announced, "In the eyes of God and before this assembly, Lachlan MacInnes and Elspeth Glendenning are husband and wife."

The crowd burst out in loud, cheerful shouts and somewhere a bagpipe started playing. Soon there was dancing, raucous and wild, men swinging other men with abandon as the women piled plates on the table. The wedding feast. Elspeth and Lachlan were seated at the head of the long table, next to Abhainn and Fiona. Mairi was there with her husband as well. He was a tall, rugged man. Elspeth found herself wondering if all Highland men were so handsome. She stole a peek at her husband. He had relaxed back in his chair. He held a goblet of wine in his hand, but he did not appear to be drinking from it.

"Does the wine not please you, husband?" she murmured.

"Aye, the wine is good enough," he answered, "but I want my wits about me when we are finally left alone."

Elspeth shivered.

A long three hours later, the couple were escorted noisily to the chamber prepared for them. There was a fire in the fireplace and food and drink on a table between two chairs in front of the fire. But Elspeth's eyes were glued on the large bed. Someone had scattered rose petals on the white bed cover. Their sweet scent permeated the room.

"Are ye hungry?" Lachlan asked "Ye ate nothing at the banquet."

"No," she replied. "I'm not hungry."

"Then I suggest we ready ourselves for bed."

He took off his shoes and high socks, removed the plaid from his shoulder, took off his jacket and unwound his kilt as she stood glued to the spot. He stood before her dressed only in his long shirt.

"Turn around," he ordered. "I know ye can no unbutton yer gown yerself, and it's a chore I've been longing to do."

Slowly he undressed her, using the opportunity to touch his lips to each new bit of flesh revealed. Soon she was standing in front of him dressed only in her thin muslin shift. She was shivering uncontrollably.

"What happens? Tell me. I need to know. What are you going to do?"

He was startled. "Do ye no ken anything of what happens between men and women?"

She sat down in the fireplace chair. Tears started to flow. "No. I know only what Mairi told me. Only that you must somehow put your seed into my body to make a child."

He gazed at her for a long moment. "'Tis naught to cry about, mo chidra. I will teach ye."

He took off his long shirt. "Observe me well, Elspeth. See what a man's body is like."

She stared at him. Her eyes wandered slowly down his muscled torso. There was a dusting of red hair on his chest and arms and his strong muscular legs. She tried to avoid glancing between his legs, but her eyes were drawn there against her determination not to do so. There was a nest of red curls and in the middle a not particularly frightening dangle. Was that the part that would go into her? Make babies?

He laughed. "I know it seems harmless enough now. But if I kiss you, even touch you, it will become verra different. Now it's your turn. Take off your shift."

She slipped it over her head, blushing furiously as she stood there, naked as the day she was born, the eyes of her husband appraising her.

"God, ye are beautiful, Elspeth." He strolled around her, close enough for her to feel his breath on her skin, but still he did not touch her.

"We are made different so we can fit together and be one."

"But how…"

"Lie on the bed and I'll show ye."

She stood, reluctant to take that last, frightening step.

He lifted her in his arms and gently placed her on the bed. Then he lay next to her, turning so his body partially covered hers. One hand cupped her breast and rubbed her nipple as he kissed her deeply. "In the marriage bed I must push myself into you, here." He cupped her mound. With one finger he rubbed her in a shockingly intimate way.

She squirmed and tried to ignore the heat he was creating in her most private place.

"Stop. Please. I don't think I can do this."

"Of course you can do this. Men and women have been doing this since the beginning of time. I promise I will not enter you until you ask me to."

"But that will not happen."

"I assure you it will."

He kissed her deeply as his hand continued to tease. Then, to her great shock, he was kissing her breast, taking her nipple between his teeth, all the while his other hand continued caressing and teasing her between her legs. She twisted and turned with the agony, the pleasure of it. Her body convulsed as she climaxed. She cried out, and he placed his body fully over hers.

"Do you want me to join with you now?"

She closed her eyes as her body throbbed under him. "I don't know."

"Not yet? Very well. I'm a patient man, although I can tell you this shaft of mine is giving me some pain. It wants to go home."

She touched him. Timidly she allowed her hand to wander, to trace the curls she found on his chest. She slid her hand lower and gasped. She sat bolt upright. Where before there had been a soft, non-threatening appendage, there was now a very large rod of steel.

"I told you it would change the moment I touched you."

"But you can't thrust that into me. It's too big. It will never fit."

"It will fit. You will come to like the pleasure it can give ye."

As he spoke, he was again touching her, tweaking the place that was so sensitive, that made her yearn for more.

She began again to be hot, so very hot and moist. She was unable to lie still; her body rose to give his hand better access… "Now," she said. "Please, now."

He centered his body over hers and drove in fast, as

far as he could go.

He muffled her scream with a kiss as a searing pain ripped through her.

He stopped moving, deep inside her. "That was yer maidenhead. I had to break through it. It was better just to do it, and not to have ye afraid and tense."

She lay still, adjusting to his weight on her, to the large thing now inside her. "So, this is what happens," she said. "I think I like you inside me. I don't want you to leave just yet."

He shuddered. "I have no intention of leaving you just yet." Slowly and with great deliberation he started to move.

This she had not expected. The heat increased. Without conscious intention her body rose to meet him, rhythm matching rhythm, faster and faster. She heard little guttural noises and realized they were hers. She was crying out with each of his thrusts. She couldn't help herself. Then her world exploded. As if from a great distance came his loud "aaah" as he fell on top of her.

So now she knew. She knew it all. How could she have been so stupid as to think she could do this just once with a man? Just to satisfy her intellectual curiosity. She wanted to do this again, and again. She never wanted to stop.

He still lay on top of her, but his thing was no longer big. It had slipped out of her, small and useless.

He roused himself to ask, "Do ye like the secrets of the marriage bed, mo chidra?"

She gave a contented purr. "Can we do it again?"

He laughed. "Give me a few minutes to recover, my love. We'll see how many times we can do it tonight."

****

In the morning, Lachlan left her to attend to his usual duties. He promised to return in the late afternoon.

Incredibly sore, barely able to walk, Elspeth wrote in her diary the most intimate details about the night that had just passed between them. She touched herself where Lachlan had touched her and was instantly aroused. How had she lived all these years without knowing the pleasure her body was capable of? It would be hard to get through the next few hours until her husband was again in her arms, in their bed.

The days and nights took on a sort of pattern. They now joined the others for dinner each evening, but the afternoons and nights were theirs. She discovered she could transport Lachlan to full arousal just by touching him. The sense of power it gave her was overwhelming.

She loved him. She loved him body and soul.

In the third week of their marriage, still in the thrall of her newfound sexuality, she began to be uncomfortable about her father. She should write to him. No. That was the coward's way. They should go to him together and tell him of their marriage. He deserved that much, at least. She should have written to him before their marriage to tell him of their plans, but the vision of him arriving, trying to stop the ceremony, was too real for her to risk.

The deed was done now. She was well and truly a wife. Her father could do nothing to change that. They should make plans to go and meet with him soon.

When Lachlan came home late that afternoon, she broached the subject to him.

"Aye. I've been thinkin' on that, too. It is long past time we should visit yer father. He'll no be happy about this."

"I know. But he can't undo what's done, and when he sees how happy I am, he'll relent. He'll adjust to the idea of a Glendenning marrying a MacInnes. After all, royalty has been marrying former enemies for centuries to create peace. How is this different?

"Well, for one thing, I am no royal. I'm a Highlander, and we are distrusted and disliked by lowlanders and city folk. I've been meaning to ask ye. How is it ye lived in Edinburgh when ye have lands and a castle south of the city?"

"My father tells me Athdara Castle is in great need of repair, hardly livable. And the house in New Town, Edinburgh, is very comfortable. It requires much less staff and it's near Papa's club, where he spends many hours."

"So, this Athdara Castle is just sitting there, empty and deteriorating?"

"Yes, I suppose you could think on it that way."

Lachlan frowned. "Ye know, we could fix it up. I have the men and boys at my disposal. I have a sufficiency of money. We could live there if ye like and if yer father approves."

"My father doesn't need to approve. Athdara Castle is mine. In my name solely. You have money? I mean enough money to undertake something like that? And you'd be willing to leave Lochleigh?"

"Leaving Lochleigh would nae be easy, but me brother is Laird. I'm like a third thumb. I hae no real place there. If ye would like Athdara Castle made livable once more, I have the men and the money to do it."

Elspeth smiled. "That might be just enough to make him accept our marriage. Even approve it. It's a wonderful idea."

They made their plans to leave within the week for Edinburgh.

****

In Keith Glendenning's study, Lachlan and Elspeth sat on straight-backed chairs rather like two children about to be disciplined by a headmaster, while Elspeth's father, on the other side of a vast desk, glowered at them.

"You mean to tell me that without my consent, or even my knowledge, you married? And worse, you married a MacInnes," he bellowed.

"Yes," Elspeth answered, unperturbed. She was accustomed to her father's bellowing.

"Sir," Lachlan said, "the decision was sudden. There was no time to get word to ye. I know I should have asked ye for the privilege of courtin' yer daughter. But wed we are. I now ask for yer blessing on our marriage. I have more than sufficient funds to support her in the manner to which she is accustomed. Yer daughter will ne'er want for anything. And if ye need evidence of that, I can supply it. It is time for the foolish feud between our two clans to be mended. What better way to accomplish that than by a wedding between a Glendenning and a MacInnes?"

Elspeth's father's face turned a deep red. For a moment it appeared he might collapse from the shock. Then he appeared to gather his wits about him. "Humph," he said. "Since it's done, there is nothing left for me but to wish you well."

"Thank ye, sir. I will do all in my power to make yer daughter happy."

Her father steepled his hands. "Where do you propose to live?"

Lachlan answered, "Lochleigh Castle. Me brother is Laird. We have a set of spacious and comfortable rooms there."

"Hmmm…" Her father appeared to doubt that any Highland dwelling could be comfortable.

"But Father," Elspeth intervened, "what if we were to restore Athdara Castle?"

"Don't be absurd. It would be a bottomless pit. No one has enough money to restore that old heap of stones."

"I have, sir, both money and access to workers."

Her father studied Lachlan speculatively. "I think before you commit yourself to such folly, you'd better make a thorough inspection of the castle. It's about a day's ride on horseback. You ride, I take it?"

"I grew up on horseback."

"Very well. I suggest you inspect Athdara Castle's condition for yourself. Go tomorrow. Elspeth can use the time you're away to pack her clothes and belongings, since I assume you will not be living here. You will spend the tonight here?"

"If ye are willing to have us."

"Of course. You are my daughter and son-in-law. We are now kin. Where else would you stay?"

Later in Elspeth's room, Lachlan said, "That went far better than I expected. Yer father appears to have accepted the fact of our marriage."

"I wonder…" Elspeth mused.

Early the next morning Lachlan set off for Athdara

Castle. His mount was not as responsive as his own horse, Bailoch, but he was a steady, reliable steed. After trying him out at a gallop and a run, Lachlan settled him into a comfortable trotting stride.

Lachlan arrived at Athdara Castle at mid-afternoon, bringing his steed to a halt in the long circular drive. He dismounted, studying the facade. There was certainly no visible sign of decay from this side of the castle. Even the roof appeared to be sound. He walked his mount around to the back and, after watering him from a nearby pump and watering trough, tethered him and entered through the kitchen, using the key his father-in-law had given him. He had been told the front entrance was both locked and barred on the inside with a thick plank fitted into L-shaped wrought iron fixtures.

He stepped into a spotless kitchen. Embers glowed red in the hearth. Someone was living here? He walked through the butler's pantry to a large formal dining room. The gleaming mahogany banquet table appeared to be merely waiting for dinner to be served. What was going on?

He crossed the large entrance hall to a drawing room. Here the furniture was sheathed in white dust covers, but a piano sat in a corner, its keys free of dust, a piece of music open as if it had been played only moments ago.

He strode on, more quickly. Why had his father-in-law suggested Athdara needed major work to be livable? He started up the grand staircase to the bedroom floor. He wandered from room to room, searching for signs of deterioration that could have made Glendenning think Athdara Castle was unlivable. He found none.

Why had he been sent on this fool's errand? Abruptly he began to fear for Elspeth. What if he had been gotten out of the way so Glendenning could spirit his wife away? He had to get back to the house in New Town as swiftly as possible.

He did not spare his mount on the return ride.

At midnight, in sight of the city gates, he was shot. He fell off his horse, hitting his head on a large rock, unconscious before he hit the ground.

His assailants came over and examined him. "Dead?

"Aye, as a doornail."

"We're to take his clan ring to Glendenning as proof. He said any money we find on the body is ours to keep."

They rifled through his clothing, taking everything that could identify him, then stripped him down to his shirt. Quality clothing was hard to come by.

****

Brother Ambrose was on his way to market at dawn with his wheelbarrow full of produce to sell. A young novice accompanied him. The boy first spied the body.

The monk crossed himself and knelt beside Lachlan.

Lachlan moaned.

"He's alive, glory be to God. Here, take these cabbages and potatoes out of the barrow. Put them in your sack. That's it. Now help me lift him into the wheelbarrow. You go on to the market and sell those. I must return to the abbey immediately and get help for this poor soul. Or the last rites, if God so wills."

****

"I don't understand what's taking Lachlan so long. It's been three days." Elspeth paced back and forth in the library.

Her father glanced up impatiently. "You are wearing a hole in the rug. Sit down, for God's sake. Mayhap when he observed the condition of the castle, he had second thoughts about his marriage."

"Don't be ridiculous, Father. Lachlan has no money concerns. If the castle cannot be made livable, we'll return to Lochleigh. I quite like it there."

Her father didn't answer, and Elspeth continued her pacing. "I wish Hamish were here. He'd know what to do. I'll send a message to Abhainn."

"Stop this foolishness!" her father bellowed. "Clearly your husband has chosen to abandon you. He has seen the wreck of a castle he dreamed about when he married you and has gone on to greener pastures!"

He got up and stormed out of the room.

Elspeth stared after her father, speechless. He had no idea of who or what Lachlan was, or what their marriage meant to them.

She had to get a message to Abhainn. Her father must have writing paper somewhere. She walked around to the other side of her father's desk and opened the top drawer. There, on top of bills and scraps of paper, sat Lachlan's ring. The ring he never, ever, removed from his finger.

She sat in stunned silence. If her father had Lachlan's ring, Lachlan was dead. He would never have parted with it while still he lived. Emptiness welled up in her. Her lover, her husband, her very life, was gone.

Her father had somehow arranged his death. Of that she was certain. He would never have dirtied his own hands.

An icy cold filled her, mind and body.

Her father came back into the library. "What are you doing at my desk?"

Wordlessly she held up Lachlan's ring.

Her father staggered.

"You arranged for my husband's death." Elspeth was white faced, her voice neutral of all expression. "You had Lachlan killed. There is no other way you could be in possession of this ring. Where is he? What have you done with my husband?" Her voice had risen to a scream.

Her father's face turned almost purple. He staggered, grabbed a chair for support and dropped to the floor.

Elspeth walked around the desk to where he lay, his breath rasping.

"My heart medicine," he gasped.

"Where is my husband?" Elspeth stood over him.

He stretched his hand to her, beseeching.

"Where?" She screamed at him.

His hand dropped to the floor and he stopped breathing.

"May you rot in hell," she said.

As she left the library, she came across the butler. "Johnstone, I believe my father may require your assistance. He's in the library."

A few minutes later, the butler knocked at her bedroom door. "I'm sorry, my lady. Your father is dead."

"Send for the doctor." Her voice was emotionless. "We'll need a death certificate. Please arrange for his burial in the family plot, where my mother is buried. I shall not be here. You will have to make all funeral arrangements. I have every confidence in you. Then send a message to my father's attorney. The reading of the will must be postponed until I return to Edinburgh with my brother-in-law."

"Certainly, my lady. But surely you will be here for the funeral?"

"No. I shall be in the Highlands with my husband's family."

She must get help. She must get back to Lochleigh. She had to see Abhainn.

She would not travel as a woman alone. She had done that once before. Too risky. She examined Lachlan's clothing. Knowing her father would probably react very negatively to his clan plaids, Lachlan had worn clothes that would blend in in Edinburgh. A well-cut, superfine navy-blue coat, doeskin breeches, and a white shirt with a cravat. She set about cutting the pants off at the bottom and hemming them to fit the length of her legs. His boots were impossible, but she had a pair of serviceable riding boots that didn't appear too feminine. His jacket was clearly too big, too wide at the shoulders. If she wore his cape, perhaps no one would notice the jacket.

She glanced in the mirror. A bit ridiculous, but it would have to do. But her hair?

She braided it tight. Then she tiptoed into the hallway. It would not do for Johnstone or the upstairs maid to find her rifling through her father's dressing room.

There was a large assortment of hats. Picking one that would cover her braids and shade her face, she slipped quickly back to her room.

In her jewelry casket she found a silver chain. Slipping Lachlan's ring on it, she put it around her neck, and hid it under her shirt.

Lachlan had left most of their money in the room. She counted it out. There was more than enough for any stops she needed to make along the way. She quickly sewed a pocket inside the jacket, at the back where it would pass unnoticed. She kept out only enough for immediate expenses. At the last moment, she took his plaid, the one he wrapped around his jacket. It would provide warmth when she needed it.

The fastest way to travel would be by coach as far as Nairn. There, she would need a horse for the rest of the journey first west and then north.

Four days later she staggered into Lochleigh castle and collapsed in the courtyard.

She came to in her own room, the one she had shared with Lachlan. Mairi was sitting beside her.

She propped up on her elbows and said, "I must see Abhainn!" Then she got up quickly and tried to get to the basin behind the screen in time, but the nausea was too severe.

Agnes was there instantly, cleaning up the floor and getting her water with which to rinse out her mouth and a cool damp cloth to wipe her face.

"Thank you, Agnes. I have missed you greatly while I was away." The child bobbed and retreated to her chair.

"I don't know what's wrong with me," Elspeth said to Mairi. "This happens every morning. I'm fine once it's over, but I've been sick every morning like this for the last week."

"Oh, my darling," Mairi said, "you're going to

have a baby. Morning sickness is the first sign."

"A baby?" For the first time since Lachlan's disappearance, Elspeth experienced the stirring of hope. Lachlan wasn't really gone. He was a seed growing in her belly. She was going to bear his son.

Mairi brought her back to the present. "You said you needed to speak with Abhainn? He wishes to speak with you, too. I'll go get him."

A few minutes later Abhainn strode into the room followed by his wife and his sister, Mairi, and Hamish.

Abhainn placed his hands on Elspeth's shoulders and kissed her on one cheek and then the other. "What's wrong, my dear?"

"I believe Lachlan is dead." Tears streamed down Elspeth's face, unchecked. "He rode out to Athdara Castle at my father's suggestion, and he never came back. It has been more ten days now."

Abhainn responded, disbelief resonating in his voice. "But surely if he was killed, someone would have found his body."

"No body was found. No murder was reported."

"Then perhaps he survived whatever attack was made, and is lying somewhere, injured."

A small flare of hope leapt into Elspeth's heart, then died. "No. My father had Lachlan's ring. Lachlan would never have given up that ring unless he was dead."

"Yer father—"

"I believe my father ordered my husband's death. And now we'll never be certain of what happened because my father is dead. He died of a heart attack when I accused him of killing Lachlan."

Abhainn sighed. "I was afraid no good could come

from a marriage between a MacInnes and a Glendenning."

"But good has come from it," Mairi said. "Elspeth is carrying Lachlan's child."

Abhainn sat back. "A life for a life. That is good. But I am not satisfied that Lachlan is dead. I must have real evidence of that before I believe it."

He gazed at Elspeth, lying on the couch, so wan and pale. "I must go to Edinburgh. Will ye stay here and let the MacInnes women care for ye? Traveling on horse's back cannot be very good for ye at this early stage of yer confinement."

"I can't stay. I need to be in Edinburgh while you seek the truth of this. Living with uncertainty is killing me."

"Very well. I put ye in Hamish's care. He has protected Lachlan since he was born. He will now protect Lachlan's son."

"I should like to take Agnes with me if I may."

"Agnes?" Abhainn appeared confused.

"The child in the corner there. She has been a great help to me."

"If her parents agree."

Elspeth was surprised to hear the child speak in a loud clear voice.

"I have no parents, sir…Please let me go with my lady."

"Of course, ye may go."

Turning again to Elspeth he said, "Ye have quite an entourage here. Clearly ye will need to go by coach once ye are beyond MacInnes lands. Fortunately, yer overturned coach is now roadworthy. Ye can travel in that."

The next day they left. Elspeth, Agnes, and Hamish. A coach driver had been found in the village. Abhainn had gone ahead on horseback. He had no patience for the slow, ponderous old landau.

Chapter Seven

The Present

"Wow. That's some story!" Iain was sitting bolt upright on the bed, his feet on the floor "She believed her father, a Glendenning, one of my ancestors, killed his daughter's husband, a MacInnes, one of yer ancestors."

"That's about the size of it," Lara answered from her chair on the other side of the room. "You still want to marry me?"

"Dinna joke about it, Lara."

"I didn't mean to speak lightly of it. But it does appear when a Glendenning and a MacInnes get together, trouble follows." Lara stood and stretched.

"It's up to us to break the curse." Iain stood and came over to her. "Elspeth spared us no details about her wedding night. Imagine, not just experiencing all that but then living it again as she wrote about it."

Lara shook her head. "What I'm having a hard time with is how she could be so unprepared. How could a girl be raised in such total ignorance about sex?"

"In the nineteenth century that was more common than you might think. Men went to brothels to be taught, women came to marriage ignorant."

Iain put his arms around her and kissed her deeply. She was melting, thinking, *why am I resisting when I know how much I want him*? Then his hand wandered to where it had certainly not been invited. She shoved him away. "Enough. Go to your own room, Iain. I'll see you in the morning.

"Yer a hard lass. How am I to sleep in this condition?"

In spite of her resolve not to, she glanced at his crotch, at his very hard, very large erection.

"I'm afraid that's your problem." She pushed him out the door and latched it behind him.

Then she smiled as she undressed and put on her oversized T-shirt. That had been fun. Let him suffer a bit. It would not hurt him.

She crawled into bed and found she couldn't sleep. She was so sexually aroused she couldn't even think straight. Before she could change her mind, she opened her door, walked across the hall and scratched at his door. He opened it a crack, then wide, and grinned at her. "Is it I have something ye want?"

"Shut up and take me to bed."

He laughed and, picking her up in his arms, kicked the door shut behind them.

****

In the morning they made love again, drowsy, coffee-flavored kisses, hands and bodies now secure in what they were seeking. Last night had been wild, neither of them in control, a long, protracted ride, both of them wanting more, more, and then still more until at the end, shattering, Iain collapsed over her as she convulsed around him, shockwave after shockwave hitting her.

"You were pretty good last night," she told him as they sat at the breakfast they had ordered in.

"Ye were not so bad yerself," he replied. "In fact, I think I can say with authority that was probably the best sex anyone in the world has ever had."

Lara laughed. "You're a world authority, are you?"

He became serious. "Marry me, Lara. I can't imagine my life without you."

"I'm not going to be pushed into a marriage until I'm ready, Iain. What I said yesterday about both of us just being out of dysfunctional relationships hasn't changed. We've just made it more complicated."

"How more complicated?"

"We've introduced sex into the equation."

"Aye, we have at that. I like this addition to the equation. Come back to bed wi'me."

"No, Iain. You promised me Edinburgh. The bed will be there tonight. I'm going back to my room now to shower and change. I'll meet you in the lobby in twenty minutes."

When she came downstairs, she found him waiting on the entrance steps, whistling *Scots Wha Hae*.

"Don't you know any other tune?"

"Aye. I know them all. I've been listening to Ewan sing and play them since I was four. But I like *Scots Wha Hae* best."

"Where are we heading this morning?

Iain took out a small pocket map of Edinburgh and showed it to her. "We'll start here at the castle and work our way downhill to Holyroodhouse." His finger slid down the map. "It's called the Royal Mile, but it's not really a mile like yer mile, it's longer. It's a Scots mile, which is 1.1 of yer miles."

"Is everything in Scotland bigger?" Her hand playfully brushed the front of his jeans.

He jumped as if he'd been stung. "Christ, Lara, have ye no modesty?"

"Not much. I never found it a particularly useful commodity. If I'd had any modesty, would I have come to your room the way I did last night?"

"Good point. I'll remember that. Now try to behave yerself for just a few hours. After that ye may put yer hands wherever ye wish."

The cab he'd ordered while waiting for Lara arrived. "Edinburgh Castle. I know ye can't take us to the entrance, just get us as close as ye can."

Fifteen minutes later they were there. The huge structure appeared to grow out of a massive, un-scalable, mountain of red rock. What an incredible defense against invading armies.

As they approached the entrance arch, Iain pointed to the two larger-than-life statues standing guard.

"Our two greatest heroes," Iain said. "William Wallace and Robert the Bruce."

"I know about William Wallace," Lara said. "I saw the movie, *Braveheart*."

"Ach, Hollywood! Americans re-inventing history again. They bend and break the truth to sell their films and thousands, nae millions, of unsuspecting—nae, uneducated—people think it is history. I'd have expected better of ye Lara. Yer a Canadian and yer a Scots-Canadian."

"So, I take it William Wallace wasn't *Braveheart*?"

"He was not. He was indeed a very brave man and an important one in the history of our country. He was an obscure, lowly knight who in the twelve hundreds led the opposition to the English occupation of Scotland. He defeated the English army at the Battle of

Stirling Bridge in 1297 but was defeated at the Battle of Falkirk in 1298. He escaped the English and was in hiding for seven years, until he was betrayed in 1305. His execution at the hands of the English was a particularly gruesome one. He was a brave man, no doubt. But he was not the one we Scots gave the title 'Braveheart.'"

"So, who was Braveheart?"

"That would be the statue here on the other side of the entrance, Robert the Bruce. While Scotland was still under military occupation by the British, he declared himself King—he had the right to the title by succession—then he went after the English. Legend has it that when forced into hiding in a cave, he was inspired by watching a spider weaving its web, never giving up over obstacles. The Bruce determined to try, try again, like the spider. Over the next seven years he led a successful campaign to drive the English out of Scotland. The two armies met at Bannockburn the 23rd of June, 1314, in what was the greatest battle in Scottish history. Scottish forces won the day and England finally acknowledged Scotland's independence. That was Robert the Bruce, Braveheart."

Lara was struck once again how immediate, as if it had happened yesterday, the history of Scotland was to Iain. The past was present to him, a part of his psyche, a deep part of who he was, who she loved.

She did love him. She had never believed she could love in this way. He was embedded in her soul. What was it Elspeth had said in her diary? Her other half. He completed her. So why was she so hesitant to give herself wholly to him, to marry him, today, tomorrow?

She was a coward. She didn't trust her own

emotions. Her mother gleefully recounted the story of how she herself had been engaged to marry one man, and then, literally, stumbled over Lara's father on an icy sidewalk, and married him within six weeks. That took nerve. "You'll know when the right man comes along," she'd told Lara.

Lara just wanted to be sure this time. She had rushed into an engagement with Edward, and look where that got her. But Iain wasn't Edward. On every score he had Edward beat by a Scottish mile. He was intelligent, generous, funny, passionate. And he loved her. Her—not what she could do for him socially, not how he would appear with her on his arm at important functions, not how people would view them as a couple—he loved *her.* With all her figurative warts and bumps, he loved her. She was as sure of that as of the sun rising tomorrow.

"Earth to Lara, earth to Lara." He grinned at her. "Back with us?"

"I think I'm going to marry you, Iain Glendenning."

He stopped dead in his tracks and stared at her. "Do I owe this to Robert the Bruce?"

She glanced up at him, confused.

"When we were in bed, making passionate love, ye wouldna' say yes. I can only assume that Robert the Bruce changed yer mind. Whatever. Yes is yes."

He glanced at the crowd around them, tour groups huddled together while their guides told them the importance of Bannockburn in Scottish history.

"Listen up, people," he shouted. "This lovely lass has just consented to be me bride!"

There was laughter and applause and there were a

few congratulatory thumps on the back and kisses on the cheek.

Lara nearly fell through the ground with embarrassment, but laughter got the better of her.

"I don't think I can give ye the castle tour right now," Iain said. "I think I need to sit doon."

"There was a café near the entrance," Lara said. "Shall we?"

Five minutes later, seated in a dark, cool corner, with espressos in front of them, Iain said, "Ye ha'e made me a verra happy man today, Lara. I've been livin' in fear ye would return to Canada and I would ne'er see ye again. Except that could no' have happened. I'd have come after ye."

A burden she hadn't realized she was carrying lifted off Lara's shoulders. She was as light as air, as free as the wind. She was going to marry the man she loved. And she was more certain of her decision than any she had ever made in her life.

Iain was babbling with happiness. "It will take a couple of weeks. There are legalities. Especially with ye nae bein' a Scot. Ye may have any rings of yer choosing, but I have me grandmother's wedding and engagement rings. Ye should see them before we shop for rings. I think they might suit ye. Sapphires they are."

"Iain, we can't be married in two weeks. I need to go back to Calgary in September. I have a teaching job, and I owe the district time to find a replacement. I'll send in my letter of resignation as soon as I'm back, but I must teach until the December break. That gives us enough time to do what I must to become a Scottish resident, to be able to live with you in Scotland. I don't expect any trouble with that. After all, Canada, like Scotland, is a part of the British Commonwealth. But formalities must be observed. And you did say Christmas is a fine time in Scotland. What better time to have a wedding?"

The frown on his face was so intense Lara expected him to bellow when he spoke.

Then he smiled. "I know what we can do," he said. "We'll be married twice. We'll pledge ourselves to each other the way Elspeth and Lachlan did. And I know the perfect place for it. We'll be wed in the eyes of God."

He grabbed her hand and threw some coins on the table.

Fifteen minutes later they were at the Botanical Gardens. They strolled through the acres of magnificent trees and manicured flowers beds.

Iain stopped several people wandering in the gardens and asked them if they'd be willing to witness a wedding. Before long they had a crowd of thirty-some, trailing along behind them.

Ian led them off the path and into a grove of blooming rhododendron. Nearby a stream flowed under an old stone bridge. Weeping willows bordered the stream, their lowest boughs trailing in the water.

"This is the place," Iain said. "Raise yer hands and place them against mine. Do ye remember the words?"

"I'll never forget them. They made me cry."

"You first then."

"I, Lara Elizabeth MacInnes, in the eyes of God and before these assembled people, do take thee, Iain Callum Glendenning, to my lawful husband, from this day forth, as long as we both shall live."

"I, Iain Callum Glendenning, in the eyes of God and before these assembled people, do take thee, Lara Elizabeth MacInnes, to my lawful wedded wife from this day forth, as long as we both shall live."

He slipped his crested ring off his finger and onto hers. He would have a smaller copy of it made for her at the first opportunity. The motto, *GHIFT DHE AGUS AN RIGH*, *by the right of God and King*, was engraved in silver and black on a gold background.

"Then, in the eyes of God and before this assembly, we, Lara MacInnes and Iain Glendenning are husband and wife." Iain kissed his bride, a lusty Scottish kiss.

The guests, picked up so randomly, applauded and crowded round with their congratulations.

Lara was married. She suspected the legality of such a marriage might not hold up in the courts of either her country or Iain's, but she was sure neither the Anglican service they would have to endure in Calgary, nor the Kirk of Scotland service they would go through at Athdara Castle, would make her more a wife than this simple swearing of fidelity to each other before witnesses in a garden in Edinburgh.

That night, Iain's lovemaking was so sweet and tender, so overflowing with his love for her that it made Lara cry.

"What's wrong, lass?" His arms around her tight. "I can no' stand yer tears."

"They're happy tears, love. I love you so much and I'm so happy to be your wife." She sniffled. "Will you tell your parents what we've done?"

"Well now, we've done a number of things I have no intention of sharin' with anyone. But pledging ourselves to each other in the gardens in front of witnesses, an old-style Scottish wedding…that I must tell them. Otherwise they might be shocked when I move in with ye, as I intend to do as soon as we're back home."

They would be living together as man and wife. Lara hadn't quite put that piece together yet. She wasn't sure…

On the other hand, Iain in her bed every night and every morning, sleepy kisses with their coffee, what could be wrong with that?

"Iain, I need to call my mother. What time is it there?"

It took him only a moment to calculate the time difference. "It would be early in the morning there. Around seven o'clock, I think."

****

She could hear her mother crying, sniffling on the other end of the phone.

"Don't cry, Mother. I'm so happy I can't bear it if you're not."

"Oh, but my darling girl, I'm deliriously happy for you. I shall start with planning the wedding right now. We'll have the service at Christ Church Cathedral and the reception here, of course. Duncan and Alison can stay with us."

"The Calgary service will need to be immediately after the schools close for the holiday, Mother, say December 15th. Then there has to be a repeat of the wedding here. You should start planning your trip now. I think we'll plan the Kirk of Scotland service for the day after Christmas. Iain and I are going to be the most married couple in all of Christendom."

When Lara hung up after talking with her mother, her face glowed with happiness.

They spent one more night at the Royal Scots Club. Iain told the desk clerk they were just married. Was there a larger room available for them? There was. A large room with a view over the park and an antique, canopied four-poster bed.

They enjoyed their few hours in the big bed, making love in a more intimate, less frantic way. They were together now and for always.

Surfeited of lovemaking in the early evening, Lara said, "I keep thinking about Elspeth. She was convinced her father murdered her husband. Is there any chance she was wrong? Could he somehow have survived?"

"One way to find out. Let's read the next pages together. You read them aloud to me. It will be more like hearing her voice."

Lara picked up where they had last left Elspeth, standing over her father's body, then arranging his funeral.

20 October 1850

"*I had Agnes dye one of my high-necked long-sleeved frocks black. That will have to do until my seamstress can make me a few more. I must at least appear to mourn the death of my father, scoundrel and murderer that he probably was. But I cannot bring myself to mourn Lachlan. Some small part of me still wills him to be alive. I think I would know if he were dead. I think if his heart stopped, mine would too, at that moment.*"

Chapter Eight

The Past

Elspeth sat at her father's desk, stunned, trying to make sense of the jumble of small bits of paper she had found therein. Every one of them had an amount on it. An amount and a name. Money her father owed one or another of his card-playing friends at his club. She totaled them again. The sum was shocking. And then there were the other unpaid bills. His tailor, his bootmaker, even the butcher and greengrocer were owed significant amounts of money. The household servants had not been paid in months. She would have to sell the house to pay off his debts.

His lawyer was to arrive this morning at ten for the reading of the will. As she glanced at the mantel clock, there was a knocking at the door.

Johnstone opened the library door. "A Mr. Fogg is here, milady. Shall I show him in?"

Elspeth perused the papers scattered all over her father's desk. "No. Show him into the drawing room. I shall be there presently. And we'll take tea, if you will."

"Very well, milady." Johnstone withdrew, and Elspeth was reminded his pay was six months overdue. And yet he stayed on. What was she to do?

The lawyer stood as she entered.

"Please sit down. Is there anyone else who should

be here for the reading of the will? Any other beneficiaries?"

"No. I don't think there will be any point in having others present."

Elspeth regarded the man who all her life had handled Papa's accounts. The man who now had a very legal document in his hands.

He cleared his throat. "With the exception of a few small bequests to long-time servants, your father left his entire estate to you. However, there is a problem…"

"I expected no less. So wherein lies the problem?"

"Put simply, your father's debts far exceed his assets. There will be nothing left for you. This house and all its contents, save for your personal belongings, will be placed on auction a week from Tuesday. You must have all your personal belongings removed by that time."

Elspeth sat back, absorbing the shock. Then she asked in fear, "What about Athdara Castle?"

"That is secure, put in your name by some discerning relative of yours. A most unusual procedure. But I investigated it thoroughly. It is yours, although I can't begin to imagine how you could manage such a large estate by yourself."

"I will not be by myself. My husband's family will see to it that I am never alone."

"I was sorry to hear of your tragic loss. Has there been any word?"

"No, none. But my husband's brother, Abhainn, is here and investigating my husband's disappearance. I have every faith in him."

Elspeth clasped once again the ring she wore on a chain around her neck. He was alive. She wasn't sure exactly when that certainty had invaded her consciousness, but she was sure in her heart he was not dead. He was somewhere beyond reach, but he was not dead.

****

Abhainn returned from his investigations with little to add to what was already known. Lachlan had been seen riding toward the castle grounds at noon by someone from the village and had been seen riding again through the village that afternoon, clearly on his way back to Edinburgh. There the trail stopped as if his brother had disappeared into thin air.

Elspeth had no doubt her father had arranged to have him waylaid somewhere between the village and Edinburgh.

"I must return to Lochleigh, my dear," Abhainn said the next day. "I think we can do no more here. Won't ye come with me? Ye are a MacInnes and ye belong with us at this difficult time. Let your family help you."

"You are so kind, Abhainn. But I must stay here. I have my father's affairs to deal with and…" Elspeth couldn't put into words the hope she still nourished that Lachlan was alive somewhere and would return to her when he could.

"Verra well. Ye must do what ye ken is right. I shall leave Hamish with ye to see to yer well-being. Lachlan would have wished it so. Hamish will continue to investigate Lachlan's disappearance. He will not rest until we have answers."

When Abhainn had left, Elspeth began the depressing job of emptying her father's house of all personal belongings not part of the settlement. The day the auctioneer descended she took refuge in her room, coming out only after everyone there for the sale had left.

She paced through the house, now denuded of most its furnishings. Her father's creditors had left the beds she and Agnes and Hamish and the remaining help slept on, but on the morrow, those too would be gone.

They must go to Athdara Castle. Her father had repeatedly told her the castle was not in livable condition, but they would have to make do. Surely, they could find enough beds and make the kitchen usable. That's all they really needed. Her income was barely enough to feed them all and to provide wood for the fireplaces. But they would manage. She put her hand on her belly. Lachlan's seed was in there, growing. That gave her both pleasure and strength.

From her own funds she paid off the servants. She sat at a scarred table in the kitchen and dealt with them one at a time, giving them their back pay and letters of reference.

She had hesitated with Johnstone. He deserved so much more than she could possibly pay him. He had been with them the since she was a child. She was fond of him, as he was of her.

When she offered him his pay, he slid the money back across the table to her. "Let me come with you, milady. I have money put aside. When you get your house in order you may pay me such salary as you can afford. And I'll bring my wife also, if you agree."

"Your wife?"

"I know it's frowned on in service, my lady, but Cook and I have been secretly married for some twenty years. Surely you can use a cook at Athdara Castle."

How could she refuse such an offer? "You have always been a good friend to me, Johnstone. I should be very happy to have you both with me, but I must warn you, my father said the castle was in great need of repair. And it may be some time before I can pay you proper salaries."

The next afternoon the five of them, Elspeth, Agnes, Hamish, Johnstone and his wife, Emma, set off in the elderly barouche pulled by two draft horses their creditors had somehow overlooked. Boxes of personal clothing and other such items were lashed to the back of the wagon. Johnstone sat on the high front seat, in the driver's place. Johnstone could drive?

Elspeth did not even give a backward glance to the house in which she had grown up. It held only unhappy memories.

They stopped for the night at a coaching inn about halfway to Athdara Castle. They had made a late start and both Agnes and Johnstone were concerned about their mistress's health. She had been nauseated during the trip and her color was wan and waxy.

Hamish, dressed in his usual Highland style, drew some unwanted comment from two rough characters seated at one of the tables in the draft room, obviously well into their cups. As he watched, one of them took a rag out of his pocket and wiped his hands on it.

Johnstone placed a restraining hand on Hamish's arm. "Milady comes first. We cannot get into a brawl, whatever the cause."

"Aye," Hamish agreed. He threw a reluctant glance at the two ruffians. "Later," he said to himself.

After all were fed and bedded, Hamish stole back down the stairs. The pub was noisy and busy, the smells of roasted meat and ale mingling with the sweat of men and women who had little acquaintance of soap and water. There were whores working the room, no doubt giving a portion of their take to the barkeep.

He eyed the corner where the two men he noticed earlier had been drinking. They were still there. He sauntered over to them and said, "May I buy ye lads a drink? I hae a thirst for some good whisky and I dinna like to drink alone." He pulled a chair up to their table and sat down.

A sullen expression passed over their faces, but the lure of free drinks was too much for them.

Hamish signaled a barmaid and ordered drinks for the three of them. "And when ye bring them," he ordered, "leave the bottle." He gave her bottom a smack and sent her off.

"Now there's a real gent fer you." One of the men elbowed the other. "A bottle no less. Thank ye kindly, sir."

"Never liked drinkin' alone," Hamish said, slurring his speech as if he'd already had a few too many. "Hamish is the name."

"I'm Luther, and this here," he said, pointing to his squinty eyed friend, "is Walton. And where would you be coming from?"

"As ye can tell from me plaids, I'm a Highlander."

"Well, Highlander or no, yer a right welcome fellow since ye come with a bottle!" He gave a hoarse laugh that turned into a cough. He took out the square of cloth Hamish had noticed when they entered the inn.

Hamish grabbed the filthy handkerchief and studied it. As he had suspected. His voice lowered to a soft, threatening hiss. "And where would the likes o' you be gettin' a fine linen handkerchief like this one?"

"Hey, there! Whatcha doin'? Leggo me arm." Luther stood as if to make for the door. Hamish pressed the sharp point of his dirk against Luther's throat, and the ruffian quickly sat down again.

"I just need information, gentleman." Hamish's voice was little more than a hiss, but the threat in it was unmistakable. "Ye can end up with extra coin in yer pockets or ye can end up dead. The choice is yers."

The bar maid approached with the bottle and three glasses. "Thank ye, mistress," Hamish said, shoving three coins across the table.

Glancing around, she pocketed them quickly.

"Go on," Hamish instructed the two men. "Pour yerselves a drink. Yer going to need it. Ye see now, I just happened to recognize that fine blue coat yer wearing, Luther, even under all the dirt and swill ye've managed to get on it. And this handkerchief…this little bit of embroidery on the corner? That would be the MacInnes crest, embroidered by me laird's own sister. So ye can understand why I might be a wee bit curious as to how ye have come by these items."

All around them were the noises of men talking and laughing, the calls of barmaids for another round, the shrieks from the whores as their bottoms got pinched. At their table the silence was profound.

"Ye will tell me, or ye'll not get up from this table alive." Hamish's voice was soft, but deadly.

"He were already dead," said the man wearing the blue coat. "Weren't no use to him."

"And where and when was this?"

Walton answered him. "'Twas about a fortnight ago. Just outside the city gates. He were just lying there, still, like. His head were all bloody. Cold his body was. We figured he didn't need his coat nor his kerchief."

Hamish didn't believe them. He wasn't sure he could get more out of them, but he was certain in his gut these men had attacked Lachlan. "I'd like to believe ye," he said, the voice of reason, "but the Glendenning has already confessed to the bailiff that ye were the two he hired to kill the young laird. Ye are looking at a hanging offense."

Luther fainted, his head banging down on the table. Walton started babbling. "He offered five gold sovereigns if we could stop the young laird. Keep him from returning to New Town. All we had to do was…"

"Keep him from returning, permanently?"

"Aye. That's it. Keep him from returning."

"And his ring?"

"We wuz to take that to Glendenning as evidence we done the deed. When we took it to him, he laughed and paid us only half as what he promised. Said we was murderers and he'd see us hang if we ever come near him again."

Hamish picked up the bottle of whisky and poured it over the head of the unconscious Luther who sat up, sputtering.

"Take me to where ye left him."

"What, now? It's dark outside." Walton whined. "How can ye expect—"

"Ye can take me to the spot and perhaps I'll let ye go, or ye can die where ye sit, right now. Yer choice. Ye have mounts?"

"Nae, we have no 'mounts.' We come on foot."

"We'll see about mounts then." He propelled

Luther to his feet. His partner lurched forward and almost fell.

"Ye are both too far gone in yer cups to be much use. Go! Out the door there. Around back to the stables."

The two did as instructed.

Hamish shook the stable boy awake. "I need a good mount for meself and a—" he glared in disgust at the two men holding on to each other for support. "Do ye have a donkey, for me friends here? One strong enough to carry the two o' them."

The boy nodded and returned a few minutes with a mare, saddled and ready to ride, and an elderly, sway-backed donkey.

Hamish patted the donkey's nose. "Sorry, laddie. Ye must bear a couple of asses on yer back tonight. Up," he instructed. It took all he and the stable boy could do to get the two men on the donkey's back.

"Now have ye some rope?" he asked the boy. Wordlessly the boy disappeared and returned with a coil of rope. Hamish handed the boy a couple of coins and wound the rope around the two unhappy men.

Then he tethered the donkey to his horse. "Now, which way?"

"Toward the city gates." Walton mumbled.

The ride was long and uncomfortable. Hamish consoled himself with the thought that if this rented mare and her ill-fitting saddle were uncomfortable, how much more would be the bare back of the donkey to those two miserable specimens of mankind.

Two hours later Luther shouted, "Here. Somewhere about here. I remember standing in the shadow of those trees. And ahead there yonder, them's the city gates."

Hamish dismounted and pulled the two roughly off the donkey.

"Where, exactly, where was he lying?"

"Over here."

Hamish stood over the spot where his master, his friend, had lain. The rock, where Lachlan must have hit his head when he fell, had a large rust-colored stain. Although faint from recent rains, it appeared to be blood.

"How did ye kill him?"

"We just found his body…" Walton began.

Hamish struck him a blow to the head that had them both, tied together as they were, on the ground.

"No more lies! If you value your lives it will be the truth from this moment." He hoisted them to their feet.

"The Glendenning gave us a loaded flintlock," Luther stammered. "He told us not to miss because we had only one shot. We ain't neither of us ever handled a firearm before, but we figured how hard could it be? Aim, pull the trigger. Walton here shot him. We know he didn't miss, because the man fell off his horse, right there."

"Where's the gun now?"

They gawked at each other. Walton spoke. "He told us to throw it in the river when we was finished."

"But ye didn't do that, did ye?"

"A gun is worth good money, it is. And with him paying us short…"

Hamish pondered. What was he to do with these two? They were the scum of the earth. No one would miss them if he cut their throats here and now. But he was no murderer. He could kill in the heat of battle, but not in cold blood. They had not killed Lachlan. They had been only the trigger. The gun was held by Elspeth's father, the Glendenning, and he was now dead and buried and, if there was any justice, roasting in hell.

"Ye are free to go," he said.

"Go?" Luther asked.

"Yes. Be off with ye. But do not let me see yer faces again or I might change me mind."

"But the ropes. We're tied together."

"Aye, so ye are. Ye can hobble along together. Mayhap some kind stranger will help ye along the way. I have no mind to."

Hamish mounted his horse and, leading the donkey, headed back toward the inn. There had been blood on the stone. But if Lachlan had been killed, why had his body not been found? Of course, there was a premium on dead bodies. Someone might well have taken his body to the medical school. They were always in need of them for anatomy classes, illegal as such practices were.

But what if the shot had missed, or perhaps just grazed him…Lachlan had a hard head. A stirring of hope rose in Hamish's breast. Could it be Lachlan was alive, could he be someplace close by? But where? And why would he not have sent a message to him or to his wife? He would surely have found a way to get word to Elspeth.

All wishful thinking. Lachlan was dead. There was no use planting false hopes in Elspeth's heart. She'd been through so much already. He had to face facts, and so must she. Lachlan had been shot. And if the shot hadn't killed him, the blow when his head hit the rock would have. Even Lachlan wasn't immortal. As for his body, well, that was a mystery, but it didn't change the known facts.

The sun was rising as he made his way back to the room he shared with Johnstone.

As Hamish crawled, fully clothed between the covers, Johnstone spoke. "You have about two hours to sleep. Then I'll expect a full accounting."

His request was greeted by an answering grunt.

In the morning Hamish related all he had learned to the others over breakfast.

"You imagine him to be dead. But what if he's alive somewhere? Perhaps held against his will?" Elspeth's voice was frantic.

"I wish I could believe that. But we must face the facts, milady. Your father hired two thugs to assassinate Lachlan. They shot him. He fell off his horse. There were blood stains where he fell. They stripped his body, taking all his identification, leaving him in only his shirt. We dinna ken who removed his body, but there are those who trade in bodies. I canna' hold out hope under the circumstances. False hope would be a disservice to us both. We must move on. And as Lachlan's widow, ye and the child ye carry are now my responsibility."

****

He surveyed his surroundings. He was in some kind of cell. His bed was a cot. High on the far wall, there was a small window. Over his head, a rustic wooden cross. The only piece of furniture, other than a small rush-seated chair, was a prie-dieu, under a wood carving of Christ on the cross. But the Catholic Church had been outlawed in Scotland, for many years. Where was he?

155

His head hurt. He raised his hand to it and found it tightly bandaged. He had been injured? Odd, he had no recollection of…

At that moment the door opened, and a man entered wearing a simple brown hooded cassock that fell to his sandaled feet. "Praise be to God, you have decided to rejoin the living. I must say it has been a long and dangerous voyage. We never thought to see you conscious again."

"What happened to me?"

"You were shot. I found you outside the city gates when I was on my way to market. The bullet cut a path across your head, but did not, praise God, actually penetrate your skull. You suffered also from blood loss and a rather severe blow to the back of your head from the rock you landed on. I carried you back here, hoping our healer might be able to help you."

"Ye are a religious order. But all such were abolished when the Kirk was established."

"We are an order that lives in poverty. We have no gold crosses or idolatrous images. We promised to observe the Kirk of Scotland services, and the people in charge of such thing agreed to let us be. I am Brother Ambrose, the man who found you. Now it is my turn to ask questions. Who are you?"

"I'm…I'm…" He frowned in concentration. Then he stared at Brother Ambrose. "I don't know who I am." His voice rose and barely suppressing his rising panic, he repeated, "I don't know…"

Brother Ambrose tried to reassure him. "It is not uncommon for there to be some memory loss after a severe blow to the head. You had not one, but two head injuries. Your memory will return in time. Now you need food and rest. We can supply those for you. You may stay with us until you are fully recovered. Now that you have regained consciousness, I'm sure that is just a matter of time."

But did he have time? He had the sense of something urgent impending. Something he had to do, someplace he had to be… "Did I no have any identification on me when I was found?"

"No. Nothing. You had been thoroughly searched and all possible evidence of your identity had been removed from you. Your assailants clearly believed you were dead. They must have stolen your outer clothing. You were dressed in naught but your shirt when I found you. There is one thing. Your first finger on your left hand—the skin is much lighter below the knuckle. You wore a ring there. A large one."

He glanced at his hand. Yes, a ring belonged there. He could almost see it. Almost…

He put his head in his hands. "I remember nothing. I do not exist."

Brother Ambrose put his hands gently on the young man's shoulders. "You do exist, my son. You will regain your memory. It will just take time and rest and food. You can stand. Are you able to walk?"

The young man took two steps and would have fallen had not Brother Amboise's arms been there to catch him.

"Not yet, then. I'll have some soup and bannocks brought to you. You need food. We have been able to get only small amounts of liquid in you. You've had no real food for," he frowned, calculating, "for ten days, since we found you."

"Ten days! But I must…" What was it he had to

do? Something. Something important. Someplace he had to be…

"Eat and sleep, my boy. God will help with the rest of it."

Brother Ambrose left. Soon after, a novice entered with a steaming bowl of soup and a warm bannock.

He was sure he was not hungry, but he ate everything in front of him. With his belly full he fell into a natural sleep. His dreams were a jumble, but always there was one face before him, a lovely face with dark eyes and hair black as a raven's wings. She was calling to him, reaching out to him, but could not move his feet. He was frozen to the spot he was standing on. He turned. There was a castle behind him. He recognized that castle, that woman. The dream faded. He was awake again. All was dark. Night had fallen. Who was he? What was he doing here?

Three days later he was strong enough to join the monks at their meals, and a few days after that he began to follow the pattern of their days. With no clothes of his own to wear, he accepted a cowl-necked brown habit and a pair of sandals. They were surprisingly comfortable. He attended morning prayers at dawn, had breakfast and dinner in silence with the monks, while one read from the English bible of King James.

He spent his days working in the garden beside Brother Ambrose, and his evenings in prayer. Had it not been for the dreams, the persistent, jumbled dreams, and the lovely young woman reaching toward him, reaching out to him and then fading, he might have settled happily into the religious life. It suited him in many ways, but there was something, something he had to do, someone he had to see…

Chapter Nine

The Present

Iain and Lara awoke entwined in the big bed. Iain ran his thumb lightly along her face from brow to jaw line. "A Glendenning has wed a MacInnes and the sky has nae fallen."

"I'm not sure of the legal status of our marriage just yet, but we'll make it official in December." Lara smiled at her lover, her husband. "And the sky will 'nae' fall."

He cupped her face in his two hands. "Have ye any idea how much I love ye, lass? I'm exhausted and yet just eye me. I'm near ready again. How much sleep have we had?"

"Not much." She slid out of the bed. "Sleep now, Iain. I'll be here when you wake."

She drew the covers over him and went to shower.

When she came back to the bedroom, he had turned on his side and was sleeping deeply. She'd let him sleep until ten-thirty. Check out time was eleven. They had to go back to face Iain's parents with a whole new world. His parents were unaware of his broken engagement to Allison, of his relationship with her…What would their reaction be to a Canadian daughter-in-law? And a MacInnes to boot? She and Iain had been making plans, but what if his parents didn't approve of their plans? Iain's family mattered deeply to him. Athdara Castle and his horses and his Highland cattle mattered. She would leave him rather than have him split between two loyalties. Tears sprung to her eyes. Leave him? How could she even contemplate leaving him? Once his parents realized how deeply in love they were, how committed to each other, they would come around.

Iain planned to live in the cottage with her. That might not be such a good idea. She pictured the shock on his mother's face, the frown on his father's.

No. Perhaps they should say nothing for the moment. Iain could tell them he'd broken up with Allison. Then perhaps slowly they could introduce the idea that there was more than friendship between them.

They arrived back at Athdara Castle just as the bus delivering the night's coterie of guests was unloading. Mrs. Murchison was at the entrance greeting them and sorting out their rooms and advising them they would meet Lord and Lady Glendenning for drinks before dinner, at seven, and that the attire for dinner was formal.

Iain took Lara to her cottage and said, "I must go change. I will be with ye at dinner, but we need a more private time to talk with my parents. We'll tell them in the morning." He kissed her lightly on her cheek and was gone before she fully absorbed what he was saying. He intended to announce their engagement to his parents at the first opportunity.

She needed to talk to him. To persuade him of the folly of rushing into this. His parents needed time to get used to the idea of his broken engagement. Then, perhaps just before she left to return to Canada, they might share their plans with Lord and Lady Glendenning.

Lady Glendenning. If she married Iain, she was someday going to be Lady Glendenning. How could she possibly do that? She was just a simple cowgirl from Alberta. Could she stand beside Iain, dressed formally, and greet people from all over the world as Lady Lara Glendenning? And what about their friends and neighbors? She had met none of them yet, but Iain had spoken about their holiday parties with bagpipes and fiddles and highland dancing. How could she ever fit into such a setting? She and Iain had been living in a dream world where nothing mattered except the way they cared for each other. But there was a whole other world out there. One in which she was a stranger. One that might well not accept her.

Dispirited, she dressed for dinner. Looking through her clothes she realized although she had come here with almost nothing formal to wear, she had somehow, on various shopping forays, managed to acquire some half dozen ensembles suitable for dinner at the castle. She had adapted without much difficulty to the requirements of acting as a sort of sub-hostess at these evening affairs. The guests accepted her as a part of the family. But would the family accept her that way? She touched the fragile silk of Elspeth Glendenning's dress. Dare she wear it? The dress of the Glendenning lass who loved and lost her highland lover?

By the time she was at the kitchen door of the castle she was chilled with fear. Nothing had changed and yet everything had changed. She was trembling as she came through to the drawing room to take her place beside Iain just as Ewan marched in with his bagpipes.

Iain glanced down at her and gasped. "Holy Mother of Mary! Yer the picture in the gallery."

Duncan smiled at her. "That's a beautiful gown. Very old fashioned."

"It belonged to Elspeth Glendenning. We found it in her trunk in the attic. I hope you don't mind my wearing it."

"Not at all. It suits you well." He murmured to his wife.

She turned to Lara with a smile. "It's the dress from the portrait, isn't it? The one you found in the trunk. It's lovely on you. And certainly lends an authentic note to this evening's dinner."

Dinner seemed endless. She was, as usual, seated on Duncan Glendenning's left, with Iain across the table from her. She chatted with the guest on her other side, a barrister from London. Somehow, she got through the meal, and was about to make her escape when Duncan Glendenning took her left hand in his and broke into a wide smile.

Lara was horrified. She had meant to take Iain's signet ring off before she came to dinner. Iain had wound string around the shank to make it fit securely on her finger. It fit so comfortably she had forgotten it.

He spoke softly to her, for her ears only. "Ach! You're wearing me son's ring. Does that mean what I hope it means?"

Flustered, Lara faltered. She had hoped Iain would speak with his parents about them first. "You hope?"

Speaking quietly with his head close to hers, he said, "'Twas clear to me from the first Allison was nae a guid match for me son. And just as clear you were a verra guid match for him. I'm that happy he had the sense to know it."

Tears threatened to spill. Iain's father approved of their relationship. He wanted their marriage. He was on their side. Now if Aileen Glendenning could just be persuaded to accept her. She had seemed so pleased with Allison as her daughter-in-law to be. And she still didn't even know their engagement was broken off.

The guests were making their way back to the drawing room. Some would settle at card tables for a round of bridge, others were heading out the door for a stroll in the gardens, most were heading for their rooms.

Iain murmured something to his mother. She nodded her response. Then he approached his father, still standing beside Lara. "Meet in the library for a few minutes?"

"Of course," Iain's father agreed. Turning to Lara he said, "Everything important happens in the library. It's out of bounds to the guests. Come, my dear." He took her by the elbow and steered her across the wide entrance hall to the quiet little room she had stumbled on her first day here. She had been reading *Waverly* when Iain first asked her to come riding with him.

Iain's mother was already there when they entered. "This was to be a family council. Should Lara be here?"

"Iain asked her to be," her husband replied.

Aileen Glendenning smiled at Lara. "No offense, my dear. It's just unusual for there to be anyone but the three of us, and sometimes Ewan, at a family council. But this summer you have become family. I'm very glad you're back. Did you enjoy Nairn? Was the inn I suggested satisfactory?"

"I loved Nairn, and the Invernairne is a charming inn."

Iain waked in and closed the door behind him. "Please sit ye doon. This may take a few minutes."

Everyone sat except Iain. He paced around the library, hands linked behind his back, his kilt swinging with every step, before stopping before his mother. "I've broke me engagement to Allison. I should hae done so months ago, years ago. It has been clear to me for a long time we do nae want the same lives. I could ne'er hae lived in Edinburgh as she expected us to, and she would ne'er hae lived here, at Athdara Castle."

"I had hoped you might find some sort of compromise," his mother began. "You've known Allison all your life. That must be worth something."

"I knew Allison when we were children. We're nae children anymore. I no ken the woman who threw in my face that she'd known for months it was over, the woman to whom keeping the ring I gave her meant more than maintainin' our friendship. No. I dinna ken the Allison I was engaged to marry." He took a deep breath. "I made a lucky escape."

"Well," his mother replied, "what's done is done. But you're going on thirty and it's high time you found yourself a wife."

Duncan Glendenning's voice was soft, with a hint of laughter in it. "I think he has, my dear. If ye'll just give him a chance, he'll get to it sooner or later."

Iain shot his father a glance of gratitude. "That's it, ye see. I need a lass who loves living a far distance from a city. Who loves horses. Who thinks a three-hour ride just to check on cattle is fun. I need someone who'd rather be outside than inside in any weather. And I found her right here. Ye might say she dropped into my lap the day I pulled her out of the gorse." He gave a laugh of pure joy. "I'm going to marry Lara MacInnes."

"Marry Lara?" His mother sounded shocked. "Are you sure?"

"That I am. And we mean to be married at Christmas."

"But you've only known each other for six weeks."

"I've searched for Lara all my life. She completes me."

Duncan spoke. "Do ye no remember, Aileen, how many weeks we were together before we decided to marry? Do ye no remember the objections our families raised?"

"Barely a month. I was here on a student tour when I met your father. I dropped out of the tour and stayed on. I remember both our families were relieved when I had to return to Calgary at the end of the summer to complete my nurse's training. They assumed that would be the end of it." She smiled at her husband.

"They had no faintest notion how much we loved each other," Duncan reminisced. "We were married three days after she graduated, first in Calgary and then a week later in Edinburgh."

Iain glanced from one to the other of his parents. "I dinna ken…"

"It appears to be a Glendenning thing," his father said. "We know when we've found the right lass. So welcome to the family, Lara. I do believe ye'll be happy here." He took his wife's hand. "We ha'e been."

"There's one other thing," Iain continued. "We've already had an old-fashioned Scottish handfast wedding where we pledged ourselves to each other in front of witnesses."

"Wherever did you do that?" There was laughter in

his mother's voice.

"In the Botanical Gardens in Edinburgh. In front of thirty strangers we picked up along the way."

His father joined in the laughter. "Are ye going to tell them, my dear, or shall I?"

"Your father and I did the very same thing. Before I returned to Calgary, we pledged our troth in this very room in front of a dozen friends. From that moment we considered ourselves married."

"So, I suppose this is by way of giving notice that ye'll be living in the cottage for the rest of the summer?" his father said.

"Aye. I'll be moving my gear out tonight and tomorrow. We'd like to live there after the ceremonies at Christmas. This fall, while Lara's away, I'll be working in my spare time on the plumbing and heating and insulating the place."

Lara said, "You do realize this will be the first marriage between a MacInnes and a Glendenning since 1850, and that last one did not end well."

"Whatever are you talking about?" Duncan frowned at her. "Surely you canna' believe that some curse follows the MacInnes and the Glendennings? Bad blood between the two clans dating from the time of Culloden? We live in another time. Such things as curses between clans are a thing o' the past."

"I hope so," Lara replied. "But Elspeth Glendenning married Lachlan MacInnes and nothing but trouble followed."

Duncan frowned in confusion.

"The diary. The journals Elspeth Glendenning kept. Lara has been reading them," his wife reminded him.

"Tell me about it," Duncan said. "Tell me about Elspeth Glendenning. To me she is naught but a portrait in the National Gallery."

Lara glanced at Iain. He nodded his head. "It's time we told them about it. We need help if we're ever going to unearth it all."

Lara started slowly, talking about Elspeth's days at home with her father in Edinburgh, then about her trip from Nairn and its consequences. About Elspeth and Lachlan falling in love and despite the long-standing feud between the Glendennings and the MacInnes, marrying in a Highland ceremony, in front of witnesses but without clergy to officiate.

"But MacInnes is not her name as it's shown in the gallery beside her portrait," Duncan interrupted. "It's another name. I can't bring it to mind. An English name."

"I'm not sure where that comes in. We're not that far into the diaries yet. But I can tell you she's in despair at the point where we are now. She's living here, in Athdara Castle, with a small handful of faithful servants. She believes her husband is dead, murdered by her father. Her father died of a heart attack when she accused him of the deed. He was deeply in debt and once his estate was settled, there was nothing left but Athdara castle, which was fortunately solely in his daughter's name and therefore untouchable by her father's creditors."

"What made her so sure her father was responsible for her husband's death?" Aileen asked, drawn into the story.

"She found Lachlan's ring in her father's desk drawer. Lachlan never took off that ring."

Aileen Glendenning sat back in her chair. "I want to know how the story ends. Keep us up to date as you read."

Iain replied. "We'd like that. You may be able to help us decipher some of the place names and references to family."

"Weel," Duncan said, "four heads are perhaps better than two…but it's late now so we'll continue on the morrow."

"Good night, my dear." To Lara's surprise, Aileen stood and embraced her. "Welcome to the family."

Duncan leaned down and kissed her cheek. "Sleep weel."

Iain and Lara left Duncan and Aileen standing in the doorway, Duncan's arm lightly around his wife's shoulder.

"I can hope for no happier marriage than my parents'," Iain said as they drove away in the Land Rover. "I can nae remember they e'er raised their voices to each other or to me. That's not to say there were never disagreements or that I was ne'er called to task for some idiocy I performed. But me father's voice, disappointed like, quiet, was enough to bring tears to me eyes as a child."

"They say that children of happy marriages are more likely to make happy marriages. My parents loved each other deeply, but I can't say I never heard a raised voice in my home. My twin brothers sometimes were just a bit too much for my mother."

"Ye never mentioned twin brothers. Ye said something about brothers, but this is the first I've heard they're twins."

"Yes. Jamie and Johnny. They were the bane of my

existence when we were children. Snakes in my bed. Mice in my school lunch box. They pulled my hair every time they walked by. I adored them. Still do. And Jamie still pulls my hair." Lara laughed.

Iain mused, "So there are twins in the gene pool."

"I hadn't thought of that. Good thing I'm on the pill."

"Don't ye want children?"

"Of course, I want children. But not before we're married."

"We are married, lassie, and don't ye forget it when ye get back to your land of cowboys and oil tycoons."

At the cottage. Iain parked and leaned over to kiss her, his right hand cradling her head as his left slid down her body. "Damn this bloody gear shift," he muttered.

"There's a bed in the house," Lara reminded him between kisses.

"Aye, so there is." He jumped over the door on his side of the Land Rover and came swiftly around to open the door on hers. "If ye don't want me to embarrass the cattle on yon hill by takin' ye here and now, ye'd better get a move on, wife."

****

The days took on a rhythm of their own. Iain was up at six every morning to help Ewan tend to the horses. Around ten he would reappear, ravenous, and Lara would feed him eggs and haggis and scones and good strong coffee. Once his hunger had been sated, he went back to work, riding out to check on his cattle. Lara often accompanied him on these rides to the distant borders of the Glendenning lands.

Her teasing him about his "Heelan'" cattle being pets was near the truth. She'd observed him more than once when he petted a newborn, while the mother stood by nuzzling him. If Lara approached, either on Flora's back or on foot, the same mother would lower her head menacingly and make decidedly unfriendly sounds.

Still, Lara had developed an affection for these sturdy, furry little beasts. She could understand why so many Scottish farms had turned to other cattle, Hereford and Simmental and Angus, all good Scottish breeds, cattle she recognized from Alberta. They were all much larger beasts, and they produced far more meat. Financially, it only made sense.

But one of the things she loved most about Iain was that his values were not based solely on making money. He cared about preserving this small part of his Scottish heritage. He had his practical side. His Thoroughbred horses produced a good income. But his "heelan' herd," that produced no income, and that, in fact, cost money to maintain, were an important part of who he was. And why she loved him.

****

The day was cold and rainy. Hard to believe it could be so cold in August. Iain had built a fire in the bedroom before he left at six, so she would not be shivering as she dressed. What had he called it? *Chittering* He'd built the fire "so she'd *no be chittering.*" She loved the odd turns of his Scottish speech. She'd asked him once how he came by it when his mother was Canadian. He'd told her he always wanted to be like his father and his grandfather. His speech came from them. He loved his mother, but hers was the foreign accent here.

The kitchen was warmed by the stove. Still, despite wearing jeans and a sweater, Lara was decidedly chilly as she set the table, baked scones, and prepared breakfast for the two of them. They would have to install some serious insulation to make this cottage livable in winter. Of course, Aileen had told her more than once they were welcome to live in Iain's rooms in the castle, with heat and hot water on demand, but until this morning Lara had never seriously considered it. She smiled at her reason. Iain's wild, unrestrained lovemaking might be somewhat inhibited by the nearness of his parents down the hall, not to mention a handful of paying guests. No, for the time being, they were better off here. She'd just go put on another sweater.

Iain arrived wet and cold. "'Tis more like November than August out there," he said as he took off his rain gear and hung it near the fireplace to dry out. "I'd prefer ye to stay here while I go check on the cattle today. It will nae be pleasant out there."

Lara nodded, relieved. She had not been anticipating riding in this downpour. She poured their coffee and placed the breakfast plates on the table, Iain's heaped with a full Scottish breakfast, hers with its single poached egg on toast. "I'll make something here for our dinner, so we don't have to make the trek to the castle tonight."

"Aye. Me mother's already suggested as such. 'Tis no day out for man nor beast. But I have a cow in the far pasture about to calve. I must see to her. I'd like to get her into the shelter, but it's sometimes hard to do."

"Why? I should think she'd want to get out of the storm."

171

"These little beasts have a long history of surviving in the wild. They're not easy to tame."

Lara spent the rest of morning cleaning the house, airing out the rooms, dusting and polishing and sweeping. She'd never done much housework. It all happened magically around her when she was a girl. She realized in retrospect her mother had always been involved more in the business of running the ranch than in keeping house. Emma had done that and the cooking. But this little house was hers for the moment. Hers and Iain's, and she took great pleasure in keeping it clean and bright.

By three in the afternoon, everything shone to her satisfaction. She had time to sit by the Aga and read for a while before she started dinner.

She awoke with a start. Her book lay open in her lap. She must have dozed off. What time was it? Good heavens, seven o'clock. Iain should have been back an hour ago. Where was he?

She opened the door to pitch black darkness. Rain was coming down in great sheets, so dense she could barely make out her gate. For the hundredth time, she cursed the fact they had no cell phone reception here. She hoped that was on Iain's list of things to do when she returned to Calgary in September. They were completely off the grid. They didn't even have a land line.

There was nothing for it but for her to saddle up Flora and find out for herself what was wrong. It could have had something to do with the horses so she'd go to the stables first. If he wasn't there, she'd have Ewan's help in searching for him. But surely, he'd be there at the stables. He was so strong. So capable. Nothing could have happened to him.

She had to pick her way through the wind and rain and the soggy ground underfoot, but Flora was sure-footed. The horse trotted on securely, even in the dark, once they started off in the direction of the stables. Lara was wearing a rain jacket, but by the time she arrived at the stables her jeans were soaked through and she was shivering.

She dismounted and patted Flora as she led her into the warmth of the stable. She found a brush and quickly rubbed her down with it, then threw a blanket over her back. It wouldn't do to leave her mount cold and wet.

Thunder was not in his stall.

Where was Ewan?

As if he had somehow anticipated her call, he appeared. "I was upstairs in me cozy flat when I heard ye. What's wrong, lass? What ye doin' out in this weather?"

Lara started to cry. "Iain's not back. He went out around noon to see to a cow about to calve, and he's not back."

Ewan held out his handkerchief to her. "Nae fash yerself, lass. Iain's strong and hearty. There's not much he can't handle. Could be it's just taking longer than he anticipated."

"No. Something is terribly wrong. I can feel it. Please, Ewan. We have to go search for him."

"Aye, well, I'm not one to doubt feelin's. I'll get the Land Rover."

"Bring a strong flashlight and some blankets, too. You have a first aid kit in the car?"

"Of course."

Moments later they were bouncing along over the

rough terrain. They could see only a few feet in front of them, through rain as dense as a waterfall.

"He'll be in the far pasture. What can have happened to him?" Lara was in tears.

"Dinna worry, lassie. We'll find him. He'll be fine. He's made of tough stuff, is our Iain." But Ewan's voice reflected Lara's. He was both tense and worried.

After what seemed like an eternity, Lara saw the first of the herd, standing stoically under the shelter of a copse of trees. But where was Iain?

"Stop the car, Ewan. We'll need to go on foot from here."

At that moment a high-pitched whinny filled the air.

"Over there, just beyond the herd. It's Thunder!"

Ewan slammed on the brakes and together they ran to where Thunder stood, trembling, rain pouring in rivulets off his flanks, his eyes rolling in fear. He was still saddled and his reins hung loose.

Lara ran to him. "Where's Iain?" she said, as if the horse could speak.

There was a rock outcropping in front of her, and a copse of trees dripping to her right. But where was Iain?

"Ewan, can you turn the car to face this way? The headlights would be welcome right about now."

She ventured a few steps. Leaves scrunched under her feet. Then the Land Rover's headlights illuminated the scene.

She stepped slowly, cautiously through the undergrowth, careful to avoid the gorse.

"Iain," she called. Then again louder, "Iain…"

Ewan was near her now, adding his voice to hers.

She was forcing back tears. He had to be here. Thunder was here.

She almost stepped on him. He lay sprawled against a rock, his long legs stretched in front of him. He was unconscious and bleeding. His left arm was at an impossible position.

"Iain," she cried bending over him.

He mumbled something. His eyes opened and focused blurrily on her, then closed again.

"It's a pretty severe injury." Ewan said. "I'll have to immobilize his arm before we can move him."

"The arm may be bad, but I'm more worried about his head." Lara said. "He hit his head on that rock outcropping."

"Nae worry aboot his head. It's harder than any mere rock. But we need to get him to the hospital."

Taking out the large medical emergency kit he kept in the Land Rover at all times, Ewan immobilized Iain's arm in a makeshift sling. He then picked Iain up gently, as if he was a babe, not 185 pounds of bone and muscle. Lara helped him arrange Iain's long body in the back seat. She was thankful he was unconscious. The pain of being handled like that could have been unendurable.

Iain was shivering uncontrollably now and moaning. Lara wrapped a blanket around him, and motioned Ewan to go.

"I'll follow on Thunder. Just help me mount him first."

"Ye can't ride that beast, Lara. Have some sense."

"Of course, I can ride him. Dammit, just help me mount him."

Lara stepped on the boulder and realized in frustration she still couldn't mount Thunder. The horse was too damn tall. "Help me up, Ewan!"

Ewan frowned, but he made a cup with his hands and Lara stepped into it and swung her other leg over the horse's broad back.

"I'll follow ye," Ewan said. "We don't need two of ye injured tonight. I'll keep ye in my headlights."

The horse headed into the pitch black of the rainy night and galloped toward the stables. Lara couldn't see three feet in front of her. Ewan's headlights bathed her in light but beyond them and all around her, dark rain blotted out the landscape as effectively as if a curtain had been drawn.

Lara was riding the horse hard, and behind her, Ewan bounced over the terrain without care for the tires. As soon as he had reception, he called the castle. Luckily Lord Duncan answered.

"Have an ambulance waiting. Iain's had an accident."

****

At the stable, Lara reined Thunder in, while the Land Rover continued on toward the front entrance of the castle.

The horse tossed his head and stamped impatiently, obviously expecting Lara to dismount. Exactly how was she going to do that? The ground was a long way down. Oh well, nothing ventured…. She threw her leg over and slid off his back, landing on the ground in an ungraceful heap.

Anxious as she was, Lara nevertheless took a few minutes to attend to Thunder. Removing his saddle and bridle, she sponged his saddle and girth areas and hosed down his muddy legs and belly. Then she used a sweat scraper, the way she had observed Ewan use it on other horses, to get him free of as much moisture as possible. When he was as clean and as dry as she could get him, she attached the lead rope to his halter and led him to his stall. She was careful to enter as she had watched Iain do, so both she and the horse were facing the door. She put fresh straw around him. He made a whickering sound. She put her arms around his neck and rested her head for a moment against his.

She left the stables at a run, arriving at the front door of the castle breathless. She came to a stop as the ambulance was driving away.

"Where were ye?" Ewan said. "I was beginning to worry."

"I was taking care of Thunder."

Ewan gawked at her.

"Iain would have wanted that," she said simply. "Has he recovered consciousness? Has he said anything? Where are they taking him?"

Duncan answered her. "No, no, and to St. Ignatius Hospital. We can follow behind. The hospital is only about 25 miles from here. But put on dry clothes first. Yer soaked to the skin. Aileen will have something ye can wear."

Lara chafed at the delay, but Aileen insisted. "We don't need two of you out of commission."

Ten minutes later Lara was dressed in warm slacks and a sweater. Duncan was waiting in the front hall. "Here." He slipped a cape in the Glendenning plaid over her shoulders. "Hospitals are always cold."

Duncan Glendenning was obviously known at the hospital. They were ushered through to the cubicle in Emergency where Iain was being examined by a doctor.

Duncan heaved a sigh of relief. "Good evenin',

John. I'm relieved ye are on duty here tonight."

The doctor nodded a greeting while continuing to examine his patient. "Could be under better circumstances."

"True," Duncan said. "This is Iain's fiancée, Lara MacInnes. Lara, Dr. John McLaughlin, a long-time friend and neighbor of ours."

"So, he's finally going to take the plunge. About time." He glanced from his patient to Lara. "Delighted to meet you, Miss MacInnes."

He turned his full attention back to his patient. "I'm ordering a CT scan for the head injury," he told them. "The arm is broken. It will have to be x-rayed then set and cast. However did he manage to do that? Iain may take chances but he's not reckless."

His father shook his head. "It happened when he was tending to cattle in the far pasture. We're not sure how long he lay there in the storm. We can thank this young lass for findin' him."

Dr. McLaughlin nodded. "We're sending him for a brain scan first. We need to know whether there's any intracranial bleeding. With a head blow like that, hemorrhaging is always possible. You can wait here if you like." Orderlies were pulling the bed out and moving it down the hall as the doctor spoke.

Lara shivered uncontrollably. Duncan hugged her and said, "He'll be fine, lass. Ye can't down a Glendenning with a simple blow to the head. We're a hard-headed lot."

The hour it took for the scan to take place and the doctor to interpret the results was one of the longest in Lara's life.

"There's no intracranial bleeding. He's had a

severe concussion and we'll keep him here until he recovers consciousness and is stable and steady on his feet. He'll have headaches, and perhaps some mild nausea for a while. I can prescribe medication for that. Meanwhile we'll get on with setting that arm. Since he's in no danger and there is nothing you can do, I suggest you both go home and try to get some sleep."

"Is it possible for me to stay with him?" Lara contemplated the still figure on the bed. "I won't be any bother, and I won't sleep at home, not knowing what's happening with him here."

"Of course, lass, if ye wish."

"I'll get on home then," Duncan said. "Aileen will be sick with anxiety and will want a full report. She's had her hands full with guests tonight or she'd be here."

Once his arm was set, Iain was taken to a small private room. He had yet to regain consciousness, but the doctor had told her not to worry. This sometimes happened with a severe concussion. He would regain consciousness in time.

There was a reasonably comfortable chair in the corner. Lara pushed it over to the bed so she could take Iain's hand in her own and put her head down on the bed. Against her will, exhaustion overtook her.

****

"Lara?"

His voice came as from a great distance. Lara shook herself awake.

"Iain, oh Iain," She burst into tears. "You're conscious. I must go get the doctor at once."

"No. Stop. First tell me. What happened? Where are we? What happened to me arm?" Iain was struggling to get out of bed.

179

Lara pushed him back against the pillows. "Lie down, Iain. You have a concussion and your arm's broken. Stop struggling. You can't get out of bed until the doctor has released you."

"Concussion?" Iain raised his good hand to the back of his head. "Jesus! There's a bump on the back of me head the size of a melon. It hurts. And somebody cut me hair."

"The nurse had to shave some of your hair off so she could dress your head wound. Your hair will grow back in time for the wedding in December."

He gave a lopsided grin. "Meanwhile I'm to tend to me horses lookin' like this? Thunder will break his neck laughing!"

"What happened, Iain? Do you remember?"

He frowned, thinking back. "I was riding Thunder. The rain was comin' down in buckets. Something ran across close in front of us, could have been a fox or a badger. Spooked Thunder. Anyway, I was holding the reins loosely and wasn't prepared for Thunder rearin' up. Off I flew, arse over tip. That's the last I remember. Is Thunder all right? Did he get back to the stable safely?"

"He's in the stable, warm and dry."

Ewan came into the room at that moment. "Guid. Yer awake and talkin'. Did the lassie here tell you what she did after we found ye?"

"No." Iain eyed Lara questioningly.

"The lass here spoke to Thunder soft like, and then he stood stock still and let her mount him and then she rode off on him into the rain like a *bean-shidh*. She rode him back to the stables."

Iain bolted straight up. "Lara rode Thunder?

Impossible! Nobody can ride Thunder but me!"

"Rode him she did. Like a bean-*shidh*." Ewan grinned at the memory.

"Like a what?" Lara asked.

"A *bean-shidh*. A supernatural being, a mischievous spirit," Iain explained. "Ye'll have to get used to *bean-shidhs* and the like if ye ever hope to be a true Scot."

Ewan continued, "Ye have no idea what a sight she was, racin' through the rain on the back of the biggest, blackest horse in all Scotland, with the wind and the rain in her face and her hair streaming out behind, and her leaning forward all the time talking to him. I could swear that horse understood exactly what she was saying. I could barely keep up with her in the Land Rover." He chuckled. "Like I said, a *bean-shidh*. Are ye sure of what ye are marrying, boy? Ye'll have an interesting life."

"I hope so." Iain started to laugh and stopped abruptly. He held his head in his hand. "It hurts to laugh."

Lara pushed him back into the pillows. "You've got to be still. Quiet. You must rest. You have a concussion. Go away, Ewan." She shoved him toward the door. "Enough. He'll probably be home later today or early tomorrow. You can scare him with your stories then."

Iain slept. It had been a rough night for her, finding him like that. But he was alive, and he was going to be just fine. Not like Elspeth when she lost her husband and didn't know whether he was alive or dead. Pregnant and without visible means.

She took the diary out of her bag and settled in to

read.

November 2, 1850

I do not know how we shall survive. I have no money other than the small monthly annuity left to me by my great aunt. And I have no home except Athdara Castle. But I do have loyal and faithful servants. They stay with me, knowing I cannot, at this time, pay them. We can but move on and hope.

I must say Athdara Castle was a surprise to us all. For so many years I was told it was in unlivable condition. My father wanted me to sell it. I suppose, in retrospect, he hoped to get his hands on the money from the sale to pay his gambling debts. One hates to think of one's parent in that way, but Papa had few redeeming graces. I shall never forgive him for taking my beloved husband away from me. Or for the lies he told me about Athdara Castle...

Chapter Ten

The Past

The coach came to a halt at the front entrance.

"From the outside, this place doesn't appear derelict to me," Hamish said, peering out the carriage window. "I'll bet those walls and towers could hold off armies."

"Drive on around to the back," Elspeth instructed Johnstone. "It will be easier to unload our household items there. And the trunks can be taken up the back stairs once we ascertain which bedrooms are livable."

"As you wish, milady."

At the kitchen entrance, Elspeth hesitated. "I have no key. Lachlan had the key on him when he…disappeared."

"Would this be it?" Hamish extracted a large iron key from his sporran. "I retrieved it when I searched those two… At the time I wasn't sure what it opened, but I took it on principle."

One more evidence of her husband's death. Elspeth's hand shook as she tried to put the key in the lock. Hamish gently took the key back and opened the door.

They wandered in and stopped short in stunned silence. The large sunny kitchen had brick floors and a long wooden table down the middle. One wall was dominated by a massive smoldering fireplace with a spit for cooking large roasts and a swinging arm with a still-warm kettle on it.

Gleaming copper pots hung along one wall.

Elspeth gazed, numb with shock. She had expected cobwebs and mice, not this clean, much-used expanse of kitchen.

Emma opened the drawers in the tall cabinet. "Everything I need. I shall enjoy cooking here." She strode across the room and opened a door. "Cold storage in here, and, glory be, some meat on a hook." She sniffed it. "Venison. I think" Crossing the room she opened another door. "A butler's pantry."

Johnstone peered over his wife's shoulder. Glass-fronted cabinets from floor to ceiling. Sets of china. And drawers that probably held silverware.

He nodded. "Everything necessary for serving large numbers of guests. Your father told you this place was derelict? We'll explore what the rest of it has to offer, but we could live in this kitchen."

A deep voice boomed at them from the direction of the dining room door. "This here's private property and I'll thank ye to be takin' yerselves out the way ye came in!"

They all stopped short, startled at the source of the angry voice. It came from a small wiry man standing legs apart, arms crossed.

"Angus?" Elspeth cried. "Is it really you?"

The old man peered at her. "Lady Elspeth? It isn't ever you!"

"It is indeed!"

To the shock of her little entourage, she grabbed the old man by his shoulders and planted a kiss on his bald head. "Oh Angus! I expected you to be long gone, like all the rest of the staff, retired or…"

"Now what would I be doin' a thing like that fer, yer ladyship? Yer father told me I had to leave when he let the rest of the staff go. But I says to meself, bloody likely. This here's me home. Somebody's got to stay on and take care of it. I was certain ye'd come home one day."

"But how did you live? With no wages."

"I live. There's rabbits and deer in the wood, and I have me own vegetable patch, and I sleep over the stables where I've always slept."

Elspeth introduced him to the others. "This is Angus McPherson. He was head groom here when I was a child. He taught me to ride."

They crowded around him, offering their greetings.

Hamish spoke. "I wondered how it came to be the place was so well maintained."

"Ach, I have to do something with me time. But ye'll find I'm not so good at housekeeping. I finally gave up tryin' to keep everything up and took sheets and covered everything I could with them."

Elspeth said, "Thank you Angus. You have done wonderfully. Our needs are simple. We just need beds to sleep in and food and a place to eat it. This kitchen table will seat us all, but we have only basic food supplies with us. We could almost live in this kitchen. Now if we can just find usable beds…"

"Ye'll no be eatin' at the kitchen table, milady," Angus replied. "Ye'll be served in the dining room as befits the owner of this estate. There's clean beds aplenty, and as for food, I have venison for tonight. And fresh carrots and tomatoes from me garden."

"Do ye now?" Emma spoke up. "Ye just fetch them for me and I'll do the rest."

Elspeth said, "Let me introduce my companions. This is Emma, she's been our cook in Edinburgh for years, and her husband, Johnstone, our butler, and my lady's maid, Agnes, and Hamish. He was my husband's companion and protector since Lachlan was born, and now he's mine. And as for the dining arrangements, there is no way I'm going to eat alone in that huge formal dining room while the rest of you eat in the kitchen. For the time being we will take our meals here together."

"That is highly irregular, milady," Johnstone said, "but perhaps under the circumstances…"

Hamish said, "Then that's settled. Now, if we can find some beds?"

"That's easy enough," Angus said, pointing. "The butler's rooms are right down that hallway. Plenty of room for you and the missus. Her ladyship's maid will sleep in the dressing room adjoining her ladyship's rooms, which are, of course, upstairs at the front of the house." He paused to ascertain if there was any argument on this. "As for Mr. Hamish…"

"It's just Hamish, not Mr. Hamish. The last name's MacInnes, of the Clan MacInnes. And wherever milady sleeps, I sleep nearby."

"Hmm. I suppose you could sleep in one of the rooms across from hers."

"Not close enough." Hamish studied the gnome-like little man.

"Well, I suppose ye could sleep in his lordship's dressing room. It adjoins her ladyship's bedroom. But it would be highly irregular."

"It will do. How is it ye know the rooms so well? Ye were a groom."

"Well, yes. At first, I contented meself with lookin' after the stables. But there weren't much to look after, ye see. All the horses was sold. Only one broken-down mare and me. We was all that was left. And so I took to lookin' after the castle. Considered myself as a *Keeper*. Each week I'd put one room to rights. Do ye have any idea how many rooms there are in this castle?"

Elspeth interrupted. "But if you were here, then you must have seen my husband. Tall, reddish hair…"

"Yer husband, wuz he? Yes, I saw him, but he didn't see me. He had a key, so I figured he had a right to be here. I was waiting for the right moment to show m'self when he ran out the door and got on his horse and was off like he were being chased by a devil. Couldn't figure out what was wrong. He were in the front rooms that I had cleaned only that very day. Everything showed good as new. Why'd he run off like that?"

Hamish answered. "Because he expected to find a castle in ruins, and instead he found it in perfect order. He was in a hurry, because at that point he was afraid my lady's father had sent him on a fool's errand…just to get him out of the way."

He turned to Elspeth. "He realized your father would stop at nothing. He feared for your life. He was headed back to Edinburgh as fast as he could ride."

"And my father was certain that was just what he would do, and had assassins waiting for him." The tears she constantly fought so hard to hold back glistened in her eyes. She took a deep breath. Her life was here now, with people who cared for her, and for whom she cared.

"Well, shall we get started unloading the carriage?"

That evening's dinner was a celebration of the new life ahead. Angus had found a bottle of good claret in the wine cellar and they toasted their new beginnings.

When Elspeth sank into her bed that night, a bed she should have been sharing with Lachlan, she thanked God for the good friends she had around her.

****

It did not take Elspeth long to realize her small staff was uncomfortable with her in the kitchen. They wanted to resume their lives as butler, cook, lady's maid, and, in Angus' case, man of all work. She frequently surprised him dusting or mopping a floor or polishing the woodwork. Without a stable to care for, Angus had turned himself into a general factotum.

The staff all wanted her to assume the role of "her ladyship," and, little though she wanted to do so, she understood their discomfort. So, it came to be that she took her breakfast in the little round breakfast room in the east tower and took her evening meal in the formal dining room, served by Johnstone. Only Hamish was always nearby.

She missed the comradery of earlier days but took comfort in the beauty of her surroundings and in the child growing within her.

One day she found a calling card in the silver tray on the hall table. She studied it.

Lord Hugh Ballantyne, Hightree Manor. On the back was written, "May I call on you?"

"Johnstone, who left this?"

"I believe he is staying with friends, the Duke and Duchess of Amsted, at Hightree Manor, on the other side of the village, Milady. He called at four o'clock this afternoon."

"If he calls again, show him in, please."

"Certainly, milady."

The next afternoon, at four sharp, Johnstone announced "Lord Ballantyne is here, Milady."

"Show him into the drawing room. And we'll have tea, please."

Lord Ballantyne proved to be a middle-aged man, a bit portly, with a ruddy face and a warm smile, and thick white hair tied at the nape of his neck.

"I observed the castle was being lived in again after many years of being closed. I must admit to being curious, so I made enquiries and discovered Lady Elspeth Glendenning was once again in residence. I wish to offer my assistance if you should need it in any way."

"That is most kind of you. However, I am no longer Lady Glendenning. My husband was Lachlan MacInnes. I am a widow."

"I am sorry for your loss. And I beg pardon for intruding at such a time."

"It is no intrusion. I must admit to being a bit lonely. It is pleasant to have someone to converse with."

Thus began the first of what would become a daily event in Elspeth's life for the coming months. An hour she always anticipated with pleasure. She and Lord Ballantyne had much in common. They discussed art and literature. They were both fond of the works of Sir Walter Scott, and Hugh introduced her to the poetry of Robbie Burns. They found they both loved the music of Mozart and he invited her to a musical soiree at Hightree Manor. Elspeth wasn't sure she should be out in public with a man so soon after her husband's death, but Lord Ballantyne insisted he was twice her age, and no one would think less of her for it. She could wear her widow's black. Surely no one could censure her for one afternoon of music.

She need not have worried. She was greeted with a warm welcome by the Duke and Duchess.

Arriving back home later, she realized this was the first day, the first hour, her melancholy had not dissolved into tears. For a few short hours she had been able to put her pain aside, to overcome briefly the numbness that was her constant companion.

"I cannot thank you enough for this afternoon," she said at the door.

"It has been my great pleasure," Lord Ballantyne answered. "Shall I see you tomorrow?"

"Of course."

****

March arrived, windy and rainy, but buds were appearing on the trees. Elspeth was beginning to settle into her new life. Her belly was increasing, but fortunately, the high-waisted gowns now in style did much to disguise the fact.

Agnes was turning into a proper lady's maid. She had proved to be gifted with a needle and had been able to make such adjustments to her mistresses' wardrobe as were needed as her pregnancy advanced. She had even begun to dress Elspeth's hair.

Johnstone and Emma had settled comfortably into their old roles, and Angus keep the rooms they were living in clean and sparkling. They had closed off all the unused rooms.

Lord Ballantyne continued to call every afternoon.

One day as they were parting, he hesitated and then said, "You will call on me if ever there is a problem…?"

"Of course," she said.

The next week the problem came in the form of an officious little man from a government office.

She inspected the paper he handed her. "What is this?"

"It is exactly what it says it is. You owe the government a hundred forty pounds in taxes. Inheritance taxes on the property in Edinburgh. We had difficulty locating you. You should have left word when you left the city."

"But the Edinburgh house was sold off to pay my father's gambling debts."

"I'm afraid that's no concern of mine. You live well enough here. A castle? You should have no trouble raising a hundred forty pounds. You have a month to come up with the money. If you can't, I'm sure the crown would be willing to take possession of this," he gestured around him, "in its place."

This was no problem her little staff could solve. What was she to do? If she did nothing, the crown could confiscate the castle and she and all her household would have no place to go, no place to live. She placed her hand on her belly. Her child, Lachlan's child. Homeless? No. It could not be. She could not allow that to happen. Lord Ballantyne. Perhaps he could help her.

That afternoon she told him what had happened. She showed him the bill.

"A hundred forty pounds? That's an absurd amount. Someone is trying to take advantage of your situation. Leave this with me. I shall investigate it. I'll go to Edinburgh tomorrow."

****

Two days later Lord Ballantyne returned.

Elspeth was sitting at the desk in the library, going over the accounts, lines of worry tracing her face as she wondered how she would ever be able to pay the butcher bill or the green grocer, let alone her small, devoted staff, when Johnstone announced him.

Ballantyne strode into the library his hands behind his back and a scowl on his face. "The matter is resolved. You need not worry about it any further."

"Did you have to pay anything to resolve it?"

"That is not the issue. There is nothing more to worry about from that quarter." His expression softened. "But you must realize how vulnerable you are."

"What do you mean?"

"A widow, of limited means, soon to be a mother, and unable to pay even her household staff? My dear, you are in a very precarious position."

Elspeth sighed. She knew what he said was true. She strolled over to the long casement window and gazed at the garden full of weeds. It broke her heart to see Athdara Castle gradually decaying around her. Her small staff, however dedicated, could not begin to keep up with maintaining this property as it should be.

He hesitated. "I have a solution."

She regarded at him questioningly.

"You could marry me."

Elspeth burst into tears and turned to leave the room.

"Wait," he said. "Wait, I beg you. Just listen." He

held his hand out to her and led her to a chair.

She gazed up at him, red-eyed.

He began pacing as he spoke.

"I am not asking for your love. I know that was given in full to your departed husband. I have heard the way you speak of him. I would never try to take that from you."

She frowned. "What then?"

"Companionship. Your friendship is enough. I'm an old man. A lonely old man. And I greatly enjoy your company. That is all I would ask of you in marriage, companionship."

Elspeth frowned. She had difficulty comprehending just what he was asking. "Companionship?"

"Let me put it another way. It pains me that you must struggle so. You haven't the money to pay your staff. That they stay with you is a testament to their loyalty. You haven't money for your basic monthly bills."

She bowed her head, twisting her hands in her lap. The tears she had been holding back began to trickle down her cheeks.

"And then there is your child."

Startled, she stared up at him. "My child?"

"Yours was a Highland wedding, was it not? A wedding performed without benefit of clergy?"

"Yes. We pledged ourselves before witnesses."

"My dear, your marriage will not be recognized except in the Highlands. Elsewhere your child will be considered…" He paused.

"My child?"

"Will be considered a bastard. A label that will

follow him throughout his life."

"No. Oh no!" Her tears now flowed, unstoppable. "The world could not be so cruel."

"Indeed, the world can be that cruel, and worse. Please my dear, my dearest, I do not wish to cause you pain. It is my deepest desire to take care of you and your child."

He sat in the chair across from hers. "I have no heir beyond a wastrel nephew. Your child would inherit my name, my title, and my estates."

He handed her his handkerchief. "Here, my dear. Dry your tears. What I offer is not so terrible. I offer you my protection. I offer you freedom from your worries about money. I offer your child my name and eventually, if a boy, he would inherit my titles and lands."

"But that's absurd," she said through hiccups. "I'm in my seventh month. How could you give my child, Lachlan's child, your name? How is that even possible?"

"Under the law, a child born in wedlock is deemed to be the child of the husband, no matter what the circumstances or how recent the marriage."

Elspeth was silent. Then she stood. "I am tired. I must lie down. I will think on what you have said."

"Do not think too long. We must act before your child is born. I shall await your answer." He rose and kissed her hand. "Good day, my dear."

The front door closed behind him as she made her way up the wide curved staircase to her rooms.

She threw herself on her bed and wept until there were no tears left. How she wished she had Abhainn's wise council. She could not make this decision alone.

Ballantyne's words came back to her. Her child a bastard? Thoughts followed upon thoughts, all jumbled like a giant jigsaw puzzle. Even if her child were not deemed to be a bastard, an outcast from polite society, what future could she give him or her? At best a life of penury. If her child was a girl, there could be no brilliant match for her, not without a sizable dowry, and if a boy, she could never afford to send him to the schools where he could build an assured future. Even if she had the money, bastards were not accepted into the best schools. *Oh Lachlan, where are you? How could you die and leave me thus?*

When the storm of tears had passed, she tried to wash the traces of them away. She would talk to Hamish. He was a simple man, devoted to her as he had been to Lachlan. He could help her make this painful decision,

She did not have far to seek. He was in his room, next to hers.

"I heard you sobbing, milady. Is there naught I can do to ease yer sorrow?

"Do you believe there is any possibility Lachlan is alive, Hamish?"

He sighed and gazed into her eyes. "Do you believe he could be alive and not come to find ye milady? I don't. If he were alive, he would move heaven and earth to be at your side. I'm afeared the evidence of his death is compelling. He was shot. We know that for a fact. He fell off his horse. There were bloodstains where he fell. The men who shot him then stole all his clothing. They took even his signet ring. Would Lachlan, alive, have permitted that? What happened to his body is a mystery, but it doesn't alter what we know as to be true."

He gave a deep sigh and his eyes met hers. "So, yes, milady. I do most bitterly believe Lachlan to be dead. And so do you. Ye have been wearing widow's weeds since we came to this place."

Elspeth was suddenly so weak she couldn't stand. Hamish steered her gently to a chair.

"Lord Ballantyne has asked me to be his wife," she said

"He's old enough to be yer father."

"True. But he is offering to give my child a name and a future. He is offering a comfortable life for us all. And all he asks of me in return"—color rose in her cheeks as she spoke of it—"is my companionship. He tells me he is too old for anything more."

"A marriage without love? For it is clear you dinna love him."

"I am fond of him, but I don't believe I am capable of that kind of love anymore, a love like I had for Lachlan. I haven't it in me to give or accept that again. That part of me died with Lachlan. A marriage based on friendship, on companionship, I might be able to manage, knowing that through it I can give Lachlan's child a future."

"Ye could return to Lochleigh, ye ken. Yer child would be cared for and loved there."

"But he or she would have no real future, as I would occupy no real place there, the widow of the laird's brother. Abhainn's son will be laird. Lachlan struggled all his life with being in second place. He was devoted to his brother, and loyal to him, but he chafed at his position. My son or daughter would be merely a dependent. I want more for my child than that."

There was silence between them for a few moments, then Hamish said, "I think ye ken what your answer must be then, and for the sake of the child ye bear. I understand and will support ye in yer decision. I have no wish to serve under yer English lord, but yer child, whatever his or her name may be under the law, is Lachlan's, and it is my sworn duty to protect that child, as I tried and failed to protect Lachlan. I dinna ken how ye will explain my presence to his lordship, but stay beside ye and yer child I will."

"What I would do without you, Hamish? You have helped me more than you know. You have cleared away the cobwebs in my mind. I will accept Lord Ballantyne's offer, with some very specific conditions. My staff, and that includes you, must remain in the positions they occupy. I have some other conditions as well. We shall soon know whether he wants to marry me enough to agree to them."

Head held high, Elspeth sailed out of the room.

The next afternoon when Lord Ballantyne came to call, he found Elspeth in the library, writing. "Good day, Lord Ballantyne. Please have a seat."

Elspeth rang and Johnstone was there instantly. "We will have tea here, please. And ask cook to send us a plate of those lovely small scones she makes, and some clotted cream to go with them."

"Of course, Milady.

When the butler had left, Ballantyne asked "Have you considered my proposal?"

"Indeed. I have contemplated little else. And I am seriously considering accepting it, but there are some conditions."

His eyebrows rose. "Conditions?"

She picked up the paper on which she had been writing when he entered. "I've written them down. If you agree to them, we should have the document drawn up legally and signed by both of us, so there can be no misunderstanding later."

He took the paper from her and started reading. "I have no difficulty with retaining your present staff in their present positions, although we shall certainly wish to augment it. You need gardeners and groundskeepers, and if we are to open all the rooms, as we should certainly wish to do, we will need more staff." He inspected the document again. "I do not quite understand Hamish's position. Exactly what is he?"

"He was my husband's companion and sworn protector, and he is now mine. When my child is born, he will also act as protector for him or her."

"What an extraordinary thing! A 'protector' no less. Hmmf. I suppose it can do no harm. I agree to this provision."

He continued reading down the document. "About the name of the child? That MacInnes should be a part of the name?"

"To honor my late husband. It can be buried somewhere in the middle of his name. I know the English practice of giving numerous family names to their offspring. I merely ask that MacInnes be one of those names in the middle."

"I hadn't quite foreseen that. I must think about it."

He read on. Then he laughed aloud. "You ask that Athdara Castle remain solely in your name and that you continue to have full authority as to its use. My dear, I would have it no other way. I have lands and houses enough. I have no need to take your castle from you."

"That may be. But under English law," Elspeth said, "when I marry you, I and everything I own become yours. For my person I accept this, but for my castle, I cannot. It must remain mine. And for that to happen there must be a legal agreement between us."

"I think I can agree to your conditions, although I must admit I didn't see this coming. I rather saw myself as rescuing you. I assumed you would fall into my arms in gratitude." He chuckled. "I should have known better. What I have always admired most about you is your intelligence and your spirit."

He rubbed his chin. "But since we are drawing lines, I should like to add a clause of my own to this document. Should your former husband ever return from the dead you must agree not to see him, and under no circumstances is he is ever to be given reason to suspect the child you bear is his."

Elspeth sighed. "Since there seems little room for doubt regarding my husband's death. I can agree to your terms."

"Very well. I shall have this properly drawn up by my solicitor and we will in due course sign it in front of witnesses. I believe I can have it ready in…in, say, three days. And on the fourth day we shall be wed. I think, considering your…" he hesitated.

"My shape?" Elspeth laughed.

"Indeed. I think we should have a very private ceremony. But to make sure it is uncontestable we should do it in a church. St. Giles, in Edinburgh. The minister there is a friend."

After Ballantyne left, Elspeth sat almost paralyzed. She had done it. She had sealed her own fate and that of her child. She had saved her child from penury and her home from gradual decay. She genuinely liked Lord Ballantyne, and she hoped she could build a pleasant future with him. Her memories veered to Lachlan and the life she had expected to have with him and for a moment she almost broke down. Then she braced her shoulders, willing herself to cry no longer. She deliberately closed her mind to Lachlan. Remembering caused only pain. She had her child to consider and a life to rebuild.

Four days later all was accomplished. She was Lady Ballantyne. And within the month, Athdara Castle was awash with new workers. There were three gardeners and there were upstairs maids and downstairs maids and footmen to serve at the table, freeing Johnstone to resume his proper role of butler. Elspeth could tell how pleased he was to have a full staff at his command. All the previously closed rooms had been opened and were ready to receive guests.

Back salaries had all been paid. The stables once again held horses, and Angus was in his glory.

Elspeth was happy. She could not have believed it possible, but she was quietly happy. Life was good. Her husband, true to his word, had never come to her bedroom at night, but was all affection and caring during the days. She loved strolling through the gardens, her arm tucked in his, while he commented on the progress being made, admiring the emerging beds of flowers. He did all he could to make her life easy and pleasant. In this he succeeded.

She discovered she genuinely enjoyed her husband's company. They had found pleasure being together before their marriage, but now they had the leisure to fully explore all the things they had only touched on previously. After dinner, they would retire to the library, he with his after-dinner scotch, she with her tea, and Elspeth would read aloud from whatever book Ballantyne selected from their library. And each night after they retired to their separate bedchambers, Elspeth recounted the events of her day in her journal.

In this way the time passed almost without notice until one morning Elspeth awoke with a terrible backache. She tried to get out of bed and would have fallen had not Agnes been there to catch her. Suddenly there was a warm rush of fluid down her legs.

"Yer water has broken, milady. Yer having the baby!"

****

Elspeth had never experienced such a surge of joy as when she first held the tiny squalling infant in her arms. A boy. She had given birth to a boy, a boy with blue eyes, Lachlan's eyes. Her heart panged as she gazed into them. She would forever have this living embodiment of the love she and Lachlan had shared.

If her husband noted his son's blue eyes and red hair, he never commented on it. He accepted the child wholeheartedly as his own, a son to follow in his footsteps, to carry his name and inherit his estates, to one day take his place in the House of Lords. He was delirious with joy.

The christening, in St. Giles Cathedral in June, was one of the highlights of the social season. In the presence of representatives of not only the best families of Edinburgh and London, but also by a representative of the Royal Family in the person of Princess Augusta Sophia, the child was christened James Edward Hugh MacInnes Ballantyne.

Elspeth, Lady Ballantyne, was overwhelmed by the attention. She had not fully realized her husband's social standing.

The summer flew by. Elspeth took great joy in attending to her young son. Ballantyne was enamored with the child, and lavished attention on him.

Late in October, Ballantyne said to her over breakfast, "We should be readying ourselves for our journey to London, my dearest. I have put off for too long taking my place in the House of Lords. And the Season is well underway. While I am not greatly into all the entertainments of the Season, you are young, and may enjoy the diversion of some of dinner parties and theater evenings and concerts the London Season has to offer."

"But…." she hesitated. "I assumed we were to live here, at Athdara Castle."

"We can certainly be here in the spring and summer, but my place is in London during the winter months. I have a duty to perform."

"Could we, Jamie and I, that is, could we not remain here?" She was sure, even as she asked, the answer would be no.

"I need you beside me, my dear. And I could not bear to miss a day in the life of our son."

"Of course." Elspeth adapted her mind to the new reality of what her life would be, married to a Peer. Somehow, she had not quite realized his importance when she married him. She understood he was wealthy beyond measure, but she had not realized he was involved in the day-to-day business of government.

Still, he had lived up to every aspect of their agreement, even to the naming of their child. She owed him the duty of any wife, to be with him and to oversee his household with as much grace and efficiency as she could muster.

"Where will we live when we are in London?" she asked, imagining coping with a small child in cramped city quarters.

"I have a fully staffed house on St. James Square. You will have every comfort, my dear."

"But what about the staff here?" Elspeth feared for her faithful employees, people who had not deserted her when she was penniless.

"The temporary workers, the extra gardeners and the local daily help, will be let go until we return. The rest will remain here to ensure everything is kept as it should be."

"I should like to take Agnes with me. And Hamish, of course."

"That will be no problem."

****

Elspeth had never been to London. She stared out the carriage window at the passing scene. The city appeared to be unbearably dirty, noisy, and smelly. People crowded the sidewalks, where there were sidewalks. At one point their carriage passed by what appeared to be a large market.

"Covent Gardens," her husband informed her. "The main source of food for the entire city."

Finally, they were in a quieter section of the city. Their coach drew up before a graceful three-story brick house facing a fenced-in park.

"We are home," her husband said.

Jamie had been sleeping soundly in his nanny's arms but was now awake and clamoring for dinner.

Against all advice to the contrary, Elspeth had insisted on nursing him herself rather than using the services of a wet nurse. It had been five hours since their last stop at a coaching station and her breasts were uncomfortably full.

The butler opened the door to greet them. "Lord Ballantyne. My Lady Ballantyne."

"Good evening, Weathersby." Ballantyne entered, his arm firmly supporting Elspeth's.

The butler stepped back, revealing the whole staff lined up on either side of the hall to greet their master and their new mistress.

Elspeth, exhausted from the journey and needing to feed her son, squared her shoulders and acknowledged the assembly with all the grace she could muster. She began to suspect life here would be far more demanding than at Athdara Castle.

Finally, she was ensconced in her rooms, sitting beside a cheery fire with her child at her breast while Agnes went about the business of unpacking her trunks. She had begged off dinner, asking that a tray be sent to her room. Idly she wondered where they had put Hamish. He would not be far away. He would never accept a room from which he could not easily guard Lachlan's child.

She glanced around quickly, afraid someone might have overheard her reflections. She must not think of her son that way. She must censor even her thoughts. She owed that to her husband. But it was difficult when she gazed into the deep blue of her son's eyes or touched the soft red of his curls.

****

The first disagreement she ever had with her

husband came when she discovered her child was to sleep in the nursery at the back of the house, on the third floor in the care of his nanny, far from her room at the front of the house on the second floor.

"I will not be able to hear him there when he cries!" she protested.

Her husband smiled at her in some amusement. "That was rather the idea."

"No," she said. "I shall not countenance it. He is an infant, still nursing. I want his cradle beside my bed."

Ballantyne regarded at her in consternation. "All the babies in our family for some generations have slept in that nursery. It's not as if he were unattended. His nanny will be there with him."

"But I am still nursing him."

"Yes. Well, that problem has not arisen before. Women of our class use wet nurses. You chose not to. But my dear, you are going to have to get used to having others care for him. You will have other duties as my wife. You cannot always be at the beck and call of an infant."

Elspeth tried to smother the rage his words aroused. She must not answer in anger.

She rose and put her arm through his, resting her head on his shoulder. "My dearest, please allow me this little folly. I would have my child beside me for a little longer. I cannot bear to be parted from him so soon. There is time enough for the nanny and the nursery when he is weaned."

He sighed. "I can never refuse you anything. But you must be aware the time will come, sooner than you realize, when he will not be with us. Jamie must be educated, prepared to take his place in society. He will enter Preparatory School at the age of six, and Eton at twelve, as all male Ballantynes have done for centuries. It will not do to mollycoddle him now, or he will never survive."

Elspeth chose not to respond to the information that her child would be sent away to a boarding school at the age of six. One battle at a time.

They had been in London only a few days when her husband's nephew came to call. They were in the drawing room, waiting for dinner to be called, when Weathersby announced, "Ainsley Ballantyne, my lord."

Before Ballantyne could respond, a young man bounded in. "No need for such formality. We're family after all."

The butler frowned his disapproval.

"Have another place set for dinner, Weathersby."

"Yes, my lord."

Her husband did not appear overly pleased at his nephew's unannounced visit.

"I learnt you had remarried." Ainsley peered appraisingly at Elspeth. "I say, uncle, you have done well for yourself. Quite a nice little piece."

Elspeth glanced at her husband for guidance.

He was glowering, his color almost purple. "You will speak to her ladyship with the deference due to her or you will leave this house now!"

"No offense intended. I say, Uncle, do you think we could have a few moments in private after dinner?"

"I can only imagine what for. You never come unless you need money. Been gambling again, have you?"

"Oh, come, Uncle. I gamble no more than most young men of my station. And I have been known to visit you on occasion without asking for money. After all, as your only blood relative, it is my duty to keep in touch."

Ballantyne smiled. Elspeth observed it was not a nice smile.

"About your station," he informed his nephew, "you are no longer my only blood relative, Ainsley. I have a son. You'd have known that if you kept in closer touch with your only family."

Ainsley blanched. For a few tense moments, Elspeth imagined he might faint.

"But…but I was told you had only just recently married."

"True. But we are not the first couple to bed before we wed."

The blood rush to Elspeth's face. She cast her eyes down to her hands clenched in her lap. How could her husband humiliate her this way?

Ballantyne at once turned to Elspeth. His tone softened. "I beg your pardon, my dear, but it is important Ainsley fully understand his position. Until Jamie was born, Ainsley was my sole heir. He now finds himself, at best, relegated to whatever small token I might choose to leave him in my will." Ballantyne sat back and smiled.

Elspeth had never observed a smile with less humor in it. Her husband was truly angry with his nephew and was taking great pleasure in deflating his hopes. For hopes Ainsley clearly had. He had anticipated inheriting it all, money, title, and lands, and now he was reduced to accepting whatever his uncle chose to leave him. It would be a pittance compared to what he had expected. And he had very likely run up many debts as the heir apparent to the Ballantyne fortune. Elspeth almost felt sorry for him.

Weathersby entered. "Dinner is served, my lord."

Later that night, after nursing Jamie and tucking him into his cradle, Elspeth wrote in her journal.

I am worried about my husband's nephew, Ainsley. I could hear them shouting at each other in the library after dinner.

True, the young man appears to be somewhat arrogant and lacking in good manners, but I gather he has grown up as heir presumptive to the Ballantyne titles and estates. It must have been a considerable shock to discover he has been replaced in that capacity by my infant son.

I gather he is addicted to gambling. It may be that once the ton becomes aware he is no longer Ballantyne's heir, his welcome in the gambling hells will be considerably diminished. That in itself may solve the problem. But it is a worry. I'm afraid I have unwittingly made an enemy of Ainsley Ballantyne through no doing of my own.

Chapter Eleven

The Present

Iain was not a good patient. He chafed over his inactivity and made himself a nuisance to one and all.

Finally, one day when he was being particularly troublesome, wanting to ride out to the far pastures alone, with only one good arm, Ewan said to him, "I'd think ye might be takin' this free time to do some of the work that needs doin' on yer cottage. Ye need to get on with the power company to get a line into yer place. Ye need electricians, and plumbers and dry wallers. And somebody needs to plan and supervise all that."

"I was plannin' on doin' all that in the fall when Lara goes back to Canada."

"Aye, but the situation has changed, and ye have the time now. In the fall we'll be preparing for the annual auction, and I'll be needin' ye with both arms functional. Right now, yer useless and in the way here and ye could be workin' on yer place."

Iain chewed on what Ewan had said, and the next morning suggested they go into town to arrange for power lines to the cottage. It would be expensive to have them laid underground, but when Iain considered how often the castle was without power because of downed lines he opted for buried lines and while he was at it, arranged for the lines to the castle to be buried also. The additional cost was minimal.

"You know we could have a wind tower put on the property," Lara suggested.

"I've considered it," Iain replied, 'but I'm worried the noise the towers produce might be a problem both for us and for the horses and cattle."

They opted in the end for electric heat on a room-by-room basis as a supplement to the fireplaces. The renovation was proving to be a bigger and more expensive job than either of them had anticipated but they intended to make the cottage livable and comfortable year-round. They hoped to live in it for some years.

Lara was thinking about color schemes and the floor coverings she wanted for each room. The stone and brick floors downstairs were beautiful, but cold even in summer. And the wood floors upstairs would be more comfortable with small rugs on either side of the bed.

"Do you suppose we could go into Edinburgh someday soon?" she asked one morning as they worked together preparing breakfast. "I can drive."

"I can drive," he said, annoyance in every syllable.

"Not with me in the car." She turned the bacon, sizzling in the pan on the Aga. "I value my life too much to risk it in city traffic with a one-armed driver. I hope to spending the next fifty or sixty years with you. Let's don't do anything that might put that at risk."

He smiled. "There is that." He came up behind her to hug her and found his cast in the way. "Damn it. I can't do anything with this cast on."

She laughed. "After last night I can hardly agree with you. You manage pretty well for a man with an arm in a cast. You stick with managing in the bedroom and I'll do the driving." She scooped bacon and haggis out of the pan and put it on the plates where Iain had just deposited their over-easy eggs.

Iain poured their coffee and they sat across from one another at the pine table to enjoy their breakfast.

"I fear I'm getting lazy. I'm usually through checking on my cattle by seven and here I am just sitting down to breakfast at eight." He shook his head. "I hate it not knowing how they are. I trust the boys from the village who come to help out but…"

"You want to see them for yourself."

"Yes."

"You know the doctor hasn't forbidden your riding, but it is just common sense you ride at a walk, not a gallop, and you not ride alone. Why don't we go out together after breakfast? You can take Thunder and I'll come with you on Flora. I worry about Thunder not being ridden. He senses something is wrong. And he feels responsible."

Iain regarded her. "Thunder *feels*…?

"Of course he feels. He felt guilt the night he bucked and you fell off. And you have not ridden him since. Oh, I know you have patted him and given him apples, but he feels abandoned. I've contemplated riding him myself, but it's not me he needs, it's you."

"Ye are a rare woman, Lara. Ye have no idea how much I love ye."

The day being sunny and bright, Lara put together a picnic lunch and they took the Land Rover over to the stables.

Ewan came out to greet them. "I hope ye aren't dropping this great nuisance off here to work," he said to Lara.

Lara laughed. "No. As a matter of fact, I'm getting him out of your hair for the morning. We're going for a sedate ride and a picnic lunch. And tomorrow, we're going into Edinburgh, shopping, so you have a two-day respite."

"Ye plan to take Thunder out? Good. He's been off his feed. Pining, I think.

Lara gave Iain an "I told you so" glance.

A loud whinny came from inside the stable. Lara walked down to Thunder's stall and rubbed his nose then put her head beside his. He butted against her. "We're going for a ride," she said. He pranced in place and she laughed. She put a lead line on him and led him out into the open area. He came and stood quiet and tame as a kitten.

"I tell ye she's bewitched him," Ewan said as he fetched the saddle and readied the horse. "He even lets *me* near him now."

Lara meanwhile saddled Flora for their ride. "I think Thunder's socialized enough now that we might let him out to pasture with the other horses for brief periods."

Iain's gaze shifted from his horse to Lara. "Ye really think so?"

"At the beginning we'd have to be there with him. It's a bit like when mothers or fathers bring their children to my kindergarten class for the first time. They watch for a few minutes until they know how other children are reacting. If they welcome the new child, or at least don't react negatively, parents go away relieved. It's the teacher's job to make that happen."

"Thunder is one big horse." Iain shook his head.

"The others may not accept him or the present leader of the herd may challenge him. We don't want that to happen."

"We'll do it slowly. Maybe just ten or fifteen minutes the first day, with us both there to intervene if things get dicey. I remember a horse being shoved against a barbed wire fence when he was introduced to the herd. We don't want that to happen."

"Can't. No barbed wire."

"Nevertheless, we'll stay and watch the first couple of times."

"Do ye ken how happy ye make me? Never in my wildest dreams did I imagine there could be a woman who would care about what I care about."

"Where shall we ride today? I know you want to check on your shaggy beasts, but after? I saw a river on the first day I was here, but never again. Can we get to it from the far pasture?"

"Nothing easier. It's just through a wooded copse and down a small embankment."

"Perhaps we could have our picnic there."

The air was sweet and clean after the recent rains as they trod through the fields. The sun had burnt off the morning mist. Puffy white clouds skittled across a fierce blue sky. In the distance, wild purple hazed mountains raised their gray and shaggy crests to the sky. The closer surrounding hills were a kaleidoscope of color, yellow gorse, purple and pink heather and another pink bush she didn't know.

"What are those lovely bell-shaped pink flowers all through the field?" she asked.

"Heath," he laughed. "They're almost as common as gorse but are considerably friendlier."

The sound of bees buzzing in clover and the gentle lowing of cattle told Lara they were nearing the far pasture.

When they came in sight of the little herd, Lara sat silent while Iain did his head count. "Nonnie is about due to calve." he said.

"Nonnie? Do they all have names?"

"Weel…"

"They all have names. They are family members. Admit it."

"Aye, they are." He had the good grace to grin. "I need to erect a better shelter here for them. A real barn. But it has to be open to the outside. They would benefit from a place where they could take refuge from winter weather. But they don't take kindly to being shut in. They have to be free to come and go. I worry mostly when they're about to calve."

"When are you thinking about building this barn?"

"At the end of the tourist season. Ye'll have returned to Alberta, and I'll be needing labor to help with rebuilding the cottage. May as well keep them on to do this."

"Have you never considered how much your B&B guests would love this? This unique little herd? You could organize trail rides. We have them for tourists in Alberta. You'd need a guide on the lead horse, Ewan, I should think, unless you want to do it yourself. A gentle guided ride through these fields and maybe down by the river. An hour or so should do it. Guest ranches near us charge big bucks for that kind of experience. As much as the cost of a night's stay."

His brow furrowed. "You don't say! We offer horses for rent to riders, and we get a few takers. But a guided 'trail ride'…I think I like the idea. It could help majorly with supporting this little herd."

He turned his horse away from the cattle, into the forest, picking his way carefully through the dappled shade of a thick wood of oak and beech. Lara followed.

"Careful," he warned her. "The ground is still muddy from the recent rains, and it's a steep descent."

"Steep is hardly what I'd call this," she replied as her sturdy little horse sidled down the wooded embankment. "It's damn near vertical. You'll have to find an easier way to the shore if you want to include it on trail rides."

"If we go past the pasture there's a place where the hills descend more gradually. I took a shortcut today."

Suddenly they were out of the forest, facing an expanse of rippling blue water glittering in the sun. A curlew uttered its plaintive cry, adding to the majesty of the scene. Lara held her breath.

Iain clicked for Thunder to stop and then waited for Lara to dismount and come help him. She tethered Flora and came to stand beside Thunder. She used her cupped hands for Iain to dismount, not an easy feat for a one-armed man. They both laughed as he staggered and then caught his balance. Thunder stood stock-still through the operation but butted his head against Iain when he was safely on the ground.

Lara set their little rug out in the shade of a gnarled oak tree. Sausage rolls, large chunks of strong cheddar cheese with a loaf of fresh home-made bread, with a couple of bottles of ale, and for dessert, grapes.

After their meal Lara shook out the little rug and they sat on it, side by side, leaning against a tree.

"Happy?" he asked.

"Deliriously," she answered. "I don't know how I can bear to leave this, to leave you. Even though I know it's only for three months."

He put his good arm around her. "I have to tell ye, I live in daily terror I will wake up one morning and find this all gone. I think about Elspeth's journal. How they expected to be together forever and then he just disappeared. If ye were to disappear from my life I don't believe I could find the strength to go on."

Lara was silent for a moment, digesting what Iain said. "It's a terrible thing to lose someone you love. I watched my mother mourn when my father died. We were all in shock and we all missed him terribly, and for a while I feared my mother wouldn't make it. But she's a strong, resilient woman, and bit by bit she came back to the land of the living. I don't think you and I are going to lose each other any time soon, but when either of us should die, the other must find a way of continuing, somehow. We owe it to each other and to life to keep going on."

"Hmm." Iain sounded unconvinced. "But I have ye here and now, and I don't think I'm going to waste this opportunity." He snuggled down on the rug, holding her close.

****

The next day they drove to Edinburgh. Lara had a list of items she wanted for the house. They took the small car, the Morris Mini, because it would be easier to park in town than the Land Rover.

Iain scoffed as she purchased fluffy white sheep skins for either side of their bed. "Tourist stuff," he said.

"Just wait until the next cold morning when you

216

put your feet out of bed and instead of a freezing floor they land in soft fleece."

She bought the fluttery white cotton curtains she had earlier imagined at their windows and a handmade rag rug for the kitchen. Eminently practical, it would be warm on the stone floor and fully washable. That is, it would be, once the house was on the power grid and they could buy a washer and dryer. Where would they put the washer and dryer? Not in the kitchen. Maybe upstairs? Use some of the second bedroom space for them? New duvets and new down pillows. Table mats and matching serviettes. And while she was at it, she bought some new stainless-steel cookware. She loved the old copper pots, but they were so heavy she had difficulty lifting them off the stove when they were full.

The vehicle was loaded to the gills as they headed out of town. "I hope you had a good time today," Iain laughed. "Remind me never to get between you and something you perceive as a bargain."

On the way out of the city they passed a large building with multiple steps leading to the entrance and an impressive larger-than-life bronze of a man on a horse in front.

"Who's the guy on the horse?" Lara asked.

"What? Oh, that's Wellington. And the building's the... Stop! We need to find a parking space, now!"

"What's going on? Why should we stop here? I've seen lots of statues of guys on horses."

"Just find a parking place, Lara."

She edged into the Morris Mini into a parking spot two blocks from the Wellington statue, and Iain started hurrying Lara down the road toward the massive building.

They stopped, breathless, at the foot of the steps. Lara gasped, "What is this place? What are we doing here?"

Iain gave a satisfied grin. "It's the Hall of Records. They will have information on Lachlan and on Elspeth. We can even research Lord Ballantyne. We have the diaries, but anything that is a matter of public record will be here. Birth and death certificates, old newspaper accounts…"

Lara have him a quick kiss. "You're brilliant!"

Inside the building there was a long desk manned by several people. Iain approached a young woman who smiled encouragingly.

"We'd like to do some research into our family histories. Can you help us?"

"Certainly. The more information you have, the more easily you will be able to locate the ancestors you are searching for. You have birth and death dates? Where born?"

They glanced at each other helplessly. "Not really. Approximate dates. Approximate places."

"That might be enough to get you started. Come with me." She led them though a stunningly beautiful room, three stories high, round in shape, and topped with a dome. Books lined multiple shelves all the way to the dome, on every wall surface.

"This room was designed by Adam," the librarian said. "It used to be our principal repository. But now, almost everything in those ledgers has been transferred to computer files." She continued through a doorway to a large room at the back of the building.

Kiosks. Individual desks lined the room, each with a computer monitor. And people. Many people busily at work, their coats slung over their chairs, scribbling in notebooks laying open on their desks.

They were not the only people seeking answers.

"Here you go." The young lady set them up in a kiosk. "The brochure I gave you should guide you through the process, but I am available for help if you need it."

"Elspeth or Lachlan first?" Iain's fingers hovered over the keys.

"Elspeth. We know her birth date."

"We do?"

"Sure. Don't you remember? Her first journal entry written in 1850 on June 30th, said '*Today is my birthday. Today I am twenty-two*.' That means she was born in 1828. Apparently, she grew up in the house in Edinburgh, although she may have been born at Athdara Castle."

They worked side by side, largely in silence.

"I've found a registration of her birth and her christening notice. And in the Scottish Thistle of 1828, there's a reference to the event in a social column."

Lara peered over Iain's shoulder. The photocopy of the old print was surprisingly legible.

"Still, it doesn't advance us much. We already knew she was born either at Athdara Castle or in the Edinburgh house in New Town."

Lara shivered. "This makes her so much more real. I think I've been reading her journal as if it's a novel. But here we are with the birth notice of a real human being. She lived and loved and sorrowed. How long did she live? Is her death notice there?"

"I don't know how to find that without a date."

"Try just writing her name and birth date and put in

death and see what comes up in the newspapers of the time."

Iain did as instructed.

Newspaper articles came up one after the other. *Noblewoman Accused in the Death of Her Husband*, screamed one headline. *Murder Most Foul,* shouted another. *The Lethal Lady and Her Lover,* still a third.

The fun had gone out of the morning. They read in shocked silence.

"I don't believe it," Lara said. "Elspeth cared for Lord Ballantyne. She would never have murdered him. I put her journal aside after you broke your arm. It had come down to an account of her daily life at Athdara Castle and then in London while her husband sat in the House of Lords. It became a bit tedious and I just put it aside."

"We've both been too busy. We need get back to her journals."

"Agreed."

The lights in the research room flicked off and on.

"That's the closing time announcement," Iain said.

All around them people started putting on coats and packing up briefcases and bags.

"Ready to head home then?" he asked. "I want to read what Elspeth says about all this."

Chapter Twelve

The Past

They had been back at Athdara Castle for three weeks in June, when Elspeth's husband announced, "I must leave for London today, dearest. I should be back in a week. Some business I must attend to myself." Lord Ballantyne was adjusting his cravat in front of the mirror as he spoke. "Is there anything you would like me to bring you when I return?"

"Some of those wonderful shortbreads from that special shop near St. James, if you have the time."

"I'll make the time. Oh, and I'm expecting a delivery sometime this week. I've ordered a case of a very special herbal liqueur made by the monks in a monastery not far from here. You might keep a watch out for it. The monk delivering it would probably appreciate some refreshment before starting on his return journey. I've already paid them for the liqueur."

"Of course, my dear. I'll take care of it."

****

The Abbot had asked him to deliver a keg of liqueur to Lord Ballantyne. He had drawn a rough map and had written out directions to the castle.

The man in monk's clothing stopped and wiped the sweat off his brow and the back of his neck. The day was warm, and he had walked, leading his donkey and cart, for some eight miles now, starting out before sunrise. He had not minded the long walk. He seldom left the confines of the monastery and even as hot and dusty as he was, he was enjoying this time alone with his reflections.

Had he been on this road before? Everything around him was vaguely familiar. The stuff of his dreams. His dreams about the beautiful young woman with the hair like raven's wings. They came less frequently now. But today, they were with him again. He was awake, not asleep and yet it was as if he were walking in a dream. He had come this way before. This road was familiar to him.

He plodded on, leading the passive little donkey. The abbot had said the castle was just beyond Glendenning Village. The name whirled round in his mind. Glendenning…Glendenning.

He put his hands to his head. The pain pounded against his temples as it always did when he tried to remember. It made him dizzy and sick in his stomach. This time the pain was almost blinding. In agony, he guided the little donkey to the side of the road, sat down in the shade of an oak tree, and put his head down in his folded arms. He would think of something else. He would not let the fleeting images and the pain invade his mind.

He started reciting *The Lord is my shepherd…*

Gradually the pain subsided. He stood and continued his journey.

He rounded a bend in the road. Athdara Castle rose before him. The buzzing in his head became louder, the pain returned, sharp as a knife, piercing, almost blinding. Stumbling along, he led the donkey and cart up the drive toward a square stone castle with turrets at each of its four corners. He knew this place. He knew it from before.

A woman was sitting on the lawn, in the dappled shade of a large oak tree, smiling as she watched a young child playing on the grassy mound. The monk observed the child, as yet uncertain on his feet, as he stood and toddled for a short distance, then, laughing, fell on his well-padded bottom, and turned over to crawl. The sun bounced off the boy's copper-red hair as he pulled off a clover flower and started to put it in his mouth. His mother jumped up and gently took it from him. "No, Jamie. It's not to eat. We'll go in soon for your supper."

Her voice rang in his head…the monk stared at the woman. "Elspeth!" he cried, running toward her, collapsing, unconscious at her feet.

****

When he came to, he was in a bed with two faces hovering over him.

Elspeth was sitting on the bed beside him, sobbing noisily. "You were dead. We all believed you were dead!"

Hamish stood slightly behind her, his face grim.

"Elspeth, Hamish," he said weakly. "Where am I?"

Elspeth answered. "You are safe, my darling. You're in Athdara Castle. But where have you been? And how do you come to be dressed in monk's clothing?"

"I…I don't know." His brow furrowed. When he tried to think, the pain stabbed sharp and brutal.

"What is the last thing ye remember?" Hamish asked.

The fog cleared. He could answer that question. "I was on horseback, returning from Athdara Castle to Edinburgh. I was in a hurry because"—he frowned with the effort of remembering, then he turned to Elspeth— "because I was afraid your father was trying to get rid of me so he could spirit you away. So he could forcibly separate us. I was afraid for your life."

Hamish grunted. "*Yer* life is what he was after. He planned to make Elspeth a widow. He hired two assassins to waylay ye as ye were returning to Edinburgh."

"Assassins? Nonsense! I remember a sudden stinging in my head. That was yesterday. But I am fine today, so it can't have been anything serious."

Elspeth sat upright, shocked. "Yesterday? Lachlan, you have been missing, presumed dead, for eighteen months. Look at yourself. You have a long beard and your hair has not been combed or cut in months. And you are wearing a monk's cassock."

Lachlan touched his beard, his long tangled red hair. He peered down at his clothing. At his dusty, sandaled feet. The pounding in his head was back. He put his head in his hands. "I don't understand."

"We were sure ye were dead," Hamish said. "Now ye came here wearing monk's clothing. Where hae ye been?" Hamish paused. "Is it possible the blow to yer head caused ye to lose yer memory? And ye were rescued by someone from the monastery?"

"Monastery? I don't remember any monastery. Do you mean to say you believe I've been missing for eighteen months?" Lachlan shook his head. "No, Hamish. That is not possible. I distinctly remember my urgency to get back to Elspeth in Edinburgh. I was worried her father would try to separate us. He lied to us about Athdara Castle."

"Aye. I believe that is what ye remember. And it is true. But it all happened eighteen months ago."

"Eighteen months ago?" Lachlan closed his eyes. For the first time he was uncertain. "How is that possible?"

Elspeth put her arms around him. "I'm sure it will all come back to you in time. You're back. That's all that matters. Oh, Lachlan, my love, my life, I was certain I had lost you forever." She sobbed softly, her arms around him, her tears wetting his cheek. "I'll never let you go again."

Hamish intervened. "My lady, I think yer forgetting something. Yer circumstances have changed."

Elspeth sat bolt upright, reality of her life striking her with the force of a blow. "Oh my God! What have I done?"

Stricken, she gazed at Lachlan for a moment. Then she put her arms around him again and laid her head against his broad chest. "I never stopped loving you. Believe that, whatever else you hear. I loved you then, I love you now, I will go to my grave loving you."

Lachlan kissed the top of her head. "I know that, lass. It is the one sure thing in my life."

Elspeth stood and gazed at him for a moment. Then sobbing, she turned to leave, stopping at the door to contemplate through tears the man she loved with all her heart. The man she had solemnly promised never again to see.

Back in her own room she threw herself across her bed and sobbed as if her heart would break. She had thrown away her life for safety and security. Deep in her heart she had never believed Lachlan dead. Why had she not followed her heart, her every instinct that told her if he were dead, she would know it?

The answer came sickeningly. She did it to protect her unborn child. She did it to save Athdara Castle. She did it to help all the people who depended on her for their livelihood. What choice had she, really?

Her sobs were replaced by a sense of dread. This was her life. She was Lord Hugh Ballantyne's wife. She had been married and she had signed a document that stated if Lachlan ever reappeared, she would not see him. She had already broken that vow. She had promised Lachlan would never know Jamie, heir to all the Ballantyne lands and titles, was his son. What had she done?

She was beyond tears. She was dead inside. She would have to tell Lachlan she was married. That she could never be with him again. Then, somehow, she would have to go on living. She had to, to keep Jamie safe and loved.

There was a knock at her door.

"Enter."

Hamish came in. "Lachlan is bathing and shaving, and fortunately, I've kept his clothing so he can change into his plaids. I am so sorry, my lady. I can only imagine yer pain. If you agree, I think I should be the one to explain to Lachlan what happened while he was away, your father's dark deeds and his death and your marriage to Lord Ballantyne."

"He can't know about Jamie! He can't know he has a child. I swore an oath."

"I know, my lady. I will speak with him. I must be

the one to tell him of the events of the last year and a half. His initial reaction may be denial. He will need time to calm down and accept the truth of the eighteen months he was missing and presumed dead. Of the dire straits ye were in when Lord Ballantyne rescued ye. And he must be convinced Jamie is Ballantyne's son. If he should suspect anything other, God help us all."

Elspeth sighed. "Very well. But I must speak with him after you."

"Of course, my lady."

Hamish left, closing the door quietly behind him.

Elspeth gazed sightlessly through the window. She would have to learn how to continue going through the motions of being Lady Ballantyne. She was a hollow shell inside, incapable of any feeling but grief, but she would have to learn to smile and make small talk, and most of all she must not let this affect Jamie. She had to go on living for Jamie.

But first, she would meet with Lachlan. She had to see him one last time.

****

In Hamish's quarters, Lachlan bathed and shaved, and Hamish trimmed his hair to some semblance of what it had been before. As Lachlan put on his familiar plaids, he began to be himself once again. He had lost almost two years of his life, but here he was. Back where he belonged. With his beautiful wife and his faithful friend.

The man who had been his guardian since his birth paced restlessly as Lachlan finished dressing in his MacInnes kilts.

"I have yer ring. Her ladyship found it among her father's things." Hamish took the crested ring out of his sporran. He had kept it safe since Elspeth found it.

Lachlan slipped the ring on his finger. With it, the last traces of the man in monk's clothing disappeared. He glanced in the mirror and said, "Am I more like meself? Am I presentable enough now to see me wife?"

"Sit down. Lachlan. There are many things ye must know first. About what transpired while ye were away." Hamish indicated the two chairs by the fireplace.

Puzzled, Lachlan did as requested. "What is it? Ye seem verra serious."

"Lachlan, ye have been missing for more than eighteen months."

"So ye keep tellin' me. I canna' help it if to me 'tis only yesterday."

Hamish leaned forward and put his hand on his friend's shoulder. "I know it must be hard for ye to believe, but I think ye must somehow have lost yer memory of who ye were and what ye were about. Do ye no ken anything of the last eighteen months?"

"I remember only riding hard toward Edinburgh, in fear for Elspeth's safety. And then waking in yer bed. I remember naught between."

"Well, ye came here wearing monk's garb and delivering a case of brandy from a monastery on the outskirts of Edinburgh. It is more than possible ye were rescued by one of the monks."

Lachlan shook his head. "I don't know. None of this makes sense to me. Hamish. Ye say I came here delivering brandy from a monastery near Edinburgh. Can ye take me there? Perhaps someone there will know me. Someone must be able to help me. I know nothing of the months ye say are missing from me life."

"Aye, that we should do, and soon. But things have

happened in yer eighteen month's absence. Important things ye must know about."

Lachlan stretched his long legs toward the fireplace. He no longer had a headache. "Then perhaps ye'd best tell me about them."

Hamish poured the each a glass of whisky. He was silent for a few moments. Then he took a deep breath and began.

"Life was bitter hard after ye disappeared. Elspeth's father, the Glendenning, died, leaving her destitute. Not only without a farthing, but deeply in debt. Athdara Castle was in her name so her father's debtors couldn't touch that, but it was all she had. The house in Edinburgh was confiscated and sold, but still there were large bills to be paid and no money to pay them. Yer lady did what she had to in order to survive and to keep those around her alive. She remarried."

"Remarried?" Lachlan jumped up and started pacing the room. "How could she? She is my wife. She is married to me."

"Ye were married by Highland custom without benefit of clergy. Under English law, yer marriage was not legal. It did not exist. Ye may recall ye intended to marry again, properly, in Edinburgh?"

"But to remarry when I was missing only a matter of months! What can have persuaded her to do such a thing?"

"She had a household of a dozen people, all dependent on her and she had naught but a small monthly income, barely enough to provide food for one, let alone the all those who came with her from Edinburgh to Athdara. Ye cannot imagine those last days in Edinburgh, the creditors hounding her for her father's debts, the house being sold from under her, the carriage and horses, the furniture, even some of her clothing…"

Hamish sighed. "She removed herself here to Athdara Castle with the lot of us. We had a roof over our heads. I hunted. Angus had a small garden. We didna starve, but there was no money to spare.

"Then she received a bill for one hundred forty pounds in taxes on her father's house in Edinburgh. They threatened to confiscate Athdara Castle if she didna pay. She had naught but her dwelling place and now even that was threatened."

Lachlan stood and paced over to the fireplace, staring into it. "Why did she no return to Lochleigh? Abhainn would hae taken care of her."

"Ye must understand. Athdara Castle was her home, all she had left in the world. She could not bear the notion of losin' that, too." Hamish took a deep breath. "A kind Englishman, staying nearby, one Lord Ballantyne, befriended her. He paid her debt and offered for her in marriage, perhaps hastily, but his intention was to save her and those dependent on her from homelessness and penury. To keep her from losing her birthright. On my advice she accepted his offer. She is married to him."

"Married? Married to an Englishman? But Elspeth is *my* wife!"

"She believed herself to be yer *widow*. We all believed that. We did exhaustive searches for ye, and everything pointed to yer death."

"But to remarry so soon…"

"I assured her we had exhausted all avenues to yer disappearance. I, meself, tracked down the two assassins hired by her father to kill ye. I learned, by their firsthand account, they had succeeded. There were no other possibility but that ye were dead. When yer widow asked me for advice, I told her to accept Ballantyne. Without that marriage, she would have lost Athdara Castle, and it would have been starvation for the lot of us. Elspeth took her responsibility toward her household verra serious."

Hamish stood, placed his hands on Lachlan's shoulder and stared directly into his friend's eyes. "She is Lady Ballantyne now. Ye must accept that as ye must accept the fact she is no longer yer wife. And if ye choose to make trouble o'er that, ye will destroy a number of lives, first among them hers."

"I want to see her. I need to hear it from her lips, that she is no longer my wife."

"Aye. That ye shall. I told her ye would come to her once I had cleaned ye up and told ye the lay o' the land. She's waiting for ye in the drawing room."

****

Elspeth stood by the long window overlooking the garden. "I cannot see you again, Lachlan. It breaks my heart to tell you so. It's as if a part of me is dying."

She faced him, tears running unchecked down her cheeks. "This is worse than when you went missing, worse even than when I believed you to be dead. To know you are alive and I cannot be with you. That I can never be with you again."

He strode across the room and took her in his arms. "Don't be foolish, Elspeth. No mere words spoken by a priest can keep us apart. We both know we are pledged to each other for life."

He touched her face, wiping her tears away with

his fingers. "I love ye and I am as sure of yer love for me as I am of the sun rising. I can understand yer sense of obligation to the man who rescued ye. From what Hamish told me, ye really had little choice. But I am here now. We both know, law or no, ye are my rightful wife."

Elspeth gently stepped back from his embrace and took both his hands in hers. "I cannot think when I'm in your arms. Come sit by the fire. We must talk."

He gave a terse nod and sat in the wing chair facing Elspeth's. "So, talk. The situation seems plain enough to me. We were married. We love each other, and we belong together."

"You must listen to me, Lachlan. I cannot come away with you. I cannot leave Ballantyne."

"Why ever not?"

"Ballantyne and I have a child." As she spoke the words, Elspeth prayed Lachlan would never lay eyes on the boy. If he did the whole pretense would fall apart. Jamie was more than a year old now, and he had Lachlan's hair, Lachlan's piercing blue eyes. Lachlan would instantly recognize the boy as his.

"A child?"

"A son who will inherit Ballantyne's land and titles. He is the next Lord Ballantyne, the next Earl of Ainsworth. He is my son and I cannot leave him. By law I cannot take him away from Ballantyne and by my love for him I cannot leave him. I cannot come away with you though every fiber of my being cries out to do just that."

Lachlan turned white as he listened to Elspeth. "Are ye saying there is no hope for us? No way we can be together? What about the vows we made? Do they mean nothing to ye?"

"They mean everything to me, Lachlan. I shall love you as long as I live. But I cannot, I will not, desert a child who is still an infant. Leave him motherless? That I cannot do. Please help me. This is the most painful decision I've ever had to make, and I cannot make it alone."

"Bring the child with you. I will raise him as me own. He will be neither Lord nor Earl, but he will have a comfortable life and learn the Highland ways. He may well have a happier life."

"I could never do that to my Lord Ballantyne. He married me to secure an heir. I cannot take his son from him." Elspeth remembered the document she had signed. She was breaking her promise merely by being with Lachlan. By talking with him.

"Weel then, we are at an impasse. I can no accept that ye are no longer me wife. But I do understand ye can no leave yer young babe. I understand, but I'm not sure how to inhabit a world where ye live and I can no see ye, no touch ye, no make love to ye." He stood and looked down at her, despair written on his face.

Elspeth threw herself into his arms and sobbed against his chest. "No more can I. But it must be thus."

Lachlan drew himself up and pushed her gently away. "Verra weel. I shall take my leave of ye now. But if ye should ever need me, ever want me to come to ye, ye have my pledge I will come."

He paused for a moment, then removed the MacInnes ring from his finger and placed in her hand. He closed her fingers around it, cupping her delicate hands in his two large strong ones. "If ever ye need me, send this, and I will come."

He gazed held hers for a long moment. Then he dropped his hands from hers and left the room swiftly, without a backward glance.

****

Elspeth's journal recounted days after that moment with agonizing sameness. Her husband returned and she arose each morning and breakfasted with him. She dealt with such organizational household tasks as were required, then her correspondence. Invitations to accept, invitations to regretfully decline, each according to her husband's wishes. She shifted like an automaton through these chores. Once they were completed, she was free to visit the nursery and be with her son. Her joy jumped off the pages of her diary as she recounted those moments with her beautiful boy, who, she wrote, grew each day more like his father.

Evenings they attended dinner parties and entertainments or they entertained. Their guests were from the highest ranks of society.

With predictable regularity, Ballantyne's nephew, Ainsley, came, uninvited, for dinner. These visits were always concluded with shouts from the library and doors being slammed. Elspeth was aware, from her discussions with her husband, that the young wastrel usually left with the money he was after. Ballantyne could not afford to allow his name to be associated with his nephew's unpaid gambling debts. And in truth, he confided to her, he carried some small guilt at having cheated the young man out of his expected inheritance.

And so the months and years passed.

In the spring of 1857, they were staying in the Edinburgh town house Ballantyne had recently acquired. "I decided it would be good to have our own place in town for your shopping forays and for my matters of business."

Elspeth was not unhappy with the arrangement. Athdara was a full day's ride away, and while she considered it a bit extravagant to maintain a town house and a country place, there was no question it was convenient.

They were in their Edinburgh house to celebrate Jamie's sixth birthday, a festive occasion, with a dozen children in attendance, accompanied by their parents, the cream of Edinburgh society. When the last of their guests had left, and an exhausted and happy Jamie had been taken by his nanny to the nursery for a nap, Elspeth's husband took her by the hand and led her into the library. "We must talk, my dear."

When they were seated with small glasses of sherry in front of them, Ballantyne spoke. "It is time for Jamie to be sent away to school."

The argument that ensued was bitter. Back in her room, Elspeth threw herself down on her bed and wept. She had no power to keep her husband from sending her child away. It had been his plan from the beginning. Every generation of Ballantyne boys had done the same. Why should Jamie be different?

But Jamie *was* different. Contract or no, he was a MacInnes, not a Ballantyne.

She took the ring Lachlan had given her all those years ago out of the small velvet bag in which she kept it and turned it over in her hand. How she wished she could talk to Lachlan about this. He would know what to do.

Before she could think further about it, she rang for Agnes and thrust it into her hands. "Take this to

Lachlan."

****

Three days later, as if in answer to her prayers, Agnes returned. Lachlan was here, staying at the Whales Tale Inn in Edinburgh Harbour.

Elspeth paced in her room. She couldn't tell Lachlan anything about Jamie's birth. She'd keep that promise. But he would know what she should do. Surely, he would never agree that a child should be separated from his parents at the age of six.

At six? Elspeth stopped in her tracks. Lachlan had never laid eyes on Jamie, but he could count. If she told him Jamie was six, he would realize the child was his. She couldn't let that happen. Even if she could skirt the truth about Jamie's age, Lachlan held no authority over Jamie's education. Should he agree fully with her, he was still in no position to interfere.

The truth overwhelmed her, immobilizing her, making her head pound and her stomach churn. She sat on the edge of her bed, hunched over in pain. She had not sent for Lachlan because of Jamie. She had sent for him because she needed him. She was desperately unhappy. She lived her life like a puppet on strings.

Now we get up and spend two hours being bathed and dressed and having our hair done; now we make endless, pointless, social calls; now we bathe and change again to go to the opera or the theater, or to a soiree given by the Duchess of someplace or other.

For six years she had fit in her visits to the nursery, her times of being Jamie's mother, around the ever-encroaching demands of being Lady Ballantyne. She was alive only in those precious moments when she could hold her child on her lap, caress him, play with him, talk to him or sing to him. Those brief times made all the rest worthwhile. If her child was taken away from her, she would cease to exist as a person. Only the puppet and the strings would remain.

She had to try once more. Ballantyne was a kind man. Surely, he could be made to see reason. No child should be torn from everything and everyone he held dear at such a tender age. Perhaps if she softened her tone, if she were more conciliatory…

She found him in the library. "I owe you an apology for my behavior the other day," she began.

"It's quite all right, my dear. I'm sorry to have been so sharp with you over Jamie's education. It pains me to deny you anything. But you must understand, family tradition…"

"Of course. Family tradition. But it occurred to me that Jamie could perhaps be tutored at home. Just for a few years. When he is ten or even twelve, he could go away to school. Would it make so much difference if we departed just this once from Ballantyne tradition? Think back to your own school years. Were you happy in that school you were sent to at six?"

Elspeth had been so engrossed in her plea she had not noticed her husband's visage changing color to red and then to an almost purple hue.

"Whether I was happy has nothing to do with it," he shouted. "Jamie is enrolled in preparatory school starting in September, and that is that! There will be no further discussion on this matter, Madam."

Matching her voice to his, Elspeth screamed, "You will not take my baby away from me at the age of six! I will see you in hell first!"

She flew out of the library and slammed the door.

Shaking, she took a few deep breaths. Weathersby appeared beside her.

"You ordered a hackney, my lady?"

"No. Yes, that is…"

"I'll ask him to wait whilst you fetch your hat, gloves, pelisse and reticule."

"Thank you, Weathersby."

She hastened upstairs. Donning her outdoor garments, she glanced in the mirror. She used a damp cloth on her tear-stained cheeks. Her hat and veil would cover the damage.

****

The hackney came to a halt in front of a dilapidated inn in a most unsavory neighborhood. The sights and sounds and smells of the bustling Port of Edinburgh assaulted Elspeth. Sailing ships lined the dock, their towering masts silhouetted against the sky. Sailors shouted and winches groaned as cargo nets laden with goods swung drunkenly over their heads. Goods were being unloaded to the shouts of rough stevedores. Carts and wagons were everywhere, vying for position. She stepped down from her hired hackney, just as two sailors were expelled from a nearby premises by an angry landlord. Why had Lachlan chosen to stay in such a part of town?

"Wait here for me," Elspeth instructed the driver.

She glanced nervously about her as she walked through the empty reception hall and up a steep flight of stairs.

Room number six, he had said. The door opened and she was in Lachlan's arms, his kisses on her lips, her hair, her cheeks, their tears mingling as they embraced.

Murmuring over and over, "My dear, my sweet, my love," he lifted her into his arms and carried her into his room, to his bed. They neither of them could remember later how they had divested themselves of their cumbersome clothing, but in moments they were naked together, locked in a frenzied embrace that did not stop until, hearts pounding, they collapsed together.

Holding her close in the aftermath of passion, Lachlan said, "Ye canna go back to him. We belong together. Ye know that as well as I."

"I don't know. I don't know what to do!" Elspeth started sobbing.

"Come, love. There is nothing so terrible that together we canna solve it. Tell me."

"It's Jamie. Ballantyne wants to send him to boarding school," she said between sniffles, "and he's so young!"

"But love, that's what the upper-class British do with their children." He brushed her hair back from her tear stained face. "It's their way. Surely ye ken that."

"But he's still a baby. I can't bear it."

Lachlan stood and started dressing. "Ye hae lost yer baby. He will be sent away and ye will have him only at holiday times and in the summer. He now begins training to take his father's place, his place in life. Ye canna change that. It is the English way. He can no run wild in the Highlands as our children might hae. He's an English 'milord' and must learn to behave as such. I canna say I agree with yer husband or the English way o' doin' things, but ye married an earl. I canna see ye have any option but to accept the life that comes wi' that. Ye'll see yer son on holidays and in the summer. I'm sorry if it seems harsh, but 'tis the reality of yer situation."

Elspeth stood and slowly started putting her clothing back on, raising her hair in her hands so Lachlan could lace and button her back into what they had so hastily divested her of.

She gazed in his small shaving stand mirror and tried to make some semblance of order with her disheveled hair. No matter, her bonnet would cover it. With the putting on of her gown she reassumed the role that was hers. The role she agreed to play six years ago. The role she would have to play for the rest of her life. She was Lady Elspeth Glendenning Ballantyne. Charming hostess, faithful companion to her husband, the Earl. Loving mother to Jamie, during the brief times each year she would be allowed access to her son.

"I have something to tell you." Lachlan guided her to one of the two chairs fronting the fireplace. He sat down in the other, his expression grim. "I am goin' away."

She stared at him, not comprehending his words.

"I'm goin' far away. To British North America, to a place called Quebec City. An outfit there, The Hudson's Bay Trading Company, is offering substantial land grants near trading posts in the western territory to anyone willing to build a house and work the land and engage in the fur trade. I sail on the tide tonight."

"But why…"

"I canna live here, where ye are so near and yet so far." His voice broke. "I can no longer do this."

Her mind rejected the words. He was going away? So far away she would have no hope of being with him again? He could not do that to her! She could not exist in a world where there was no Lachlan.

"Ye could come wi' me."

For a moment her heart jumped with joy. To sail away with Lachlan. To leave it all far behind. To begin again.

Then she remembered Jamie. She remembered the agreement she signed. She could not do this. Not to her husband, not to her child.

She tried to pull the shreds of her dignity together. "I cannot," she said simply. "I would rather be with you than anyplace else on earth. But I cannot."

"I know, my love. I understand."

He placed her pelisse over her shoulders. "If e'er ye need help, me brother has promised to act on me behalf. Ye hae but to send for him." Lachlan took the signet ring off his finger once more and pressed it into her hands. "Send this and he will come to ye."

He cupped her face in his hands. "Ye carry me heart wi' ye always. Try to be happy. Remember me and that we ha' loved well. I shall ne'er forget ye, ay it be ten thousand mile."

Then, somehow, she was in her carriage on the way back to her husband and child, the life sentence to which she had agreed so long ago. She was no longer crying. There were no tears left. In their place was a deathly silence, an emptiness deep in her soul.

The carriage arrived at their townhouse. She reflected on her husband. He was a good man who had not deserved her infidelity. It would not happen again. Henceforth there would be an ocean separating her from the temptation of Lachlan's arms. She would concentrate on her roles as wife and mother. She owed her husband that. She had the solace of her beloved child, who with every passing day was more like his father. Lachlan would always be present in her life through his child. With that she must be satisfied.

Assisted by the driver, she stepped down from the carriage. She put a few uncounted coins in his hand and trod slowly up the broad marble steps to the doorway. She must do her best to make a home for her husband and child. She had duties to perform. And first among them, she must speak to her husband.

Weathersby opened the door. As she stood in the entrance hall, handing him her gloves, pelisse and bonnet, she considered how she should proceed.

Perhaps with soft words she might be able to persuade Ballantyne to allow Jamie to remain at home with a tutor for another year or two. And if not, she must bow to the inevitable with as good grace as she could muster. Jamie would one day be Lord Ballantyne, Earl of Ainsworth, with a place in the House of Lords, and responsibility for overseeing her husband's vast interests and estates. Hugh Ballantyne surely had a clearer notion than she of what the best education for that role must be. She admitted to her fear of losing Jamie. Her strong maternal instinct urged her to keep him close, in no small part because of his resemblance to Lachlan. But she could not fight generations of tradition. He would be educated as all the male Ballantynes had been educated. She would have to be satisfied with such crumbs of his time as that tradition allowed.

"Is my husband at home?" She asked Weathersby.

"I believe he is still in the library, my lady."

She should speak with him now. She owed him an apology. She walked down the hall and tapped lightly on the library door before opening it.

She did not immediately see him sprawled on the floor in a pool of blood. When she did, she uttered an ear-piercing scream and ran to kneel beside him. She cradled his head in her arms. Blood seeped from a deep wound in his head. A bloody fireplace tong lay beside his body.

"Hugh, oh Hugh!"

Weathersby appeared in the doorway; others of the help clustered behind him, drawn her screams. She was now moaning and rocking back and forth, clasping her husband in her arms.

"Get a doctor quickly! Lord Ballantyne has been injured." She turned back to her husband. "Wake up, Hugh. The doctor is on his way. Please, my love, stay with me."

"You, James," Weathersby said to the footman standing behind him gaping at the scene. "Fetch Lord Ballantyne's physician immediately. And you, Ensworth, run find a constable."

He then strode over to Lady Ballantyne, who was rocking back and forth, cradling her husband in her arms and making inarticulate noises, oblivious to the blood soaking her gown and streaked across her face where she had wiped tears away.

"My lady, come. You cannot be found this way. Your husband is dead. There is nothing more you can do for him. Come." He placed an arm under hers and attempted to get her to her feet. "Come, my lady. You must bathe and change. You cannot meet the constables in blood-soaked clothing."

She did not hear him. She shrugged him off and continued rocking back and forth, her husband's bloody head cradled in her arms, murmuring to him. "Not you, too. I cannot bear it if I lose you, too. Please my dear, speak to me."

A blue-clad constable appeared in the doorway. "What have we here? Crikey! She's done 'im in!"

Elspeth sat on the floor, holding her husband's bloody body in her arms. "Hugh, Hugh, dearest, speak to me."

She was unaware of the policeman entering. Of Agnes and Weathersby gently forcing her away from her husband's body. Of Weathersby telling the policeman Lady Ballantyne was in shock at having found her husband dead or dying and urgently needed to be attended by the Ballantyne physician.

She was taken to her room and undressed. She allowed herself to be lowered into a warm tub. Agnes washed the blood away. Even Elspeth's hair had traces of her husband's blood.

The next afternoon, the police arrive to question her. That evening, she wrote in her journal:

My position is precarious. The police appear to believe me guilty of my husband's murder. The law firm who have always handled Hugh's affairs say they cannot defend me. They are not, they claim, accustomed to the procedures in a criminal case such as murder. They recommended as counsel one Gilbert Billingsgate, who came to visit me and asked me a few questions, but I sense he is not convicted of my innocence. If the man appointed to defend me believes me guilty, what hope have I with a jury?

Chapter Thirteen

The Present

Iain glared up from the screen. "These newspapers have made hay over the tragedy. They convict her without benefit of trial. We need to know what she says in her journal. And, if there was a trial, how that trial ended."

Lara flipped ahead on the screens. "Yes. There was a trial and it appears to have made Elspeth notorious. Poor thing. There are pages and pages of inflammatory rhetoric here."

The lights flickered again in the room.

"The signal for us to close down. These offices close at five. And this being Friday we won't be able to continue until Monday, or whenever after that we can get back to Edinburgh."

"But I can't leave things like this. I have to know what happened to her!" Lara glanced around her. All the other people in the room were gathering up coats and stowing iPads and notebooks into bags and briefcases.

"We have her journals. We can read what she has to say about all of this." Iain stood and started helping Lara on with her coat. "I think we should do a little more investigating where she lived. She spent considerable time in Athdara Castle. Perhaps she is buried in the church yard at St. Timothy's in the village."

"We can check. We haven't really visited any of the places where she lived except for Athdara."

They trooped through the door, surrounded by other seekers of the past. Three blocks farther on, they found the Morris Mini had a parking ticket under the windshield wipers.

Iain put it in his pocket, uttering a Gaelic curse. "I'm afraid we've exceeded our time."

Lara slid in behind the wheel of the little car. She didn't immediately start the motor. "I'm deeply disturbed at what we read in those papers. It just can't be true. Not of Elspeth."

"Maybe we could take a trip up north, to where Lachlan came from. Where Elspeth met him and fell in love with him." Iain said. "Surely the story will have been passed down in some fashion. Star-crossed lovers and a murder. That should make for a good Highland tale."

"I came to Scotland hoping to locate other MacInnes'. Maybe talk to someone from the MacInnes Clan. After all, they're my history. So yes, I'd love to take a trip north. We need to go back to Athdara first to unload this lot of shopping and to make sure we aren't needed there. But I'd like to go as soon as possible. And I'll bring Elspeth's journals with me. We'll can read what she has to say about all this. Maybe we could get an early start tomorrow morning? I'll do the driving. You can be navigator."

Iain sighed. "Another two weeks before this cast comes off. I hate being so useless."

"You are far from useless, *mo chridhe*." She smiled

a self-satisfied smile. "I love you. *Tha gaol agam ort.*"

Iain sat back in surprise. "Ye are learning Gaelic?"

"I've been studying it a little bit. Just getting the essential phrases. Searching for words to say when you're making love to me and whispering things in Gaelic to me. I love the sound of the words, even though I don't know what you're saying. I can't find them in my English-Gaelic dictionary." Lara leaned over to him, kissed him lightly, and brushed his crotch with her hand.

His physical response was instant. "Stop that unless you want to get us arrested. You do it again, I'm going to pull ye over to me, gear shift notwithstanding, and ride ye here in the car on a public thoroughfare. We shall no doubt be arrested for lewd behavior and our pictures will be in the papers kept in the Hall of Records for our great grandchildren to read."

"Ne fash yerself. I can wait until we get home." Lara started the car and steered deftly out into the rush hour traffic.

"Nae, yer unlikely to find me words in an abridged English-Gaelic dictionary. They are, ye might say, a bit randy. Not proper language."

"I've learned what some of the things you say mean. When I'm fussing about something you always tell me not to *fash m'self."* And when we're making love you call me *mo chridhe,* my dearest." Lara grinned. "And you shout *Oh Dhe* when you come."

He shook his head. "I'm not conscious of saying anything. When I'm inside ye I'm the most powerful man on earth. Alexander the Great and Attila the Hun and Augustus Caesar all rolled into one. I'm God himself." He gave a deprecating laugh. "I hope that

247

never changes. I don't ever want to be like those married people who schedule sex once a week on Saturday night."

"Considering that we've now made love in every room in the house and every wooded area around it, and pretty much in every position in the Kama Sutra, I don't think we have to worry too much about becoming bored with sex."

"Ye exaggerate." He gave a low suggestive chuckle. "There are at least a dozen we ha' yet to try."

****

That evening when the guests had retired to their rooms, Iain told his parents about their shocking discovery in the hall of records.

"It can't be!" Duncan replied, stunned. "A scandal like that would be part of the family lore, surely. I've ne'er heard a word about it."

Aileen put her hand on her husband's arm. "What family was there, Duncan? Elspeth was married to Lord Ballantyne. He had no family except his infant son and a nephew. They were Ballantynes, not Glendennings. Athdara Castle was Elspeth's, but Glendenning was her maiden name. Whether or not she murdered her husband, someone must have appeared on the scene to continue the Glendenning name after Elspeth's death. A male Glendenning had to have come from somewhere for the line to continue. For there to be a *you.*"

Duncan shook his head. "I can't believe I don't know, but I don't. If my parents were aware of this family scandal, they never told me. As for who inherited, it is not uncommon for a distant cousin to inherit if there is no closer blood relation. Such an heir would assume the family name along with the titles and lands. That was a fairly common practice. Elspeth's son was by birth a Ballantyne, not a Glendenning or a MacInnes. The Ballantynes were far more important, their English titles far grander than those of our Scottish Glendenning ancestors."

"The portraits might tell us something" Aileen said. "I think every laird and a quite a few of the lady Glendennings since the fourteen hundreds are on the wall somewhere. Let's go check them out."

The four of them trooped upstairs to the portrait gallery, Lara with pen and notebook in hand. They were searching specifically for dates around the mid-1800s, the dates of Elspeth's journals.

"I can't believe it," Duncan said as they came to the end of the portraits, some thirty-five in all. "How could we not have noticed the gap in time before?"

"Elspeth's portrait in the National Gallery covers some of that time period." Lara said. "But who continued the Glendenning name?"

Duncan pointed to a portrait of a gentleman dressed in the formal attire of the late- nineteenth century. "Laird Elbridge Glendenning comes the closest. His dates appear to overlap with Elspeth's. He's probably my ancestor."

Lara glanced at the notes she had jotted down. "It would help if we could locate a family tree. I assumed families like yours always kept family trees."

"If there is one, I don't know about it," Duncan replied.

Iain deliberated. "Why don't we construct one? It shouldn't be too difficult. We'll start with the portraits here and fill in the gaps with whatever information we can garner from the Hall of Records. And while we're about it, we'll check out Lara's ancestors."

"We're going to visit the church graveyard here," Lara added. "And then we'll take a couple of days up in the far north, in the Highlands. We'll try to locate Lochleigh Castle and talk to any of the MacInnes still in the area."

Lord Duncan nodded his approval. "Except for the coastline, that's pretty desolate country. Ye'd best take the Land Rover. Some of the roads are nae more than stony tracks."

The next morning, after a hearty breakfast of eggs and bacon and haggis, of which Iain ate everything on his plate and half of what was on Lara's, they left Athdara Castle. Their first stop was the little church on the top of a hill at the end of Glendenning Village. Like many of the churches Lara had observed on her trip to Nairn, this one was deserted, its windows open to the elements, its little graveyard overgrown.

Some of the gravestones were still legible but many were so eroded as be completely unreadable. They found one dating from 1780, but like the portraits on the wall in Athdara castle, there was a gap in time. The next grave was Elbridge Glendenning's, and gave his birth date as some years later than Elspeth's.

"He must have appeared on the scene when Elspeth died. He could be that 'distant cousin' me Da' said must have been sought to continue the line."

"If so, Elspeth died young. She's only have been what? Forty, forty-five?" Lara conjectured.

"If she was convicted of murder, she died even younger." Iain's voice was grim.

Leaving the little church, they headed north toward the ring road around Edinburgh.

"I think we should take the highway as far as it goes," Iain suggested. "We'll be on one-lane roads much of the way after that."

Late in the day, they arrived at Belter, the closest village to where they hoped to find Lochleigh Castle. They agreed that it would be pointless to set out in near darkness to search for the ruins of the MacInnes stronghold. The little pub in the middle of the village offered accommodation as well as food, so after a hearty supper accompanied by good strong ale, they settled in for the night in a tiny room under the eaves, cossetted with down pillows and a deep down duvet.

Over breakfast they chatted with the innkeeper, who introduced himself as Graeme Maclean.

"I dinna think there be any MacInnes left around here, but then I'm a newcomer. Been here only forty-five years, since I married me wife Betsy and she inherited this pub. It's her ye need to be speakin' to. She knows quite a bit about the history around these parts. Here, Betsy," he called. "Folks who would speak wi' ye."

A plump, pleasant-faced woman emerged from the kitchen, wiping her hands on her apron, and at their invitation, joined them.

Iain introduced himself and Lara to the innkeeper's wife and asked, "Would ye know if any MacInnes still live about, Mrs. Maclean? We're tryin' to trace me wife's family."

"The only MacInnes around here now is old Balfor. Eighty-nine, and a widower, he lives in the village and is frequently here of an evening."

Lara could hardly contain her excitement. "You mean there is a MacInnes still living here?"

"Aye. But don't get yer hopes up, lassie. He may have yer name, but that dinna mean ye are related. The families who lived on the Laird's land oft-times took the name of the laird. They paid him land rent, worked the land, and fought alongside him in battles, in the way o' the time. Do ye ken what yer ancestor's position was in the clan?"

"He was brother to the Laird. Lachlan MacInnes, brother of Abhainn MacInnes."

The innkeeper's wife studied her with renewed interest. "Ye come from old stock. If ye go to the ruins of the MacInnes stronghold, ye'll find Abhainn's tombstone still readable. But I know nothing about Lachlan. Ye could take a good gander at the other grave markers. See what ye can make out."

"I believe Lachlan is buried in Canada, where I live." Lara reflected on the little hillside graveyard dating from the 1800s on the ranch. She had never studied the names of her ancestors buried there. When she returned to Canada she would certainly do so.

"Is it near here, the castle?" Iain asked.

"Aye, the ruins of Lochleigh Castle are not far. About five mile down the road and then another seven or so on a rough, unmarked trail. Unless ye have a four-wheel vehicle ye'll have to park and hike in. I can draw ye a map. The graveyard's there too, up a hill behind the castle. Some of the markers are nigh onto seven hundred year old. Unreadable, they are. But ye can still make out the words on some of the ones from the seventeen- and eighteen-hundreds. Mind ye, I ha' not been there in many years, not since I were a girl. At one time, this were all MacInnes land. This village and all the land around it. Times change."

They thanked the innkeeper and his wife and returned to their room to prepare for what promised to be a long day.

"Take all our rain gear. This far north the weather can turn in an instant. And wear yer hiking boots and that heavy sweater. I think we may be in fer a long day over rough terrain. I only wish I could do the drivin'."

"I can do this, Iain." She smiled. "And besides, I'll have you beside me all the way, backseat driving."

"There is that."

When they came back down the narrow winding stairs to the pub, the innkeeper was waiting for them. He handed Lara a large bag. "Me wife supposed ye might need some sustenance along the way."

"Thank you so very much." Lara took the proffered lunch. "I'm sure we'll enjoy it."

"And she's drawn ye a rough map. Here"—he pointed to a large X on the map—"there's a boulder here as big as a house. That's the beginning of the trail. There's no marked trail but ye can see on the map here, the river runs on one side and a high hill is on the other. Once ye've surmounted the hill, ye'll be on a high plateau. It'll be easy goin' after that. The moor will be stretching out afore ye, and in the far distance, a line of trees. On the other side o' the trees is the loch." His finger pointed. "Here on the map. And at the far end of the loch, the ruins of Lochleigh Castle. It's a full day's hike but in the Land Rover ye should be able to do it in less time."

They had not been driving long before they came to the river the landlord mentioned. Lara parked the car and got out.

Iain followed her. "What's wrong?"

"The curving road, the river…"

"Ye think this is where Elspeth's carriage overturned?" Iain studied the terrain.

"I do. Lachlan would have come down that steep cliff to rescue her."

"Aye. It seems likely."

Lara peered at the cliff. "Is that what we have to drive up to get to the trail to Lochleigh Castle?"

"Perhaps not," Iain replied. "The landlord's map shows a huge boulder. We're not there yet."

They got back in the Land Rover. Around the next bend, there before them was a massive rock outcropping—the boulder the landlord mentioned. And beside it, winding erratically up the hillside, lay a narrow, overgrown track.

Lara cautiously edged the Land Rover up the almost vertical hill. She could sense Iain beside her, trying to hide his frustration at being passenger rather than driver, tensing as the trail switched back and forth. Keeping the vehicle upright as it ascended was a challenge. When she finally arrived at the summit, with the tall grasses of the moor stretched ahead of her, Lara was weak with relief. She stopped the car and got out.

"Well done, lass." Iain joined her and gave her a one-armed hug. "Don't think I could hae done it better m'self!"

"Where is the line of trees shown on the map?"

Iain opened the compartment and took out a pair of binoculars. He held them to his eyes, adjusted the focus and passed them on to Lara.

"Brilliant. You are brilliant." She hugged him and then studied the distant green. "How safe is it to drive across the moor? I've read stories…"

"Aye. There can be surprises. The ground is not as smooth and flat as it appears. But if there were any real danger, Mrs. Graeme would hae warned us. Her map indicates we should stay on the far right and keep our eyes on the tree line ahead of us."

"Right you are. Straight she goes." Lara down shifted to accommodate the rocky terrain as they bumped along the barely discernable track.

An hour later, with the tree line now visible to the naked eye, Lara stopped the Land Rover and got out.

"Somethin' wrong?" Iain jumped out and came around to her.

"My back hurts from all that bouncing over rocks. I just need to stretch."

He rubbed her back as she nestled in against him.

"Mmm, that's so good."

"That it is." His hand wandered lower.

"Okay. That's enough. Back into the car with you!"

A half hour later they were into the trees. The wide trail stopped abruptly. There was a narrow path, wide enough only for a horseman or for someone on foot.

Lara parked the Land Rover. "We'll have to hike in from here. No wonder the king's men never sacked Lochleigh Castle. They couldn't find it."

Iain retrieved the lunch bag Mrs. MacLean had prepared for them. "Take your rain gear. I know it's sunny now, but it may not be by the time we head back. The weather can change in an instant this close to the North Sea."

"That's why I travel with a backpack," Lara replied. "Just don't forget the food."

"Not likely!" Iain laughed.

The path was seldom used, so overgrown in some places that it was hard to find, but the walking was easy, with pine needles underfoot. The occasional low branch had to be navigated, and sometimes a root would trip one or the other of them, but an hour later they found themselves in a clearing.

Lara gasped. The scene before them was magical. The loch glittered in the sunlight, and at the end of it, the ruins of Lochleigh Castle were reflected in the deep blue of the water.

"I can understand why they chose this location to build their stronghold," Iain said. "It's not only strategically sound, it's also beautiful, set there at the end of the loch."

They picked up their pace.

In front of them stood a high wall with an archway in the middle. On the far right most of the wall had fallen away, but Lara could imagine how it must have been in earlier times. "They said this was a ruin. Just rubble."

"Weel, it is a ruin. But there's more here than we've been led to believe." Iain strolled over to the archway. "The MacInnes crest is still visible here over the entrance. See? In the center stone of the arch, *Ghift Dhe Agnus An Righ,* By the Grace of God and King. And the two lions holding the crest? Of course, the problems for the MacInnes clan came because the king they supported was the *one over the water."*

Lara studied the crest. Her family's motto. "The king over the water?"

"That's how the Jacobites referred to King James, who was in exile in Italy, hence, 'over the water.' They believed, with some merit, James the Seventh of

Scotland should hae been James the Second of England, the rightful king of both England and Scotland. But James was Catholic, and the powerful families in the English court refused to accept a Catholic king. They chose instead, a Protestant, Prince George of Hanover. He could barely speak English and could be easily manipulated by his courtiers."

Lara shook her head. "Politics never change, do they? Those in positions of power manipulate outcomes, wherever they are."

They stepped carefully through the archway. Before them was a rubble-strewn courtyard, and on the other side of the open space, a partial wall with a doorway still intact. Lara headed for it, Iain following.

"This might have been the great hall. A section of roof is still covering a part of it."

Lara took a sharp breath. "This is where Elspeth and Lachlan were married, I know it is." She pointed. "At that end would have been the Laird's Chair."

"Ye may be right. It's possible. Have any other rooms survived?"

They picked their way through fallen stone and rubble to the only doorway still intact. Most of the interior was covered with fallen debris.

"Hard to believe this is all that's left of what was once the heart of a thriving clan," Lara said, "but it's more than I hoped for. It's easy to imagine it as it must once have been."

"What say we have our lunch now?" Iain, ever hungry, suggested. "Here in the ruins of the great hall."

"Sure. I like the idea of eating where once there must have been great banquets like the one Elspeth described on her wedding day."

They sat on blocks of fallen stone and ate the cheese and ham sandwiches Mrs. Maclean had prepared for them. They didn't dally over their lunch; there was still more to do here, and the sun was already low in the sky.

"Let's go find the graveyard." Lara headed outside.

Iain followed, Mrs. Maclean's roughly drawn map in hand. "Here. She shows it behind the castle, on the top of the hill. The family burial site."

They trudged around the ruin. Before them was a very high hill. There were trees, pines and larch, on the lower slopes, but the upper half on the hill was bare. On the crest they could just make out the small enclosed plot of land they were seeking.

"That's a pretty steep climb. Are ye up for it?" Iain put his arm around Lara's shoulder.

"Sure. We'll leave our excess gear in the castle. No point in lugging it up the mountain."

"'Tis nae a mountain, Lara. Tis only a Scottish hill."

"I know," she giggled. "Everything in Scotland is bigger."

The sun was low in the sky when they came to the little graveyard. Lara stepped through a break in the wall surrounding the site. She began examining the stones. Most were so worn as to be unreadable, but even those were interesting. One had a death's head, another, a pair of cherubs carved into it, and still another, a circle of leaves carved around a faded name that might have been Edmund or Edward, hard to be sure. The dates of his life were still readable, 1760 to 1790.

"He only lived to be thirty," she said.

"'Twas not easy, life in the eighteenth century. But over here." He took her hand. "This is what ye were hoping to find."

There they were, side by side in death as they had been in life, Abhainn and his wife Fiona. The dates were still readable. Abhainn was born in 1818 and died in 1874. Fiona died only a few weeks after her husband.

The graves were choked with weeds. Iain attempted to pull some of them away with his one good hand. Lara knelt down and joined him in the effort. It took a half hour to clear away the area of just one grave. "Next time we'll come with gardening tools," Lara said. "I'd like to clean up this whole graveyard."

"Aye. I'd like to come back properly equipped. It's a fitting thing to do."

"But Elspeth isn't buried here." Lara's disappointment colored her words.

"She was married to a Ballantyne, remember? We were unlikely to find her here."

"Do you suppose we could gain access to the Ballantyne family graves?"

"We can try."

When they got back to the pub. Lara asked Mr. Maclean if Balfor MacInnes was there.

He nodded. "Over there, the corner table by himself. Come." He took her by the arm and led her across the small floor.

"Guid evenin', Balfor. The young miss here would like to talk to ye."

The man regarded her, bleary-eyed. "Well, sit ye doon, lass. What is it ye think I might be able to tell ye?"

"I'm Lara MacInnes. I'm from Canada and I'm

trying to locate any relatives I might have here. My very great grandfather was Lachlan MacInnes."

"Aye. I've heard tell of him and his brother Abhainn. They were the last of the great lairds of the clan. After Lachlan left and Abhainn died, people just drifted away. Many emigrated to the Americas or to Australia. There was no livin' to be made here by that time, with droughts and crop failures and the English always wantin' to put sheep on the land."

"But you're a MacInnes."

"Aye, me family stayed. They was farmers on MacInnes lands. In the way of the time, we took the Laird's name. But I'm sorry to tell ye if yer descended direct from Lachlan MacInnes, ye are no blood relative of mine."

Lara sat back, close to tears. She had so hoped…

"Dinna fash yerself, lass. We may not be blood kin, but we are of the same Clan. We are both Clan MacInnes."

Lara smiled. "So we are. Thank you, Mr. MacInnes."

Getting ready for bed that night, Lara said, "We've studied every gravestone that's still readable. Elspeth was not buried here." Lara was despondent. "What had happened to Elspeth? Where was she buried?"

"Ye ken if she was convicted, she would not be buried in consecrated ground."

"What?"

"The last we read of Elspeth, she was on trial for the murder of her husband. If convicted she would most certain hang, and her body would nae be returned to her family for burial."

"But that's ridiculous. We know she was with

Lachlan when Ballantyne was murdered."

"Aye. We know. We've read her diary. But who was there to speak at a trial on her behalf? Her alibi was sailin' across the Atlantic. He was unaware of her plight. And if Lachlan had been there to speak, do you think the court would ha'e believed him? Her lover?"

"We must return to the Hall of Records on Monday morning when they open," Lara said. "There was one newspaper, the *Scottish Thistle*, I think, with a day-by-day verbatim account of the trial."

Chapter Fourteen

The Past

15 September 1856

My trial has been set for six weeks hence. I have so far fared better than many in this horrid place. Because of my husband's rank and station, I do not have to share my cell with other prisoners. It is above ground and I can see daylight through my one small, barred window. They allowed Agnes to provide me with clean bedding and a small table and writing materials, and a folding screen so I may take care of my ablutions unobserved.

I cannot comprehend how I alighted here, in a prison cell. How could anyone think I would have ever harmed, let alone murdered, my husband, a man who rescued me, who saved me and my child from a life of penury? I respected and cared for Hugh Ballantyne. Our union may not have been a marriage in the fullest sense, but we were genuinely fond of one another.

Yet here I am, in prison, awaiting trial. My greatest fear is for Jamie. His legal next-of-kin is Ainsley Ballantyne, who lives a life of debauchery and is always in want of money. If I am convicted, all that stands in the way of Ainsley and the vast Ballantyne fortune will be a six-year-old boy. The mere notion terrifies me. On the day I was arrested, I instructed Agnes to take the child secretly to Lochleigh, to Abhainn and Fiona, and to let no one know where she was going. Jamie will be safe there. Knowing he is safe makes the rest of this nightmare easier to bear.

All too soon it will be my first day in court. I shudder with dread at the prospect. Alone in the prisoner's box, all eyes on me, condemning me.

****

The Lord Justice Clerk addressed the court.

"Lady Elspeth Glendenning Ballantyne, lately prisoner at Edinburgh, you are now indicted and accused, at the instance of John Barleysmith, Esquire, Her Majesty's Advocate for Her Majesty's interest: that by the laws of this and every other well governed realm, you wickedly and feloniously did strike your husband with a fireplace poker with intent to murder, a crime of an heinous nature, and that you, Lady Elspeth Glendenning Ballantyne, are guilty of said crime on the seventeenth of June, eighteen hundred fifty-six, at your residence in New Town, Edinburgh. Relevant documents are lodged in the hands of the Clerk of the High Court of Justice before which you are to be tried."

Turning to the jury, he instructed, "Lady Elspeth Glendenning Ballantyne should be punished with the pains of the law, to deter committing like crimes in all time coming."

In the prisoners' box, Elspeth stood, her head bowed, her hands tightly clasped, immobile as the charges were read. She wore the black of deep mourning, her face obscured by her hat and heavy black veil.

Three judges in their long, curly white wigs sat on the highest benches, their solemn faces, their down-turned lips, their frowns, all evidence of their condemnation even before the trial began.

Elspeth read contempt and disapproval in the faces of the jury of twelve men who sat across the room from her. Twelve men ready to believe her capable of murder.

She forced her attention back to the proceedings. The Clerk of Court was now reading out the names of the witnesses who would be called to testify. It included most of her household staff and few names she didn't recognize.

The day passed in a blur. She was barely able to focus as the Clerk of the Court outlined what was to happen in the coming days. Her mind kept wandering back to that horrible day. The day when she had said a final farewell to the love of her life and then come home to find her dear husband dead, murdered.

Finally, the ordeal was over, and she was returned to her small cell. She took off her hat, threw herself down on her cot and sobbed. She was guilty. She had not taken the poker to her husband, but she had betrayed him in thought and deed. Hugh Ballantyne had been nothing but kind and considerate to her. She may not have wielded the weapon that killed him, but she had broken every promise she made to him. She should be hanged for her crimes. It was no more than she deserved.

The jailor approached her cell door, rattling his keys. "You have a visitor. Ten minutes, sir."

Abhainn strode in, and she flung herself into his arms. "Is Jamie safe?"

"Safe and having a fine time playing with his cousins. Did the lad ne'er play with other children afore?"

"No. Not really." Elspeth had not considered how isolated her son had been. She spent as much time as she could with him, but there had been no other children in his life. No one to play with. She vowed to herself if she survived this ordeal, their manner of living would change. She would make sure her little boy had a happy, carefree, childhood.

"But it's not Jamie I'm here for. It's you." Abhainn put his hands on her shoulders and stared directly into her eyes. "Did ye kill Lord Ballantyne?"

She stepped away from him, incensed. "No. Of course not. How can you ask such a thing?"

"I just needed to hear from yer own lips that ye were innocent. So if ye are not guilty, who is?"

Elspeth drew in a sharp breath. She had not asked herself that question. "Who, indeed?"

"The motive for murder is generally either love or money. If the court can make a case that ye were having a love affair and wanted to get rid of yer husband, ye will most surely hang. But ye had just bid a final farewell to yer lover and sent him on his way. What reason would ye have fer then murderin' yer husband?"

"Would the prosecutor even know about Lachlan?" Elspeth asked.

"Aye, he'll know. Lachlan told me ye wrote nightly in yer journals. They'll have taken yer journals as evidence. Of that ye may be sure."

"Oh, no." Elspeth sat down on her cot, shocked. Her journals. Her closest, most personal feelings. Lachlan was in them on many pages. Vivid descriptions of their lovemaking, of her passion for him. How could she hold her head up if they were read out in court?

"If they have yer journals, the court will surely use yer own words to convince the jury this was a crime of passion. But we know ye sent Lachlan away, when ye could hae gone with him. That information must be conveyed to the jury."

"Must it?"

"Aye, lass, if ye are not to hang. We both know we can eliminate a love affair as the reason for this murder. We must bring this to the attention of any witnesses who might be kindly disposed toward ye. Who would they be?"

"Most of the household staff." Elspeth reflected for a moment. "If we could get them to include Hamish in their list of witnesses…but I suppose he sailed with Lachlan."

"He did not. He said he was too old to be embarking on such a venture, and Lachlan released him. How do ye think Hamish could be of help?"

"He never left Lachlan's side. He could testify that Lachlan was never with me except for the afternoon before he sailed. That in all the years of my marriage, except for the day he recovered his memory, we never saw each other. They are going to try to prove I killed my husband to be with my lover. If I am not to hang, we must somehow show Lachlan and I were never alone together after my marriage until that afternoon before he sailed."

"I'll exert what influence I have to make that happen." Abhainn paced the small cell as he considered what to do next. "Then there's the other piece of the puzzle. If it wasn't a crime of passion, it must have involved money in some way. Who stands to gain if ye hang?"

Elspeth shuddered. "Immediately upon my husband's death, Jamie inherited his titles and all his vast estates and holdings. He is now Lord Ballantyne, the thirteenth Earl of Ainsworth. I inherit only a widow's portion, a modest allowance on which to live, and the dower house at my husband's family home at Ainsworth."

She paused. "Of course, Athdara Castle is mine, and my husband left an endowment to cover its expenses in perpetuity. If I...die," she stumbled over the word, "my son inherits that as well."

"He is a very wealthy little boy. You said there was a nephew?"

"Ainsley. My husband must have been very angry with him. I never expected him to be left such a pittance in my husband's will. His inheritance is a small yearly stipend, barely enough to live on, if he does not gamble or drink. He can certainly no longer live in the style to which he has become accustomed."

Abhainn slapped his knee. "There ye have it. The *other* most common reason fer murder. If ye were to hang, there would be naught between this Ainsley and a massive fortune except a six-year-old boy. And in the natural course o' things, if ye are convicted of murder, the courts would assign Ainsley Ballantyne, the next of kin, as the boy's guardian." He shook his head. There are so many ways a young child can die."

Elspeth blanched. "You think Ainsley Ballantyne murdered his uncle over money? And could also be planning to murder my son?"

"Aye. It's the only thing that makes sense. Now all we have to do is convince someone to draw that fact to the court's attention. It might help if it were to surface that there was a history of disagreements between Ballantyne and his nephew."

"But there was. Ainsley's visits inevitably ended in loud quarrels over money. He was always in trouble over his gambling debts, and his uncle always bailed him out, but not before there were ugly arguments between them. The whole household could hear them."

"Better and better. Who on the staff do ye trust to tell the truth?"

"You might start with Weathersby, the butler. And, of course, Agnes, my lady's maid. When my husband and Ainsley started shouting, everyone in the house could hear them, all the way down to the kitchens."

"Guid, lass. I'm not sure it's enough to prove ye innocent, but it may be enough to muddy the waters."

****

The next morning, the Lord Advocate, William Anthony, began calling witnesses. First to take the stand was a young parlor maid Elspeth recognized as only recently hired.

After swearing the witness in, Lord Anthony began questioning her. "Did you ever hear your master and mistress arguing?

"That I did." She threw a malicious glare at Elspeth. "I was dustin' in the hall when she come flying out of the library, yelling at the master. 'I'll see you in hell first!' Them was her very words."

"And what did she do then?" Lord Anthony prodded.

"She slammed the library door. Then, shortly after, she went out. She was in a murderous rage."

"A murderous rage." Lord Anthony raised his eyebrows and glanced tellingly at the jury. "Did you happen to hear the address she gave the driver?"

"Someplace in the port. I didn't hear the street or the number. But she was going by public conveyance, a hackney. Now, I ask ye, why would she do that, with three carriages at her beck and call, if she wasn't trying to hide something?"

"Why indeed? Did you ever hear your master and mistress argue at any other time?

The girl's chin came up and she pursed her lips. "No. But that's not to say as they didn't. I only been with the Ballantynes for two weeks."

"No more questions, my lord."

The young woman flounced out of the witness box, smirking at Elspeth.

Elspeth remembered telling Weathersby she didn't care for the new parlor maid. She had caught her listening at doors more than once when she should have been about her duties. Had Weathersby spoken to her about it? Why else should she exhibit such hatred for her?

Elspeth glanced at the jury. They had believed every word. But then the words the maid recounted were true. Elspeth had indeed shouted them at her husband. They were, to her everlasting sorrow, the last words she ever spoke to him. The memory of them made her cringe with shame.

Over the next three days, it seemed to Elspeth every upstairs and downstairs maid, every footman, every cook's assistant, and every scullery maid was asked to tell what they knew or surmised about her marriage. Most commented Lord and Lady Ballantyne appeared to be a devoted couple. But those who overheard that fateful argument repeated Elspeth's last damning words to her husband: "I'll see you in hell, first!"

Weathersby, their butler, was the last member of the household staff to be called to the witness stand.

To counsel's question about arguments overheard, he answered, "Indeed. There were many loud disagreements. Every time Lord Ballantyne's nephew, Ainsley Ballantyne, came to call, the arguments over money were so explosive no one in the household could fail to hear them. The young man had a history of gambling and always expected his uncle to cover his losses. He and his uncle were often at odds. More than once his uncle loudly threatened to disinherit him."

"No, no." The barrister appeared flustered. "My question was about disagreements between Lord and Lady Ballantyne."

"They were a devoted couple. Only once, in all the years I was in their service, do I recall ever hearing them raise their voices to one another."

"And that once would have been?"

"On the day Lord Ballantyne died. Just before my lady went out, they had a heated exchange. Lady Ballantyne wished to keep their young son at home with a tutor, while Lord Ballantyne insisted he be sent away to school. Hardly the kind of disagreement one would commit murder over."

"Your opinion has not been solicited. The jury should be instructed to ignore that last remark."

The Judge concurred. "Restrict your testimony to answering the questions."

"Did you see her ladyship go out shortly after that exchange?"

"Yes."

"And why, with a stable full of carriages, did she choose to take a public conveyance?"

"It is not my place to question her ladyship's actions. I can only surmise she did not wish to wait while a carriage was prepared."

"And how long was she gone?"

"A bit over two hours. Just long enough for Lord Ballantyne's nephew, Ainsley Ballantyne, to come and go, asking for money to cover his gambling debts, as usual."

The courtroom erupted in babble.

"Silence." The first of the three judges ordered. "Silence in the court."

Peering at Counsel, a judge asked, "Is Ainsley Ballantyne listed among the witnesses?

"No, my lord. I didn't know… I had not considered it necessary…"

"See that he appears tomorrow."

"Yes, my lord."

Back in her cell that night, Elspeth smiled at the unexpected turn of events when Weathersby testified. Her smile turned to a worried frown. Why had nothing had been said about her journals? Nothing could be more damning than her written declarations of love for another man, her plans to meet him on that fateful day, and yet her journals had not been introduced into evidence.

The next morning, taking her place in the prisoner's box, Elspeth studied the spectators. Every seat was filled. A sensational murder trial always brought out people seeking morbid entertainment. Did they believe her guilty of murdering her husband? Difficult to tell. Most would not meet her eyes when she glanced at them. That was not a good omen.

All rose as the judges entered and took their places at the bench. Court was declared in session.

"The Prosecution calls Ainsley Ballantyne to the stand."

Elspeth took a sharp breath. The young man threw her a vicious glare, then ambled to the witness box and took the oath.

"Would you characterize your uncle's marriage as a harmonious one?"

"Hardly."

"Expand on that, please. What did you observe to make you suspect theirs was not a happy marriage?"

"Well, just think about it. She married him for his title and money. Anyone can see that. She's half his age. And she tricked him into marriage."

The prosecutor eyed the jury. "Just how did she trick him?"

"By the oldest trick in the world. She told him she was going to bear his child."

There was an audible gasp from the gallery.

"And just how did you come by this information?"

"Well, it wasn't hard to surmise. The bastard was born barely two months after their marriage. Furthermore, he has red hair. No one in the Ballantyne family has red hair."

The Lord Prosecutor waited for the babble to die down. "You visited Lord Ballantyne on the afternoon of his death?"

"Yes. My allowance was late. I was short of funds."

"Were you frequently short of funds?"

"A man in my position must keep up appearances."

"And exactly what *is* your position?"

"I *was* his only heir until he married that woman!" he pointed dramatically to the prisoner's box.

The Lord prosecutor smiled. "You may step down. The court may wish to recall you."

"The court now calls Hamish MacInnes to the witness stand."

Elspeth's head jerked up. How had Abhainn found Hamish so quickly? And how had he maneuvered to get him on the witness list?

"You were in the employ of one Lachlan MacInnes?"

"No, m'lord. As a member of the clan, I was charged with the honor of protecting him. I was his gilly for thirty years."

"His gilly?"

"Aye, m' lord. I was his constant companion. I was charged wi' keeping the Laird's brother safe. It's the way in the Highlands. Ye should know the custom if ye profess to be a Highlander, m'lord."

There was a twitter in the courtroom. Lord Anthony waited for silence. "Was Lachlan MacInnes Lady Ballantyne's lover?"

Hamish frowned, as if puzzled by the question.

"Let me phrase the question another way. Were Lachlan MacInnes and Lady Elspeth Glendenning ever alone together, to your knowledge?

"After her marriage to Lord Ballantyne? Only once, m'lord. She came to bid him goodbye on the day he was leaving for a far country. I gave them privacy for their farewells."

"I see. And how long did these 'farewells' take?"

"I couldn't say, m'lord. I was engaged in a game o'

273

cards with the hackney driver, and we were no keepin' track o' the time. But this I can swear to. That afternoon was their only meeting in some many years."

The prosecutor frowned. "You may step down. I should like to recall Mr. Weathersby to the stand.

"You have been with Lord and Lady Ballantyne all the years of their marriage. Was Lachlan MacInnes ever in their home?"

Weathersby frowned. "Only on one occasion."

"And when was that?"

"Three years ago. He was delivering a supply of liquor from the nearby monastery when he collapsed on the front lawn and was carried into the house to recover. He left later that afternoon and was alone with the mistress in the drawing room for only a few moments before he left. And I might add, in contradiction to Master Ainsley Ballantyne's testimony, there are six portraits of past Ballantynes with red hair!"

The court broke out in raucous laughter, and the judges called for order.

Court was adjourned for the day.

The next morning, Elspeth saw a slight change in the way the spectators eyed her. Yesterday's testimony must have given them some pause for thought. The jurymen, however, were as dour as ever. She braced herself for what was to come.

The Prosecutor approached the Judges' Bench. "New evidence has come to light, My Lord, which makes it necessary to recall certain witnesses."

The judges conferred. The one in the middle glowered at Lord Anthony. "You had ample time to question witnesses last week when they testified. Is your 'new evidence' compelling enough to prolong this already too long trial?"

"I believe it is, sir."

"Very well. You may proceed."

"Gilbert Weathersby to the stand."

"You understand you are still under oath?"

"Yes, my lord."

"How long were you in the employ of Lord Ballantyne?"

Weathersby huffed and frowned, calculating. "Some thirty years, m'lord."

"Did you ever in all those years know Lord Ballantyne to lose his temper?"

"Quite regularly, sir. Every time his wastrel nephew, Ainsley, came demanding money."

There was a loud buzzing from the spectators.

"And did Lord Ballantyne ever lose his temper with his wife?"

"Quite often with the first Lady Ballantyne. With the present Lady Ballantyne, only once in all the years they were married."

"That disagreement was characterized as a 'murderous rage' by one witness. Would you agree with that characterization?"

"Most certainly not, my lord."

Counsel paused and glanced toward the jury. "How would you have characterized it?"

"As a simple marital disagreement over the education of their child."

"You may step down."

Lord Anthony approached the judges. "My lords, I'm afraid I have been unable to locate Ainsley Ballantyne."

"Unable to locate? Is his testimony crucial? You have already questioned him once." The first judge's voice was sharp, demanding more information.

"I am sorry, my lord. There is some question about the timing of his last visit to his uncle. It appears he may have been leaving as her ladyship was being admitted to the house by Mr. Weathersby. A new witness has come forward…"

"A new witness? Then add him to your list and call him. If his testimony contradicts that already presented, you must give Mr. Ballantyne opportunity to refute that new testimony."

"We are trying to locate him. We left a message at his lodging house."

The judge waved his hand airily. "Call your next witness."

The young man, hardly more than a boy, approached the witness stand warily, cap in hand.

Elspeth smothered a gasp. Thomas, the coach boy Hamish rescued when her carriage overturned. The half-starved child he'd carried back to Lochleigh. A young man now. The last she'd seen of Thomas, he'd been in the Highlands, healthy and happy, growing up with the MacInnes children.

Thomas took his seat in the witness box and was sworn in.

The prosecution queried, "Where were you on the afternoon of August ninth?"

"I was drivin' the lady's hackney," he nodded toward the witness box as he spoke.

"And when she descended from the carriage and into the inn in the port, what did you do?"

"I waited, like she told me to. I was gettin' paid to

wait, so wait I did. I whiled away the time with a game o' cards."

"And how long did you wait?

"Hard to say. Maybe two hours. When she came out her face was all blotchy and she was crying." The boy glanced at Lady Ballantyne, sympathy in his eyes. "All she said to me was to take her home. Back to where I picked her up."

"What happened then?"

"Well, I took her back like she asked me to, and she paid me extra because of the wait."

"And then?"

The boy squirmed. "I stepped around the side o' the house to take a…"

"Yes?" the prosecutor encouraged.

"Piss," he answered.

The courtroom exploded in laughter. The boy turned beet red.

"And what did you see?" The prosecutor asked in the suddenly tense, quiet courtroom.

"I saw a bloke climbin' out the window. He 'ad blood all over him. I got out o' there as quick as possible."

"And would you be able to identify this 'bloke' if you were to see him again?"

"Aye, that's why I'm here. I seen his picture in the paper, in the *Scotch Thistle*. I 'ad to come. I couldn't let you think her ladyship—"

"Thank you. I have the paper in question here. Is this the picture?

"Aye. That's him."

Lord Andrews spoke directly to the jury. "The picture is of Ainsley Ballantyne."

There was a hushed murmur in the gallery.

"Thank you." The prosecutor spoke to the boy. "You may step down."

"The court recalls Ainsley Ballantyne to the stand."

"Ainsley Ballantyne!"

"My Lord, he doesn't appear to be here."

The judges conferred.

"Court is adjourned for today." The first judge addressed the prosecution. "Ainsley Ballantyne is to be in court when we resume tomorrow morning at nine!"

Back in her cell, Elspeth took off her veiled hat and stepped behind her privacy screen to remove her mourning dress with its high neck and long tight sleeves, and to unlace her uncomfortably tight stays. Near impossible to undo stays without a lady's maid, but she had no choice. When she was down to her chemise and petticoats, she heaved a sigh of relief. She emerged from behind the screen wearing a long, loose, comfortable wrapper. A few weeks ago, she would never have chanced a man viewing her in this state of undress, but she was fully covered and no longer cared if someone observed her without her stays.

She was seated at her writing desk, detailing the events of the day in the new journal Agnes had provided her with, when a jailor approached. "You have a visitor, my lady. Ten minutes, sir."

Abhainn entered, a basket over his arm. "Your cook has sent an offering. You have a very devoted staff."

"How kind of her, and of you for bringing it."

"We have very little time. The evidence of young Thomas this morning was helpful. Of course, Ainsley Ballantyne will refute it, but at least there will be some measure of doubt in the juror's minds. Ballantyne annoys the jurors with his pretentions, while Thomas gives the impression of honesty."

"I don't know how you did it, Abhainn, but thank you. Today's proceedings give me hope. But on to more important things. How is my son?"

"Happy and healthy and running wild with the rest of the Highland lads. For the present we're not worrying overmuch about lessons. Oh, he's being taught reading and numbers for a couple of hours every day. Fiona is teaching him along with our boys. But if it's Latin and Greek and higher mathematics ye want, ye'll just have to wait until ye can hire a tutor."

"What would I do without you and Fiona, Abhainn? Thank you."

"Weel, it *is* me nephew we're talkin' aboot. Even if we can never acknowledge him."

Elspeth stared at Abhainn in shock. "How long have you known?"

"Since the day I first set eyes on him. He's the spittin' image."

Elspeth bowed her head and a tear splashed on her hand. She took a deep breath. "I took an oath…"

"Aye, I know, lass. I know the whole sorry story from Hamish. Ye did what ye had to. No more need be said. On my honor this will go no farther."

"Have you heard from Lachlan, Abhainn? Has there been any word?"

"There has not yet been time. His ship will be sighting land sometime in the next few days if the voyage was a good one. He'll write when he can. And I'll answer. Do ye want him to know about all this?"

"No. Please. We came to an ending the day he left.

Do not open that raw wound again. Even if I am declared innocent of all charges, there is Jamie to consider. One glimpse of him and Lachlan would know the truth of his parentage. It could destroy Jamie. My first responsibility must be to my child. I must shield him as much as possible from all this ugliness. And I must rear him in a way fitting to a peer, a lord of the realm."

Abhainn put his hands on her shoulders. "My dear, that may be hard to do. Even if you should be declared innocent of these scurrilous charges, the scandal will follow you for the rest of your life. And in those schools the upper-class English are so attached to, the other boys will attend to their parents' gossip and Jamie will be made to suffer for it."

Elspeth turned white and her knees gave way. Abhainn caught her and placed her on her bed. He took some water from the pitcher behind the screen and wetted his handkerchief with it. This he placed gently on Elspeth's brow.

As she regained consciousness, the vison of her future and the future of her young son hit her with the force of a blow. "What am I to do?"

"For the moment, nothing. Your son is happy and safe. When ye are free, as I am sure ye will be, I suggest ye join us at Lochleigh. There is a saying, 'out of sight, out of mind.'"

The next day Elspeth studied the jurors as they filed in. Did they appear a little less intimidating? Had they believed Thomas? How would they react when Ainsley took the stand? He would surely deny Thomas' allegations.

The judges took their places at the bench. Court

was in session.

"The prosecution calls Mr. Ainsley Ballantyne to the stand."

There was a deafening silence in the courtroom.

"Mr. Ainsley Ballantyne."

"My Lords," prosecution addressed the bench, "I was with him only yester evening. He assured me he would be in court today to answer these scurrilous charges."

"Yet he is not here! Has anyone in the courtroom information as to the whereabouts of Mr. Ballantyne?"

Abhainn stood. "I believe I may be of some help, yer Honors. Mr. Ballantyne was involved in a high stakes card game last evening in the Pennyworth Hotel. Sometime after midnight he was accused of cheating. He drew a gun, meaning to leave the game with his illicit winnings, but his gaming partners threw themselves upon him. Mr. Ballantyne died of a gunshot wound at three in the morning."

There was a sudden intake of breath among the spectators.

"May I ask you how you came by this information?" The third judge peered at Abhainn.

"I was there, idly watchin' the games. There were a number of them going on in the hall. It is what I believe you call a 'Gambling Hell.'"

"Thank you, sir, for your information. I take it the proper authorities were sent for?"

"The police were arriving as I left."

The three judges conferred. The third judge spoke. "The evidence of the hackney driver, Thomas, must be taken into consideration when the jury retires to consider a verdict, but the jurymen must also consider there has been no corroboration of the hackney driver's evidence. Mr. Ainsley Ballantyne is not able to be here to clear his name or to refute that testimony."

He turned to the prosecutor. "Now, Lord Andrew, are you prepared to continue?"

"Yes, my Lord."

As his last witness, the Prosecution called the accused, Lady Elspeth Glendenning Ballantyne, to the witness chair. Elspeth took her heavy veil in her two hands and arranged it on the back of her hat. She wanted the jury to see her face clearly as she testified. She placed her hand on the Bible and was sworn in.

"Did you, on the afternoon of the ninth of August, have an argument with your husband?"

"Yes. Married people do sometimes disagree."

Her response caused a twitter from the observers.

One of the judges admonished, "Answer the questions, madam. Do not express your opinions."

Elspeth nodded meekly. "Yes, my lord."

"And this disagreement was about?"

"My husband wished to send our six-year-old son away to boarding school. I wanted to keep him at home with a tutor for a little longer. I thought it cruel to tear so young a child away from all he was familiar with at so tender an age."

The prosecutor glanced at the jury. "The argument must have been very heated for you to have screamed at him the words, 'I will see you in hell, first.'"

"We had a very heated argument. And I shall regret to my dying day those words were the last I ever spoke to my husband."

"And then you left the house. You traveled by hired conveyance although you had your own carriage at your disposal. May I ask why that was?"

Elspeth hesitated only briefly. "I was late for an appointment."

"Where and with whom?"

"A dear friend was leaving Scotland to sail to British North America."

"And would this 'dear friend' have been a gentleman?"

Elspeth reflected for a moment, then opted for some version of the truth. "I wished to say farewell to a man, Lachlan McInnis, who saved my life when I was in an accident in Scotland six years ago."

The prosecutor raised his eyebrows. "You were alone?"

"Yes."

"You met this man in his rooms, without your lady's maid or any other companion?"

"Yes."

"And how long were you alone with this man, your Scottish friend?" The Prosecutor observed the jury to be sure they understood the implications of his question.

"I returned home two hours later."

"Two hours? That seems a rather protracted farewell for someone who was only an acquaintance. He *was* only an acquaintance?"

"No. He was a dear friend. Someone who saved my life when I was in a perilous carriage accident. He and his whole family took care of me until I was once again able to travel."

"I put it to your ladyship that you were more than friends. I have here a document that shows that that barely a year before you entered into a marriage agreement with Lord Hugh Ballantyne you were married in a Scottish ceremony to Lachlan MacInnes."

There was a palpable gasp from the gallery.

The Judge intervened. "Has Lachlan MacInnes been called as a witness?"

"No. my lord. We have been unable to locate him."

Elspeth started to speak. "He—"

The judge admonished her. "You will speak only in response to the prosecution's questions."

The prosecutor continued. "While your Highland marriage might not have been considered legal in any other part of the British Isles, it is legal in the Highlands. I put it to you that, before his disappearance, you were living with Lachlan MacInnes as husband and wife. Is that not so?"

Elspeth clenched her hands until her knuckles were white. "Yes," she whispered.

"Please repeat your answer. The jury must hear it."

Elspeth squared her shoulders and raised her head to stare directly at the jury box. "Yes." Her voice was strong and clear.

"Let me be clear about this." the Prosecutor leaned toward her, menace in his very posture. "You were married to two men at the same time?"

Elspeth took a deep breath. "Lachlan MacInnes was presumed dead when I married Lord Ballantyne. Lord Ballantyne was fully aware of my first marriage. We both believed I was free to marry. Two years after our marriage I discovered Lachlan MacInnes was alive."

"And did you share this 'discovery' with Lord Ballantyne?"

"At the time, I did not deem it necessary to do so."

The Prosecutor gazed at the jury significantly. "Not

necessary. So, you then secretly resumed your relationship with Lachlan MacInnes?"

"I most certainly did not. I sent him away on that very day, four years ago."

The Prosecution paused dramatically and regarded the jury. "And yet, four years later, you were with him on the day of your husband's murder."

Elspeth did not respond.

"You have no answer to that?

"I was unaware you asked a question, my lord."

The gallery once again twittered, causing the judges to glower at them.

The prosecutor leaned toward Elspeth, his posture intimidating. "I put it to you Lachlan MacInnes was your lover, and in order to be with him, you did most heinously murder your husband. You planned to be with Lachlan MacInnes when he sailed that night." His voice rose, "Is that not so?"

Elspeth raised her head and spoke directly to the jury. "It is not. On returning, I went immediately to the library with the intention of apologizing to my husband for my earlier unforgivable behavior. I found him…" Elspeth's iron control broke as she remembered holding her husband's blood-soaked head in her arms.

The prosecutor pounded her with his words. "I suggest you found your husband alive in the library. Did you not?"

"No. That is a vicious lie."

"And when he refused your plea yet again, in a rage of anger, you struck him over the head with the closest weapon at hand, the fireplace poker."

Through sobs Elspeth said, "I ca-cared deeply for my hu-husband. I could never have ha-harmed him. I found him dying."

"So you would have us believe." He turned to the Judge. "And yet we have the evidence of the blood on your gown and on the instrument of his death."

Finally, she was allowed to step down from the witness box.

The judge spoke to the jurymen. "You are allowed a free day tomorrow so you may attend church. Court will resume on Monday morning."

****

Abhainn visited Elspeth in her cell on Sunday afternoon.

"I believe there is some reason for optimism," he said, handing her a basket of food. "While we may not have conclusively proved yer innocence, considerable doubt has been thrown on Ainsley Ballantyne's evidence. Pity he had to die before testifying again."

"I'm not sorry he's dead," Elspeth replied. "I've been sick with fear for my child ever since Hugh was murdered. Ainsley would sooner or later have found some way of eliminating the only barrier between him and the Ballantyne title and fortune."

"Ye may possibly have the right of it. In any case, that danger no longer exists."

Elspeth sat on her bed, indicating Abhainn should take the desk chair. "I hope to walk free tomorrow," she said, "but there is no way of predicting what those twelve men may decide.

"If I am found guilty…" Her voice trembled. She took a deep breath and continued. "In the event that I am found guilty, I have written a letter to be given to my son on his twentieth birthday. I have told him everything about this trial and my earlier marriage to

Lachlan. To honor my pledge to Hugh Ballantyne, I've not told him about his parentage. Hugh considered him his son and I will do my best to raise him in a manner befitting the son of Hugh Ballantyne. I believed it would be better for him to know the truth of the trial than to be plagued all his life by rumor and innuendo."

Abhainn sat for a moment in silence. Then he sighed. "I believe ye are doing a guid thing. There will be no way of keepin' this trial and all the newspaper accounts from him. Far better if he has the truth of it in yer own hand. I will undertake to give him yer account at the right time."

"Thank you, my dear friend."

****

In his summing up to the jury, the prosecutor reminded them of the conclusive evidence of a loud quarrel between Lord and Lady Ballantyne overheard by most of the household. He recalled to them Lady Ballantyne had then rushed out of the house into the arms of a man to whom she had previously been married. He suggested she murdered her husband with the intent of joining her lover that night when his ship sailed and suggested only the presence of bailiffs in the house prevented that from happening. He reminded them of the evidence of her blood-soaked gown and the blood-stained fireplace poker.

He spoke dismissively of the evidence of the hackney driver and reminded the jury that Ainsley Ballantyne had been unable to appear in court to refute that evidence due to his untimely death.

After some ponderous pronouncements from the bench about their duty, the jury was sequestered to deliberate their verdict.

Elspeth was taken to a small side chamber to await the verdict. To her surprise, Abhainn was allowed to join her as "next of kin." Spectators and newspapermen hovered in the outer halls.

Two tense hours later they were ushered back into the courtroom. The jury had reached their verdict.

"How find you in the charge of murder against the defendant, Lady Elspeth Ballantyne?"

"Not proven, my Lords, by a majority of eight to four."

The courtroom erupted in babble.

The judges stood. "Not proven. The jury is hereby dismissed. The prisoner is free to go."

Newspapermen pushed through the crowd toward Elspeth, but Abhainn was by her side instantly, shielding her with his body, edging her toward a door at the back of the courtroom. A burly policeman stepped aside and opened the door for them. They were in a hallway leading to a back entrance.

Outside a hackney awaited. "Thomas," Elspeth cried.

"Inside my lady, quickly."

Abhainn picked her up, deposited her on the seat, and followed her. The carriage took off with a spray of dirt and pebbles as a crowd of spectators and newsmen rounded the corner.

Elspeth's nerves, already tight as a bow string, shattered. She started sobbing uncontrollably. Abhainn put his arms around her and allowed her to cry herself out.

Finally, she sat upright. "I'm sorry," she hiccupped.

"If anyone had reason to cry, ye have, my dear."

"What does it mean, 'Not proven'?"

"It means the jury had some doubt about yer guilt, but no enough doubt to declare ye innocent. It is a peculiarly Scottish verdict. A bit nasty, since innuendo and gossip will continue to hound ye all yer life. But it is certainly preferable to being declared guilty and hanged. Ye are free."

Elspeth sat back and took a quavering breath. "I'm free. But what about Jamie? The scandal! I have ruined his chances!"

"Nae. Nothing of the sort. Gossip has a short life. Ye are most certain the topic of today's drawing rooms, but in five years, nae, five months, it will be forgotten. Besides, I have some ideas aboot young Jamie's education. But first we must get ye to Lochleigh. Ye are in need of rest and fattening up. Yer thin as a rail. And young Jamie is anxious to have ye back."

Chapter Fifteen

The Present

They were in the Hall of Records, engrossed in the word-by-word account of Elspeth's trial in *The Scottish Thistle.* Lara jumped up, incensed, from the last lines of the newspaper story. "What the hell kind of verdict is that! 'Not proven'! I've never heard of such a thing!"

"It's a peculiarly Scottish verdict, love. Would ye rather have had her hanged?"

"No. Of course not." Lara had tears in her eyes. "It's just so unfair. We know she was innocent and yet suspicion will follow her for the rest of her life. And what about her son? I shudder to think of the problems he would have encountered in school. Children can be so cruel in circumstances like these."

"We don't know what Elspeth chose to do about Jamie's schooling. We need to go back to her journals."

"Speaking of her journals, why do you suppose the prosecutor never entered them into evidence?"

"The only possible answer is he didn't have them. My guess would be Agnes took them away with her when she took young Jamie."

"But—"

"Let's go home, love. We need to be there when the workmen arrive. The electrician is due on Monday and the plumbers on Wednesday. We can spend the next few evenings catching up on what Elspeth has to say for herself."

They were at the castle for dinner that night. After the tourists had dispersed, they retreated to the library. Lara told Iain's parents about Elspeth's trail and verdict.

"Not proven," Iain's mother said. "That's a harsh sentence to live with. Her son would have been hounded with it throughout his school years. I can't imagine Elspeth, from everything you've told me, allowing that to happen."

"But she returned to Lochleigh with Abhainn after the trial." Lara answered. "Perhaps she stayed on there. No one there would have cared a fig for a 'not proven' verdict. They all loved Elspeth. They all were aware of the whole story. And Lachlan's child would have been loved and cherished there."

"True as far as it goes," Duncan intervened. "But Lachlan's child was legally Hugh Ballantyne's child. He was Lord Ballantyne, Earl of Ainsley and a Peer of the Realm. And Elspeth must have borne a strong sense of obligation to the man who rescued her and her child and all her dependent staff from a life of penury. A child who, in the eyes of the outside world, might otherwise have been considered a bastard."

"I understand," Aileen said, "but how did she manage to prepare him for that life? The schooling her husband expected would have been out of the question. In the first place, I'll bet none of the schools where he was enrolled would have accepted him after that notorious trial."

Lara smiled. "Knowing Elspeth through her journals, I'm sure she found a way. She was a clever and courageous woman." She reflected for a moment. "The Ballantynes. We haven't explored the Ballantyne family yet. We should be able to find out something about Jamie there. And perhaps about Elspeth. There must be a Ballantyne graveyard. And perhaps Jamie's descendants would be willing to talk with us."

Iain was skeptical. "We could try. But I'm not sure the heirs will be willing to talk to us about a scandal that happened two hundred years ago. And even if they're willing, I doubt they could add much to what we already know."

"I know how we can find out." Duncan laughed. "It's so obvious. Why didn't I think of it before? *Burke's Peerage*. We can find the Ballantynes in Burke's Peerage. Surely they'll be there."

Lara was confused. "Burke's Peerage?"

"Burke's Peerage is the definitive guide to the genealogy and heraldry of the peerage, baronetage, knightage, and landed gentry, established in London in 1826 by John Burke. The Ballantynes are sure to be listed. Jamie will be in there."

"Do you have a copy of it here?"

"No. But the library in Edinburgh will."

Iain put his arm around Lara's shoulder. "I guess we're in for another trip to Edinburgh. We can go on Monday."

A half hour later, when they walked into the cottage kitchen, Lara shivered. "I can't imagine how cold it must be here in December when it's this uncomfortably chilly and damp in August. You grew up in this house with only fireplaces for heat. How did you manage?"

"I don't remember being cold except in the

292

mornings. Me da' kept the fireplaces going durin' our waking hours. But they died down overnight, and I remember chitterin' in the morning chill until the fireplaces were lit. Sometimes there was ice on our wash basins in the mornings."

Lara shivered at the very idea. "In Alberta our winter temperatures can hover as low as minus twenty. Most houses have natural gas heat, but the outside temperatures can go so low they warn us on the morning news as to how long it will take for human flesh to freeze. Sometimes less than two minutes. We have to bundle up so very little skin is exposed. And we have to plug our cars in at night to keep the oil from freezing."

Iain knelt to light the fireplace in their bedroom. "By that standard, ye'll find Scotland almost tropical." He started undressing. "Nae fash yerself. I know how to keep ye warm."

A moment later he dived into the bed, taking her with him. "Ye take too long getting out of yer clothes, mistress. Clearly ye need help." He edged her long skirt up and started to pull her panties down.

Lara wanted to be angry but instead, burst out laughing and nudged him aside. Imitating his speech, she said, "Ye'll just have to wait until I hang up this very expensive dress. Then, *maybe* I'll consider yer kind offer of warmth."

He stretched out on the bed and gazed at her as she stood and undressed. Slowly she took off her dress and hung it up, then unhooked her bra and slid it off, cupping her breasts with her hands as she did so. Finally, slowly, she slid her panties down her legs, waving her bottom before him.

She stood, naked in front of the fireplace, lifting her hair in her hands. "Nice fire. I don't believe I'll need any more heat than this, thank you."

He growled and was off the bed in a flash. He stood before her, mere inches separating them. He brushed her nipples with his fingers, light as a whisper. His lips sought hers, soft, inviting. He rubbed his erection against her belly, barely touching. Then he crawled back into bed. "Guid night, love. Hope yer warm enough."

"On second thought," she laughed, "maybe I'm not." She slid into the bed, wrapping herself around his hot, inviting body.

****

The week passed quickly. The plumber and electrician came and went, and dates were established for their work.

Iain spent increasing time in the stables with Ewan. The fall Thoroughbred sale was now only weeks away and decisions had to be made as to which horses were to be sold and which kept. Iain, although inconvenienced by his cast, was able to ride Thunder for a short time every day. Introducing Thunder to the herd, allowing him to pasture with the other horses, had gone as smoothly as Lara predicted it would. Lara had worked some magic on the creature. He was no longer the skittish, dangerous beast he had been two months ago.

As the time neared for Lara to return to Canada, the hours they spent together were more precious. Lara worked daily in the stables beside Ewan and Iain, grooming and exercising the horses.

Weekends they continued their investigation into the mystery left by Elspeth Glendenning. They found the Ballantynes in Burke's Peerage as Duncan had said they might. Jamie, at nineteen, had married Lady Alicia Henderson, the daughter of an Earl. He had sired four children, three boys and a girl, ensuring that the Ballantyne lands and titles were secure. He had taken his place in the House of Lords on his twentieth birthday and had lived a long life, dying in his eighties.

There was no mention of his mother beyond her marriage to Hugh Ballantyne.

Lifting her eyes from the volume in front of them, Lara said, "What happened to Elspeth?"

"There's nothing in here to help us with that. I think we should ask the Ballantynes whether we could visit their family graves. She might be there."

****

Iain and Lara sat in the library, tense as Duncan placed the call. "This is Duncan Glendenning. I believe we met at a dinner given by Sir Alexander MacLeish...Well, thank you. I'm calling to request a favor. My future daughter-in-law, Lara MacInnes, is tracing her family history. One of her ancestors may have been Elspeth Glendenning, who married Hugh Ballantyne. Would you be willing to grant her access to your family graveyard? ...That is most gracious of you. Tuesday at ten? I'm sure that will work well for them. Thank you."

He put the phone back on the table. "Done. Now all you have to is get there. The Ballantyne estate is in Cornwall, on the South Coast."

"Thank you, Duncan," Lara sighed. "I hope

we'll find Elspeth there. After all, she was legally a Ballantyne."

Duncan considered what Lara said. "Perhaps, but it's not a certainty. Her earlier marriage to a MacInnes might well be considered legal today. Still, it is one more avenue to explore."

The visit to the Ballantyne Estate was pleasant if not informative. The present Earl, a soft-spoken, tweedy kind of man and his blonde, very English wife, were gracious, inviting them to have tea before they traipsed up the hill to the family graves.

Iain told the Ballantynes Lara believed it possible Elspeth Glendenning Ballantyne was one of her ancestors and was hoping to locate Elspeth's grave.

"I'm quite sure no Elspeth Ballantyne is buried here, but you are welcome to visit the family graveyard. Emmett"—she nodded to her husband—"will take you there after our tea." Turning to Iain, she said, "How are your mother and father? I so enjoyed chatting with them at the MacLeish's house party last month."

"Doing very well, my lady. They send you their respects. We're all busy right now getting ready for our Thoroughbred show and sale in September."

"Ah, yes. It is on our calendar. A highlight of the season."

As they trudged through tall grass up the steep hillside at the end of the formal gardens, Lara was grateful she had worn her hiking boots. They had been out of place in the Ballantynes' drawing room, but they were necessary for this trek. She noticed their host had changed to boots also.

The air was moist and soft with the scent of moss and damp earth. A massive yew tree stood guard at the entrance to the cemetery, its branches heavy with last night's rains. The grave site was large and beautifully tended, like the rest of the Earl's gardens. The oldest graves were nearest to them, moss encrusted stones barely legible, going back to the 1600s.

"This property has been in your family since the sixteen hundreds?" Lara asked, in awe.

"The fifteen hundreds, actually. A land grant from Henry VIII, held onto through both Catholic and Protestant regimes through our family's canny ability to shift with the times. It is not so easy today. Taxes on such properties are gradually making them less and less possible to keep. We open all but our private living quarters for viewing to the public during the tourist season. That helps. Your family, I believe, has converted their castle into a hotel. We all do what we must to maintain these vestiges of history. They should not be lost."

Lara viewed their host with new respect. Somehow, when he had greeted her, so much Lord of the Manor, she had not suspected that he, too, had to work hard to hold on to this history his family had built.

"Ah, here we are. The eighteen hundreds. Hugh Ballantyne? His is the rather grandiose one with the cherubs and angels. Very nineteenth century. His first wife, Emma Hartsworth Ballantyne, is buried with him. Here's her name carved in the marble. There is no second wife buried here. Elspeth Glendenning, you said? Most odd that she isn't here.

Perhaps she remarried?"

"We don't really know. We're just doing some research. They were married in the mid-eighteen hundreds."

"I recall hearing something mysterious about his death. He was murdered, I believe. But my parents never talked about it."

Lara opened her mouth and then closed it. Perhaps if the earl had never taken the time to investigate that dark chapter in his family's history, it would not be welcome from a stranger.

Later as Iain and Lara drove away, Lara said, "Don't you find it odd, that he has never investigated that chapter of his family's history?"

"I wondered about that also," Iain replied, "but you know, I think he may be very well aware of it but isn't about to discuss it with strangers."

Lara shook her head. "I hadn't considered that. But it makes sense. I suppose no one would want to discuss a family scandal with outsiders."

"So, we're back at square one." Iain shook his head. "What became of Elspeth?"

When they returned home and reported on their visit to Iain's father and mother, Duncan asked, "What about her journals? Have ye finished reading them?"

"All but the last one. I'm sorry to say we haven't gotten back to them since we read about the trial and the 'Not proven' verdict. We stopped at the point where she had been three years in Lochleigh after the trial. Her days there took on a sameness that I suppose I just tired of reading. Jamie took his lessons with the rest of the MacInnes children for a while, then, cognizant of what her husband would have wanted, Elspeth hired a special tutor for him in Latin and Greek and mathematics. Our suppositions were correct. Jamie was no longer on the admission list of the preparatory school he had been enrolled in since birth."

Iain added, "Where we stopped reading, she was considering whether to travel with him to school abroad. Whether he should spend some years at Heidelberg before coming home to England to finish at Eton as Lord Ballantyne always intended. She was determined he should be a well-educated man when he took his rightful place in the House of Lords."

Lara added, "Elspeth threw herself into ensuring her son's life was all Lord Ballantyne would have wanted, in spite of the obstacles she faced in the aftermath of her trial."

Duncan nodded. "Heidelberg is one of the oldest and finest universities in Europe. Under the circumstances it would have been a good choice."

Lara added, "I skipped forward a bit from those early days at Lochleigh. They appear to have been good ones for both Jamie and his mother. Perhaps not happy ones for Elspeth, but peaceful ones. She was slowly recovering from the death of her husband and the nightmare of her trial. Abhainn and Fiona accepted them both in as family, almost as if her intercepting marriage to Lord Ballantyne never happened."

Iain picked up the story. "The most interesting bits are her references to letters from Lachlan to his brother, first that he safely arrived in British North

America, and then later, his travels westward. Lachlan spent some two years seeking the land he wanted, and finally found it in the shadow of what, today, we call the Canadian Rockies. He describes it as a desolate place with the closest community a trading post called Calgary. He said it remind him of Scotland."

Lara smiled. "That quarter-section of land was the foundation of the ranch my family still lives on. He received the original land grant from the government."

"Did he know Elspeth was with Abhainn and the rest of his family? Did he ever know about her trial for murder?"

"Apparently not," Lara replied. "Elspeth was adamant that he should not be told of her troubles. She expressed guilt at the sorrow she had caused him and wanted him to find peace in his new life. Abhainn and Fiona agreed with her. Still, she lived from one of his infrequent letters to the next."

"But he must have married. Otherwise your family would not exist." Duncan suggested.

"About three years after he settled there, he a married a widow whose property adjoined his, and a year later they had twin boys. They would be Lara's ancestors. His wife died when the boys were still young."

"It must have been a lonely and difficult life, running a huge ranch and raising motherless twin boys. Why didn't Elspeth go to him then?" Duncan asked. "Did she never consider joining him?"

"How could she?" Lara replied. "She had made a contract with Hugh Ballantyne, and she was honor bound to see it through. She could never be free until her son had taken his place in the House of Lords."

****

The days of summer dwindled down. Soon Lara would be leaving. She and Iain were too busy, between working on the cottage and readying the Thoroughbreds for the coming show and sale, to think much about their coming separation. They still had dinner most nights at the castle, relieving Iain's mother and father of some of the pressures of running a hotel.

Iain's lovemaking took on an almost frantic note as the day of Lara's departure approached.

"Come with me," she whispered in the aftermath of passion.

"Stay with me," he replied.

"I'm not Elspeth, Iain. I'll be back, I promise."

"And just to be sure, I'll be in Calgary to fetch ye on December fifteenth."

****

December came. The months had been endless but finally Lara and her mother were at the arrivals area at Calgary Airport, waiting for the plane from Edinburgh via London to disembark. Crowds thronged through the double doors, pushing carts piled high with luggage.

Then she spotted him, towering over most other passengers, his red hair a beacon, with Duncan and Aileen close behind.

Weaving her way through the flood of people, she threw herself into his arms. He kissed her soundly and people around them paused, laughed,

Blair McDowell

and applauded.

"We're holding up traffic here, son. If ye can wait five minutes, ye can do that properly."

"Right, Da." He continued maneuvering their cart through the crowd until he was out of the narrow exit area.

"Aileen, Duncan, how wonderful to see you again. Welcome to Canada. I hope your trip wasn't too tiring?" Lara's mother hugged them each in turn. "And this, I take it, is Iain." She kissed him on the cheek. "You are the young man who intends to spirit my daughter away to Scotland."

Iain laughed. "Aye, that I do." He cupped Lara's face in his hands. "God, I have missed ye, lass." He kissed her a smacking kiss again.

Tears came to Lara's eyes. She was almost afraid to be so full of joy. Until he came through the doors, she had been afraid something might go wrong.

He leaned down and whispered to her, "'Tis naught to cry about, lass. We're about to make our marriage legal in Canada. As far as I'm concerned, 'tis already legal. But I'm lookin' forward to seeing ye in yer white wedding dress. And I'm lookin' forward even more to takin' it off ye."

She laughed in spite of herself. His behavior was so incorrect in almost every situation. He never said or did the expected. And she loved him wildly.

Christ Church Cathedral in Calgary was full to overflowing for their wedding. Lara walked down the aisle in her mother's wedding dress, on the arm of her brother Jamie. Iain was resplendent in his kilts.

302

At the reception at the ranch, there were fiddlers for the dancing.

Iain watched with interest. "'Tis not unlike our dancin'."

"Of course not." Lara's mother said. "That's where we came from. These parts were settled largely by the Scottish and Irish, and not all that long ago, a hundred, or maybe a hundred fifty years ago."

Iain took Lara by the hand and joined in the fun.

It took hours for the crowd to thin out enough for Iain and Lara to take their leave. They would stay at the ranch tonight. Tomorrow they would drive to Banff for a short honeymoon before returning to Calgary to fly out to Scotland for their next wedding celebration.

Lara took Iain aside. "Go take off those togs and put on your jeans and riding boots. I've something to show you."

Five minutes later she led him out through the kitchen to the mud room. There they put on down jackets before going out to the stable. Two horses were saddled and waiting for them.

"There is something you must see."

They rode in comfortable silence. Lara led the way up a steep hillside about a half mile from the ranch house.

At the top of the hill they came to a small graveyard enclosed by a wooden fence. "I didn't even remember this place," Lara said. "It hasn't been used as a burial ground in a hundred years,"

Iain dismounted and helped Lara to dismount. She unhooked the gate and together they entered.

The oldest graves were in the back of the little cemetery and had stone markers. The names of the dead were chiseled deeply into the stone. Lara led Iain to the oldest.

Iain read aloud.

Lachlan MacInnes
1823-1899

"Your very great grandfather."

Lara stepped to the grave beside Lachlan's.

Elspeth Glendenning MacInnes
Beloved wife of Lachlan
1828-1901

Tears trickled down Lara's face. "She was here all the time and I didn't know. She found him. And they were together again to the end of their lives."

Iain enfolded her in his arms. "They were together against insurmountable odds. We are fortunate. We are married, a Glendenning and a MacInnes like Lachlan and Elspeth, and the sky has nae fallen in."

Chapter Sixteen

The Past, 1873

Elspeth, wearing the gray of half mourning, her hat swathed in a concealing veil, watched with great pride from the gallery as her son took his place in the House of Lords. How happy Hugh would have been. His son was married to a well-born young woman; they had one child, a boy, and another on the way. There were adoring grandparents on his wife's side.

As much as Elspeth would have loved to be an adoring grandmother, every time she appeared in public, the old scandal was resurrected. There was no place for her in society here. While her son and his wife ignored the slights and direct cuts when she was with them, and had repeatedly asked her to live with them, her presence in their lives could only have a detrimental effect on her son's career and marriage. The old adage "out of sight, out of mind" was more truth than fiction.

This was the last time she would see him for a very long time, perhaps forever. Her eyes brimmed with unshed tears. By the time he received her letter, she would be on the high seas.

*****

Abhainn and Fiona came to see her off. "Are

305

you sure you want to undertake this long and possibly dangerous trek?" Fiona queried her yet again.

Elspeth smiled and told them indeed she was sure.

Abhainn pressed a letter into her hands. "To give him when you arrive. *Beannacht leat*, our blessings go with you," he said as Fiona hugged her.

The voyage was long. The seas were stormy and many of the ship's passengers were sick, but Elspeth reveled in every nautical mile that took her farther from her former life. She stood on the deck, the wind blowing her hair loose from its pins, her cloak whipping around her. For the first time in twenty years she was free. Free of responsibility, free of the constant shadow of gossip and innuendo.

Not that she didn't have moments of doubt. She was forty-two. Would he still want her? She studied the image in her glass. Her face was unlined. Her breasts were firm. She was still slender. Then she smiled at her insecurity. She loved Lachlan. She had aged in the last years as she was sure he had aged, but she was as certain of his love as of the sun rising in the east. She remembered a song she had sung when she was young. How did it go? "*As the sunflower turns on her god when he sets, that same look that she gave when he rose.*"

The journey ahead of her was long and arduous. By boat to Quebec City, by train until the tracks ran out. Information about what would happen after that was sketchy. By river and on horseback. If she was fortunate, she might be able to join a wagon train for part of the way. From Lachlan's letters to Abhainn,

Elspeth was aware the closest trading post to his ranch was Calgary. He lived somewhere west of Calgary, in the foothills of the Rocky Mountains. He would have to come to the trading post for his supplies. Someone there would know where he lived.

And now, after four months of arduous travel by boat, by train, by canoe, by wagon train and finally on horseback, she was here. She gazed at the little log house nestled into the hillside. It was early evening and snow was falling. Flickering light shone through the cabin windows.

The Blackfoot guide she had hired in Calgary helped her dismount. Snowflakes brushed the fur hood of her cloak and landed on her eyelashes. She stood, suddenly fearful, unable to move. Her guide regarded her, then knocked on the door.

Lachlan opened the door and stared in surprise at the guide. "Asatsista, what are you doing here on such a snowy night? Come in, come in out of the cold!"

The guide stood back.

Lachlan swayed and grasped the doorframe. "Elspeth?"

Then she was in his arms.

The guide quietly closed the door behind them.

"Oh Elspeth, I never thought to see you again. I hoped, I despaired, I did not think it possible... Are you here, are you really here? Here to stay?" Lachlan laughed through his tears, his tight embrace leaving her breathless.

"I'm here, my love. I'm here to stay if you still want me..."

"I have never stopped loving ye, wanting ye." He pushed her fur hood back and smoothed his hand over her hair. He then unfastened her heavy cloak, allowing it to fall in a puddle on the floor. He stepped back and surveyed her. "Oh, my dearest, my beautiful love, if anything, ye are lovelier than when I first met you."

Elspeth smiled into his beloved face. "I have but one request, dearest."

"Anything. Anything that is in my power to give, lass."

"I want us to be married. In a church, by a preacher. I want you to make an honest woman of me."

His laughter rang out. "We'll ride into town and set a date with the preacher and post the banns tomorrow." He turned her around and started undoing the tiny buttons at the back of her dress. "But tonight..."

"Tonight?"

"Tonight ye may have to teach me as I once taught ye. It has been so long I'm not sure I remember how..."

A word about the author…

Blair McDowell's first career was as a musician and teacher. She studied in Europe and, during the course of her academic career, lived in Hungary, the United States, Australia, and Canada, teaching in universities in the latter three countries. She has always loved to write and has produced six widely used professional books and numerous articles in her field.

A voracious reader, Blair decided when she retired from university teaching to turn her talents to her first love, writing fiction. She moved to Canada's scenic west coast and, with a friend, opened a bed & breakfast. Mornings she makes omelets and chats with guests from far and near, and afternoons, she writes. From March through September, the world comes to her doorstep, bringing tales that are fodder for her rich imagination, but once the tourist season is over, she packs her bags and takes off for exotic ports: Europe in the fall, the Caribbean in the winter.

Her novels are set in some of her favorite destinations.

http://www.blairmcodowell.com

~*~

Other Books By Blair Macdowell

ROMANTIC ROAD ~ Romance, murder, mystery, and mayhem, in Germany, Austria, and Hungary.

DELIGHTING IN YOUR COMPANY ~ And solving a 200-year-old mystery on a Caribbean island.

WHERE LEMONS BLOOM ~ Love, danger, and intrigue on Italy's Amalfi Coast.

FATAL CHARM ~ A theft from the Louvre, and a heroine in peril in Paris.

Thank you for purchasing
this publication of The Wild Rose Press, Inc.

For questions or more information
contact us at
info@thewildrosepress.com.

The Wild Rose Press, Inc.
www.thewildrosepress.com

To visit with authors of
The Wild Rose Press, Inc.
join our yahoo loop at
http://groups.yahoo.com/group/thewildrosepress/

CPSIA information can be obtained
at www.ICGtesting.com
Printed in the USA
LVHW042140040919
629986LV00005B/28